RUSH

Praise for LAMBDA Literary Award Finalist Carsen Taite

"Real Life defense attorney Carsen Taite polishes her fifth work of lesbian fiction, *The Best Defense*, with the realism she daily encounters in the office and in the courts. And that polish is something that makes *The Best Defense* shine as an excellent read."—*Out & About Newspaper*

"Taite is a real-life attorney so the prose jumps off the page with authority and authenticity. [*It Should be a Crime*] is just Taite's second novel...but it's as if she has bookshelves full of bestsellers under her belt. In fact, she manages to make the courtroom more exciting than Judge Judy bursting into flames while delivering a verdict. Like this book, that's something we'd pay to see."—*Gay List Daily*

"Taite, a criminal defense attorney herself, has given her readers a behind the scenes look at what goes on during the days before a trial. Her descriptions of lawyer/client talks, investigations, police procedures, etc. are fascinating. Taite keeps the action moving, her characters clear, and never allows her story to get bogged down in paperwork. *It Should be a Crime* has a fast-moving plot and some extraordinarily hot sex." —*Just About Write*

In *Do Not Disturb*..."Taite's tale of sexual tension is entertaining in itself, but a number of secondary characters...add substantial color to romantic inevitability."—Richard Labonté, *Bookmarks*

In *Nothing but the Truth*..."Author Taite is really a Dallas defense attorney herself, and it's obvious her viewpoint adds considerable realism to her story, making it especially riveting as a mystery. ...I give it four stars out of five."—Bob Lind, *Echo Magazine*

Visit us at www.boldstrokesbooks.com

By the Author

truelesbianlove.com

It Should Be a Crime

Do Not Disturb

Nothing but the Truth

The Best Defense

Beyond Innocence

Rush

The Luca Bennett Mystery Series:

Slingshot

Battle Axe

RUSH

by
Carsen Taite

2013

RUSH

ISBN 10: 1-60282-966-7
ISBN 13: 978-1-60282-966-4

This Trade Paperback Original Is Published By
Bold Strokes Books, Inc.
P.O. Box 249
Valley Falls, NY 12185

First Edition: December 2013

CREDITS
EDITOR: CINDY CRESAP
PRODUCTION DESIGN: SUSAN RAMUNDO
COVER DESIGN BY SHERI (GRAPHICARTIST2020@HOTMAIL.COM)

Acknowledgments

Thanks to all the readers who buy my books, show up at events, and write to encourage me to keep telling stories. Special thanks to fellow authors VK Powell and Ashley Bartlett for lending me their skills—they read and critiqued several versions of the manuscript before I shipped it off to editor extraordinaire, Cindy Cresap. Cindy, thanks for everything you've taught me. I can't imagine a better mentor.

Sheri, thanks for another excellent cover. Thanks to Len Barot and everyone else at Bold Strokes Books—you all make the business of writing fun.

To my wife Lainey, thanks for everything you do to make it possible for me to pursue this dream. You are amazing and I love you.

Dedication

To Lainey. Life with you is the best rush ever.

CHAPTER ONE

Danielle Soto strode into the room, careful to step around the marked off areas, the blood splatter, and the once attractive older woman who lay on the floor with a noose around her neck. Like the last time, three weeks ago, she struggled to contain her mixed reaction of nausea and sorrow. It was a challenge. She wasn't used to seeing dead bodies. Not in person, anyway.

"Danny!"

She turned toward the loud voice and smiled at the big burly man who waved from the doorway. "About time you got here, Ramirez."

Detective George Ramirez pointed at the body. "What, like she would've been any less dead, if I hadn't stopped for donuts?" Before Danny could respond, he added, "And, I've been here. I was just out back, talking to the first on scene. You would've done well to stop somewhere and change. You're already getting your fancy suit all messy."

Danny followed his pointing finger to her pant leg and shook her head. She'd come directly from the courthouse, not even considering her clothes. Too bad, since she was wearing her best and most favorite suit, which was now sporting splotches of black fingerprint powder. The dry cleaner better be able to work a miracle. George was right; she should've changed, but she hadn't really had a choice. Her cell phone had started buzzing with texts during her morning hearing, and it had taken every ounce of restraint she possessed to make her arguments to the judge and appear to patiently address his concerns before running from the courtroom to this crime scene.

"Whatever," Danny said. The ruined suit didn't seem like such a big deal compared to the fate of the woman lying on the floor. "Who was first on the scene?"

"Patrol officer out of the West Precinct. Baxter. Dispatch got a call from a nosy neighbor saying she thought she saw a prowler. Baxter responds. Doesn't see anything in the area, but he knocks on the door and it swung wide open. He called for backup. While he was waiting, he took a look around. Bet he won't do that again. He's out back, still throwing up."

"You're such a nice guy. Like you never threw up at a crime scene."

"And waste a good lunch?" He shook his head. "Never gonna happen."

Danny placed a hand on her stomach. "Okay, stop talking about food. I haven't eaten yet, and after this I may never eat again. Walk me through what you've got so far."

"Martha Lawson, white female, age fifty-nine. Shot once in the chest. Fatal. The rest of the stuff came after."

Danny forced her gaze back to the victim and took in "the rest of the stuff." The distinct pattern of slash marks across her abdomen, the elaborate staging of the body, and finally, the same coarse rope tied into a hangman's noose pulled tight around her throat. Just like the two victims before her.

She'd seen enough. "Flowers?"

"Yep. Come on, I'll show you."

She followed Ramirez, appreciating his ability to know what she would want to see, what would be important to her. He treated her like a colleague, when a lot of cops with his experience thought the trial attorneys who prosecuted their cases didn't get the system. When she'd started with the district attorney's office seven years ago, she'd quickly realized she wouldn't get far if she didn't make friends with the cops she had to put on the stand. Many of her fellow prosecutors never got the memo, choosing instead to act like they knew everything and the cops who worked their cases were just like any other witness instead of a valuable resource. Ramirez was an asset and a friend besides. Didn't hurt that he'd been her brother's best friend since they were in preschool.

"Looks like she was going to put them in a vase." Ramirez pointed to the green wax paper bundle of white roses on the floor, next to a tipped over thick glass vase. "A dozen here and one by the body. Same as the others."

"You think he followed her in?"

"Yep. No sign of forced entry. Maybe she was going to get him a tip after she put the flowers away." He pointed at the sink. "Water was still running when we got here."

"You'd think after we released that detail, people would learn not to open their doors." After the second kill, the DA's office and police department tipped off the local news outlets that flower delivery had been linked to several assaultive attacks. They hadn't wanted to hold a big press conference and scare the community, so they'd been purposely vague, not even releasing specific details about the type of flowers connected to the crimes. It looked like the subtle approach wasn't working. She shook her head. "Show me what else you've got."

He walked around the room, pointing out various areas marked by the crime scene unit. A purse was sitting open on the kitchen table, but it appeared the contents were completely intact.

When he finished his tour, Danny asked, "Okay, what do you need me to do?"

"Subpoena phone records, bank records, whatever else we can get to piece together a pattern. No way this guy is picking these women at random. They are all in the same age range, but there's another connection. I can feel it in my gut."

"I'll do whatever you need, but you should know I may not be on this much longer." At his raised eyebrows, she added, "This is number three, and you know as well as I do, this sicko's not going to stop. If we don't get a solid lead soon, your boss and my boss are going to start considering other options."

"This is our case. No way am I handing it over to a bunch of cowboy feds. Guess we better move quickly. I'll get you an affidavit in an hour."

Danny looked at her watch. "Great, but make it two. You can't type for shit, especially when you're in a hurry. I'll be at the courthouse and we can walk it over to Judge Amos."

"Thanks for coming out."

"No problem. Gory murder scenes are great for my waistline."

Danny waited until she was several blocks from the scene before she pulled over, opened the door, and dry heaved in the direction of the road. In her career as a prosecutor she'd gotten used to the sight of maimed and bloody bodies in autopsy reports and crime scene photos, but she'd never get used to the sight of atrocity in the flesh. She couldn't let the aversion handicap her; she had to channel it so when they finally caught the monster who did these horrible things, she could use her emotion to paint a picture for the jury that the flat, glossy photos never would. What she'd just seen fueled her desire for justice like no written report, no pictures ever would. The wrenching pain would fuel her arguments to the jury that the person who committed these crimes didn't deserve freedom. She lived for the opportunity to bring this monster down, and no amount of personal discomfort would get in her way.

CHAPTER TWO

"Ellen, Mrs. Lawson's daughter dropped this off for you. She said you wanted it delivered directly to you."

Ellen Davenport took the plain brown envelope from her assistant who stood waiting at the edge of her desk. "Thanks, Jill." She slit the envelope open with a lapis handled letter opener and carefully removed the photograph inside. "She didn't have a digital version of her favorite photo so she sent this over. I promised to guard it with my life." Marty Lawson sported crazy plaid pants and a collared pale yellow shirt. She held a golf club in one hand and a tee in the other. Happy, sporty. Alive.

Not anymore. She'd been killed in her home by an intruder just last week. Her vibrant life cut short. A tragic waste and a huge loss. Marty had been an active alumna of Alpha Nu, and the organization wouldn't be the same without her. In the over thirty years since she'd graduated from college, Marty had continued to be an active member of the sorority, working on numerous regional committees, mentoring young women in the university chapters, and eventually serving on the national board. Ellen, executive director for the sorority's national organization, enjoyed working with her on a daily basis and planned to write the tribute for the website herself.

"I'm headed out for lunch. Do you want me to bring something back for you?"

Ellen looked up from the photo on her desk. She'd forgotten Jill was still there. "Actually, I think I may go out, stretch my legs. Thanks, though." She ignored Jill's curious look and handed the photo to her. "Could you scan this and e-mail it to me? I'll send it to the webmaster as soon as I've written the tribute. And then send the photo back to Marty's daughter as soon as you're done."

The time she'd spent working on Marty Lawson's tribute left her feeling empty. All that life, suddenly gone. Cliché, but true—life was indeed too short to take precious moments for granted. She glanced at the clock on her computer. She had lots of work to do, but no more appointments for the rest of the day. Anxious and unsettled, she decided a walk wasn't going to calm her nerves, but a visit to one of Marty's closest friends might. She stuck her head out of her office and watched Jill disappear down the hall. When she was out of sight, Ellen grabbed her purse and keys. She scrawled a note on the stack of Post-its on Jill's desk, letting her know she had a personal matter to take care of, that she'd be back in a couple of hours. She wasn't quite sure why she hadn't told Jill face-to-face she'd be gone longer than a stretch of her legs, except that Jill already thought it was strange she was deviating from her usual lunch at her desk routine. Ducking out now would avoid her inevitable questions. She didn't like having to explain her personal life.

The drive was about thirty minutes. As many times as she'd taken this route, the way the steel and cement of downtown Dallas suddenly burst into rolling hills and wooded forest still amazed her. She'd picked the place carefully. Had to be close to the city, but had to be serene. Had to be secure, but hospitable. Luckily, cost hadn't been an issue. She'd found the perfect place only miles from Dallas.

She pulled into the broad circular drive, handed her keys to the valet, and strode over to the large glass doors of the main building. The doorman smiled and greeted her.

"Good afternoon, Ms. Davenport. Nice to see you early in the day."

Ellen heard no judgmental inflection, but her failure to schedule regular visits during the day tugged at her conscience. "Nice to be here. Do you happen to know if Mrs. Patterson is in?"

"I saw her just a few minutes ago. Would you like me to call her for you?"

"That would be great. I can wait here." She pointed to a sofa in the lobby.

"Your mother's outside on the veranda if you'd like to join her."

She didn't, but she knew she should. "Thank you, Virgil. When you see Mrs. Patterson, you can let her know I'm out there."

"Will do."

Ellen took a deep breath and headed out to join her mother. The older female Davenport was seated in a wicker chair, facing the lush grounds. She didn't move as Ellen approached from behind, but just as Ellen wondered whether she should clear her throat to keep from surprising her, Vivian Davenport spoke. "I hear you, trying to sneak up on me." She turned in her chair and Ellen pulled up short. And waited. She hated this part.

"Why, Ellen. Whatever are you doing here in the middle of the day? Did you lose your job?"

Judgment. Ellen was relieved rather than annoyed at the familiar trait. "Hello, Mother. Nice day, isn't it?"

Vivian waved a hand at the great outdoors. "Nice enough, I guess. I'm bored though. Sit and talk to me. There aren't enough intelligent people to talk to around here." She pointed to the chair next to her, and Ellen dutifully took a seat.

"How are you feeling?"

Vivian bristled. "I feel fine. Who wouldn't feel fine with people waiting on you hand and foot? Did you bring me any books? I'd like the new John Grisham."

"I think I brought that to you last time." She was certain she had. "Maybe it got misplaced in your room. I can help you look for it."

"I don't misplace things. Hell, I don't have enough space to lose anything. I've been thinking about getting a bigger place."

"Sure, maybe there's a bigger suite available. I can check with Mrs. Patterson, if you want."

"I mean something like a townhouse. Smaller than the house your father picked out, but big enough for me to have more private space. I might even do something crazy, like get a roommate."

Vivian looked so happy at the prospect of living somewhere else, Ellen didn't have the heart to burst her bubble. "We can definitely look into that. In the meantime, I'll get you another copy of the book. Deal?"

"Deal. Are you hungry? I'm ravenous. Why don't you go sneak us some sandwiches from the canteen?"

Ellen glanced around. The director, Mrs. Patterson, was standing in the doorway to the veranda. Seizing on the perfect opportunity to speak to her alone, she said, "Will do. I'll be right back."

As she approached Mrs. Patterson, she signaled she wanted to speak to her inside. Once they were safely out of hearing range from her mother, Ellen asked, "Do you have a few minutes?"

"Of course." She walked them over to a sofa near the lobby. "I'm so glad you could make it by. She's having a good day."

Ellen pushed aside the exchange about the lost or stolen Grisham book and considered the reason for this visit. Her mom looked healthy. She was focused. She was indeed having a good day, but before she did anything ill-advised, she wanted Patterson's advice. "She does seem to be doing really well, and that's what I want to talk to you about." She paused. The subject of Marty's death was still difficult to discuss. "A good friend of my mother's died this week. You may have seen her here. I know she came to visit when she could. Marty Lawson?"

"Of course. Ms. Lawson was a devoted friend. Your mother loved her visits. They talked for hours. I'm sorry to hear that she died."

"Actually, she was murdered. I know that under normal circumstances, mother would want to hear about it. From someone she knows, not on the news or some other less personal method. I want your advice about what, if anything, I should tell her."

"That's a tough one. How long were Marty and your mother friends?"

Ellen laughed. "Forever. At least it seems that way to me since they met before I was born. They went to college together. They were in the same sorority and they were both active alumnae until…" her words trailed off into sadness. Marty would never be part of that world again, and her mother? Well, Vivian probably never would be either.

"Does your mother ever mention Marty to you?"

"No, but…" Her mother tended to focus on one subject during her visits, and it wasn't her sorority sisters. Familiar guilt crept in. If she'd visit more, especially during the day, she might be able to talk about more pleasant things. But the visits she made time for were hard enough. She pushed the guilt aside. "Well, I know from Marty that she enjoyed their visits. I just don't want her to see something on the news, read it in the paper and not understand why I didn't tell her first."

"Valid concerns. However, I think it might be best to wait until the issue comes up. The likelihood that she will be exposed to the news is minimal, and even then she might not make the connection."

Ellen caught the unspoken implications. If her mother didn't remember Marty between visits, hearing about her death on the news might not strike a chord. Bringing the subject up was borrowing trouble. It wasn't necessary to put her mother through the drama. Relief washed her guilt away. "Okay. That sounds like a good plan." She stood. "Mother keeps talking about moving out, getting her own place. Normal or not normal?"

"Well, that's all relative, but for the most part, everyone here has gone through a phase like that. She's perfectly healthy, and on good days, those kind of thoughts are perfectly natural."

"It's hard to know what's natural anymore."

"I understand. You know if you ever need someone to talk to, we have several great counselors on staff. They are always available to talk to you."

She shuddered inwardly. Sharing was not a family value. Not in her family anyway. "I'm fine." To soften her abrupt response, she added, "I do appreciate everything you do for Mother. I'm sure she appreciates it too." That last was a lie, but like her mother had always said, a little lie can save a lot of hurt. "I only have a few minutes before I have to get back to work. I should go say good-bye. Thanks again for your time."

Ellen felt Patterson's gaze on her back as she walked away to get the promised sandwiches. She'd have to take hers to go. Her impromptu visit had already eaten a chunk out of her day. Time to get back to the office. She purchased two California clubs from the small deli/shop and headed back to the veranda. Her mother was no longer seated in the chair where she'd left her. She spotted her at the far end of the balcony, leaning over the rail, pointing in the distance. Ellen set the food on a nearby table and stepped cautiously toward her mother, anxiety growing with every step. When she was close, she called softly, "Mother?"

Vivian didn't turn, didn't move, her gaze transfixed on the lush lawn below her. Ellen walked closer and opened her mouth to call out again, when Vivian spun toward her.

"Did you see it?"

"What? Did I see what?"

Vivian grabbed her arm and gripped tight. "I need to get down there and check it out. Go wake my husband. Tell him we've found the perfect spot. He'll want to sleep longer, but tell him it's critical. He needs to come now."

"Mother, let's go sit down. I got your favorite sandwich."

"We don't have time to eat. Someone else may find it first." She shook Ellen's arm and pulled her toward the railing. "See for yourself."

Ellen stepped closer to the railing. Green grounds. Colorful flowerbeds. Active fountains. Whatever had Vivian so agitated wasn't in plain view. But it never was. Not anymore.

She tried once more. "Mother, please. Let's go sit down."

Vivian's eyes were glassy, but it didn't dim the animation in her voice. "My name is Vivian. Why are you calling me mother? I don't have any children. Please go get Bill and tell him to get down here now."

Ellen nodded and walked away. If only it were so easy, she'd get Bill in a heartbeat. But her father was halfway across the country and neither he nor her mother was ever coming back.

Chapter Three

Danny looked up from her desk and waved George into her cramped office. "Hey, it's been a week. Any chance you found any decent evidence in the stuff you got from Lawson's place?"

"Nice to see you too, Danny." He placed a Starbucks cup on her desk. "Oh, and thanks for the coffee."

She reached for the cup and pulled off the lid. "Americano? Quad shot?"

"Just the way you like it."

"Leave your wife and marry me."

"She'd probably be okay with that. At least she would this week since I've been working round the clock. Too bad I'm not your type."

Danny downed a third of the cup. "I might be able to overlook your manly ways if you brought me coffee every day."

"Wouldn't last. Eventually, coffee wouldn't be enough and you'd step out on me with some hot broad who made you forget your addiction to caffeine."

"Never. Okay, well, maybe." It had finally been long enough that she could find humor in jokes like that. George, on the other hand, looked contrite about his careless remark. She smiled to signal she was okay, and then changed the subject before he felt the need to offer an awkward apology. She held up her cup. "Tell you what, while I inject this dose of caffeine, why don't you give me an update on the Lawson case?"

George pulled a small notebook out of his jacket and thumbed through the pages. "Martha 'Marty' Lawson, age fifty-nine, retired from her career as an analyst at Raytheon last year."

"Any connection to Sally Jones or Joan Gibson?" She referred to the first two victims.

"Other than the fact they're all around the same age? No. Not yet." He consulted his notebook again. "Marty does, make that did, a lot of volunteer work, charities and such. Spent a lot of time working with her college sorority, Alpha Nu."

"She seems a little old to be hanging out with sorority girls."

"I guess it's an alumni thing."

"Alumna."

"Huh?"

"Female alumni are alumna. Plural, alumnae." Danny saw George's eyes start to glaze over. He didn't give a damn what female graduates were called. "Sorry, never mind. Not important. So, what else can you tell me?"

"She was supposed to be at a meeting at Richards University the day she was killed. They were hosting a meeting of alum…whatever. She's on the national board for the sorority."

"What does that even mean?"

"Like I know anything about sororities? Anyway, she seemed to spend a lot of time on this stuff. Might be worth checking into."

"Sure, okay. Sounds like a good idea although I doubt our killer is a psycho sorority chick." Danny didn't get why anyone would spend time on a college campus with a bunch of party girls, let alone extend the party into her adulthood. She'd scratched and crawled her way into academic scholarships for college and then law school, and she hadn't had a second to spare on frivolous crap like sorority rush, initiations, and heavy social calendars. Those activities were for students with money and connections, two things she'd never had and done fine without.

"I assume you want to go with?"

"I should. Alvarez has a bad feeling about these cases and wants me involved at every step." After the first murder carried signature signs of a serial killer, staging and mutilation of the body, DA Frank Alvarez had assigned her to be a liaison between the DA's office and the homicide unit. Although it was unusual, she didn't mind. Early involvement meant she'd have firsthand knowledge when it came to getting an arrest warrant from a judge for the sick fuck who'd committed these crimes, and it put her first in line to try these cases whenever they actually made an arrest. Like Alvarez, she believed that the killer who'd inflicted such a horrible death on these three women wasn't done yet, and she wanted to be part of stopping him. "I have a hearing this morning. Do you have some time this afternoon?"

"Sure. I already got the name of the executive director for this sorority Lawson was part of. Ellen Davenport. I'll call her and make an appointment. Pick you up at two?"

"Perfect. See you then." Danny finished her coffee and reviewed the file in front of her. Most of her docket had been shuffled off to other prosecutors, but she'd hung on to a few cases she'd already worked on for a while. This case involved a felony DWI. Wasn't much to it. Defense counsel was challenging the stop. The officer who'd made the stop was a seasoned veteran who'd be able to articulate a valid reason for pulling the guy over. All she had to do was walk him through the questions and wait for the judge to rule her way.

A couple of hours later, she walked out of the courtroom, another win under her belt. The defense attorney shook her hand and said he'd talk to his client about the deal she'd just offered. She had no doubt he'd take it, since she'd just eviscerated his only defense. As he walked off, the number two in her court, Molly Howard, asked, "You ever feel bad about beating them all the time?"

"Not a lick. You?"

"Nope, but I don't have as many wins as you do."

"I've been at it a little longer." She handed the file to Molly. "Here, finish this one and take the stat. And there are a few more files on my desk. I have a feeling things are going to heat up on my other project. Do what you can while I'm out running around with DPD."

Molly grinned. "Thanks, boss. What happens when you catch the guy?"

"Hopefully, I'll be lead prosecutor at his trial and send him to death row."

"And after that? Do you think Mr. Alvarez will promote you?"

Danny knew there was lots of speculation around the office about her assignment to the task force and what it would mean for the prosecutors left in her court. Would they leave her chief spot open or fill it on the premise she'd probably get a bump up whenever they caught this killer? *If* they caught this killer. She did her best not to focus on the future since there were too many contingencies. "Who knows? Maybe. You bucking for my spot?"

Molly grinned. "Who knows? Maybe."

"Okay, superstar, let's go over these cases. You rock them and I'll put in a good word for you."

They spent the next hour reviewing the details of her remaining caseload. At two sharp, George appeared at her door, jingling his keys. "Your chariot awaits."

She grabbed her briefcase, packed full of material she needed to review for the following day, and followed him to the car. The ride downtown was short. The Frank Crowley Courts Building was just close enough to downtown to be convenient for private practice lawyers, but far enough away to keep the riffraff who glutted the system from being an eyesore to the Dallas business community. George parked in a vast underground parking structure, and the two of them rode a series of elevators to the twenty-third floor of a high-rise office building.

George groused during the ride. "I hate coming down here. So damn confusing. You park underground and enter the building from underground. Hard to tell if you're even in the right place since they all look alike from the inside. Did you know Dallas has a whole series of underground tunnels? So the people that work in these buildings never have to go outside to eat lunch, get their shoes shined, go to the bank. Hundreds of grunts in prison who'd give ten years off their life to see daylight, and these stiffs live in a goddamn cave."

"You're such a philosopher, George." Danny laughed when he stuck his tongue out at her. "You're not wrong. It is crazy, but it's not like I understand anything about the people who choose these regular jobs anyway. Do you?"

"No, you're right. Money changing hands. Analysts. Accountants. Bankers. Whatever. None of it really matters."

"Lots of lawyers in these buildings."

"Not the good kind." He grinned at her. "Not the kind who keep the system working, keep our streets safe."

"I suppose."

"You ever wish you'd gone into some other type of law?"

"Not usually. Must admit it crosses my mind when I pay my monthly student loan payment. Don't think I'll ever get that paid off. Some folks in my class got deals that included having their loans paid off as a hiring bonus."

"Sweet. You'll probably be paying on those loans the rest of your life if you keep working for the county."

"I call it the happy tax. Instead of pushing paper, I get to put away bad guys. Money well spent."

The elevator stopped and they both walked the halls in search of Alpha Nu's suite number. Danny tried to connect the fancy reception areas they passed with the binge drinking Greeks of her college days. Guess everyone has to grow up sometime. At the third door, George consulted his notes. "This is it."

Plush, but not huge. The reception area was crammed with heavy furniture and lots of fragile-looking knick-knacks. She sat down, careful to avoid bumping into any of the breakables, and let George tell the receptionist about their appointment. She pictured Ellen Davenport, sitting in a plush office full of antique furniture, pouring tea from old china and reminiscing about her sorority days. "*Marty and I used to party hard back in the day, but lately all we ever did was sit around and tell stories of our misspent youth over afternoon tea. I can't believe she's dead. Would you like another scone?*"

A few minutes later a trim, sharply-dressed woman who introduced herself as Jill led them to a corner office. Plush yes, but definitely modern. If Davenport was an old biddy, she was hip at least. Fancy, but with a comfortable feel. At Jill's urging, Danny and George sat in chairs across from the large desk.

"Ms. Davenport will be right with you. Can I get either of you something to drink?"

"We're good," Danny answered, but she couldn't resist looking around for the tea service.

When Jill left, George leaned over and whispered, "Guess we both picked the wrong line of work. I don't know jack about art, but I'm thinking these walls are filled with stuff that should be in a museum."

"Damn, I've been found out." A tall blonde walked through the doorway and stuck both wrists toward them. "I confess. I looted the museum. Take me in, but please be gentle."

Danny laughed while George, red-faced, scrambled to his feet. "Ms. Davenport?" He stuck out his hand. "I'm Detective George Ramirez and this"—he pointed to Danny who stood beside him—"is Assistant District Attorney Danielle Soto."

Ellen Davenport shook George's hand, but her eyes were on Danny. Her gaze was penetrating, and Danny couldn't look away from the piercing blues.

"Nice to meet you, Ms. Soto. I'm Ellen Davenport."

The words broke the trance and Danny looked down to see Ellen's outstretched hand. She reached out, touched, and held. "Danny. Call me Danny."

Ellen's eyes twinkled, which didn't do much for Danny's ability to focus. "Danny, it is. Shall we sit down?"

A few beats later, Danny realized she was still holding Ellen's hand and reluctantly let go. "Sure, absolutely. Thanks for seeing us on such short notice."

As she settled into her chair, Danny took a deep breath to calm her nerves. She was thrown, and not just by the revelation that Ellen Davenport, Executive Director of National Alpha Nu, wasn't a little old lady. No, Ellen was model tall and beautiful. And young. Well, not college young, but young enough.

"How old are you?"

What the fuck? The question had tumbled out of her rambling thoughts and into spoken words. Rude, crass, and none of her business.

"Thirty-five. Am I under investigation?"

Well, you weren't until I met you. Now, I want to know everything about you. Danny pushed her inappropriate thoughts away. No way was she ever going to know anything else about this captivating woman now that she'd blown her opening by asking the dumbest question ever. Too bad, since her long dormant libido had come to full attention. She didn't need to look over at George to know he was staring at her like she'd grown an extra head.

"No, you are not under investigation. I'm sorry for being so blunt. When I learned that Mrs. Lawson was on the board, I guess I expected..."

"You expected an office full of old biddies sitting around planning tea parties?" Ellen asked.

"Guilty as charged. Why don't you explain how this office works?" Safe subject. Danny vowed to keep the rest of the meeting purely professional.

"I'd be happy to. Alpha Nu has forty-three chapters at various college campuses around the country. In addition, we have twenty-four regional alumnae chapters. I run the national office, which sets policy, issues credentials, and serves as the hub for the various chapters. It's a pretty active position and I think they wanted to make sure whoever got the job was young enough to handle the high energy atmosphere."

Danny laughed at the well-intentioned dig delivered with a straight face. "Well, then you certainly seem to fit the bill."

"Glad you think so."

George cleared his throat and Danny felt the tips of her ears begin to burn with embarrassment. For a minute, she'd completely forgotten he was in the room. That she was here on a case. To talk to a potential witness. A beautiful smile, a teasing manner, and a refreshing bluntness—everything about Ellen Davenport made her forget who she was, why she was here, and most importantly, why she'd been avoiding beautiful women.

Unacceptable. Time to get to the point and then get out. "We understand Martha Lawson had a board meeting scheduled the day she was…the day she died. Detective Ramirez has some questions for you about that." She turned to George and willed him to take the lead.

"Ms. Davenport—"

Ellen held up a hand. "Ellen, please. Ms. Davenport brings to mind old biddies, don't you think?"

He grinned and Danny was glad and a little jealous she wasn't the only one captivated by Ellen. "Okay. Ellen, we're trying to track all of Mrs. Lawson's activity on the day she died. Sometimes that includes looking into what she was scheduled to do, but didn't wind up doing."

"So, your investigation isn't focused on the sorority itself?"

"Excuse me?"

George appeared genuinely puzzled, but Danny read the scene and interjected. "She wants to know if the sorority is in any kind of legal trouble. You know, so she can consult with their lawyers. Am I right, Ellen? I imagine the sorority has a fleet of lawyers."

"Fleet is probably an overstatement, but you've got the point. Just doing my job."

"We have no reason to believe that Mrs. Lawson's death is connected to the sorority in any way." Danny conjured a mental image of tea-sipping sorority alumnae plotting the demise of one of their own, but her humor was quickly tempered by the dark memory of the torture inflicted on Martha Lawson. "Piecing together her activity on the day she died is a standard part of the investigation."

"Is it standard for someone other than the police to be conducting the investigation?"

"Not sure what you mean."

"I thought I heard Detective Ramirez introduce you as a prosecutor, not a police officer."

Beautiful and smart. Ellen Davenport was proving to be very interesting. Danny scrambled for a response that didn't give away the real reason for her involvement. "I'm part of a pilot program where a prosecutor is assigned to the homicide division. Theory is I can do a better job prosecuting the case if I'm in on the investigation from the beginning." She conveniently left out the part about how these particular murders were the impetus for the pilot program. She watched Ellen's face to see if she was buying it. Why wouldn't she? What did a woman who ran a sorority know about criminal procedure?

Ellen's expression settled into acceptance. "Sounds efficient and I'm happy to help. I'll tell you everything I know."

For the next few minutes, Ellen answered George's questions without hesitation. Danny watched their exchange, but she only heard about every other word, distracted as she was by Ellen. Her composure, her wit. Her legs. Damn, her legs were long. And fit. And bare.

"Here's a copy of the agenda for the meeting she missed." Ellen handed a sheet of paper to George who Danny realized was standing again. The interview was over and she hadn't said a word. Ellen probably thought the pilot program was bunk, or more likely, that she was a dolt. As George thanked Ellen for her time, Danny pulled a business card from her pocket, scrawled her cell on the back, and waited for an opportunity.

Ellen turned from George and winked at her. Winked. Unable to resist the signal, Danny thrust the card her way. "You can call me anytime. I mean anytime you have information. About the case. If you think of anything else."

Ellen took one end of the card and held it for a moment before Danny let go. Their fingers were only an inch apart. "Thank you. I think we covered everything, but you never know what might come up. Rest assured, you will be the first person I call."

As Ellen tucked the card away, Danny silently prayed something would come up.

Chapter Four

Wow. Ellen sank into her chair and let out a deep breath. When she'd gotten the call from Detective Ramirez, she'd envisioned a couple of burly cops in uniform showing up to ask questions. Never in a million years did she think Detective Handsome and his beautiful Latina attorney sidekick would appear instead. Those two should hang out together all the time—they made a striking couple.

No, Danny had the edgy feel of a truly single woman. Ellen flashed on the way Danny had stared at her legs through the entire interview. And then her verbal stumbles when it came time to focus on actual work. She'd bet her life savings that Danny Soto wasn't involved with Ramirez or anyone else. Which was dangerous because Danny intrigued her. She'd be crazy not to be attracted, and it was obvious Danny returned the compliment. She'd put aside her own personal life when Vivian had gone into Cedar Acres. Maybe it was time for a little extracurricular activity.

She glanced at the calendar on her desk. Alpha Nu alums had a regular mixer every other month, and the next one was in a few days at a new club in a hotel downtown. Maybe she'd buy a new dress, shoes—something to show off her legs, and check out the scene. She leaned back in her chair, closed her eyes, and imagined Danny at the club. Leaning against the bar. Dressed in a more casual version of the tailored suit she'd worn today. Her collar open wide, offering a tantalizing view of her cleavage. The same electricity that had pulsed between them in the simple exchange of a business card now surged off the charts.

"Ellen, are you okay?"

Ellen opened her eyes and lunged forward at the sound of Jill's voice. "Um, yeah. Guess you caught me napping."

Jill gave her a puzzled look. "Sounded like you were in pain. You need anything?"

She was in pain, but not the kind Jill meant. "No, I'm good."

"You look tired. All work and no play, yada, yada. Why don't you take the rest of the afternoon off? I can handle any calls that come in."

Ellen looked at her watch. It was four o'clock. Maybe a couple of extra hours of downtime would be good. "Okay, I'll take you up on it." Jill started to leave the room, but Ellen called her back. A thought had been nagging at her ever since Danny and the detective had left her office. "How much trouble would it be for you to get me a list of alumnae that have died in say the last year?"

"No trouble at all. I keep a running list for the slide show memorial at the annual board meeting. You want me to print you a copy?"

"Sure. I'll take it with me if you have a second to print it now." To cover the odd request, she added, "I might do a feature for the next newsletter."

Ellen waited until Jill left before looking through the list. So far this year, seven alumnae had died, most of the tedious stuff of getting old like heart disease. But one name stood out. Joyce Barr had died a brutal death a few months before. Ellen remembered talking to the family who hadn't been shy about sharing the details. Detective Ramirez and Danny had been pretty circumspect about the exact nature of Marty's death, and Ellen hadn't asked her family, not wanting them to relive the tragedy, but perhaps there was a connection. What were the chances that two alumnae of the sorority had both been killed so close in time?

She reached into her pocket and retrieved Danny's business card. Danielle F. Soto, Assistant District Attorney. It looked so official, completely at odds with the looks Danny had been giving her during the interview. Danny had scrawled her cell number on the card, her handwriting bold and sure. Before she could think her way out of it, Ellen punched the numbers into her cell and waited through the rings.

"Soto."

Brash, abrupt. This voice was all business. Ellen considered hanging up. Then she remembered business was why she called in the first place. "Danny, it's Ellen. Ellen Davenport."

The voice warmed. "Hi. Didn't I just leave your office?"

"How far away are you?"

"Not far. George, I mean Detective Ramirez, just dropped me off at the courthouse."

"Oh."

"Oh?"

Ellen had held out some hope Danny would still be in the building. That she would come back upstairs. They would talk. Then maybe grab a drink. Dinner. And whatever else might follow. Ridiculous. If Danny had still been in the building, Detective Ramirez would be with her. They'd come together. She'd let her mind wander past the bounds of reality. Time to get grounded.

But reality whooshed past. "I thought of something that might be relevant to Marty's, Mrs. Lawson's, case. If you were still around, I was going to suggest we grab a drink and discuss it. But you probably don't drink on the job, right?"

Danny's laugh was delicious. "That's mostly TV. And mostly cops. Actually, it's kind of late in the day and a drink would be terrific. Shall I pick you up?"

She'd said yes. Thrown off balance by the quick acceptance of her invite, Ellen struggled to maintain control. It'd been so long since she'd done anything for her own personal fun, but she didn't want to be without her own car. Having Danny pick her up sent a stronger signal than she wanted. "Pick the place and I'll meet you."

"Perfect. Meet me at Adair's in Deep Ellum. In about a half hour? Do you know it?"

"I've never been, but I recognize the name. Half hour's perfect."

"Great, see you then."

She set her phone on her desk and immediately considered calling Danny back, and canceling. What had she been thinking? She could barely remember the last time she'd been on a date. Probably last year when her friend Diane had set her up with an engineer who spent the entire evening talking about circuits and bandwidth. Surely it hadn't been that long.

Maybe it had. She wished she had a change of clothes at the office, since her suit was wrinkled and the coffee stain on her shirt wasn't going anywhere. But if she changed, then Danny would know she'd dressed just for meeting her. And it wasn't really a date. She'd called Danny to talk to her about the case. Anything more personal would be spontaneous, incidental. Careful and cautious as she usually was, she found herself hoping for spontaneity.

Chapter Five

Ten minutes had already passed. If she didn't hustle she'd be late. Ellen grabbed her keys, phone, and purse and dashed out of the office.

Deep Ellum was only a few blocks from downtown. She drove by the hotel where the Alpha Nu mixer would be held later in the week. Sleek and trendy. Typical Alpha Nu. She continued east on the downtown streets, crossing into the eclectic neighborhood of Deep Ellum. She looked hard for Adair's, but she circled the block several times without a sighting. Finally, she pulled over and consulted her phone for directions. Chagrined to learn she'd driven past the bar more than once, she focused on finding a place to park.

When she finally pushed through the doors at Adair's, she felt more rumpled than when she had left her office. She took a deep, calming breath and looked around the crowded room.

"Can I get you a beer?"

She turned to face Danny, who did not look rumpled at all. She'd taken the time to change out of the suit she'd been wearing earlier. Tight, dark blue jeans, a crisp white shirt, and a fitted black leather jacket transformed Danny from lawyer to date.

Business. She was here on business. Business with beverages. "How about a glass of red wine?"

Danny shook her head. "Some other time. Actually, make that some other place. I'm fairly certain that if they have wine here it'll be poured from a box."

"Beer then. Whatever you're having." Ellen was determined to be a good sport even though beer wasn't her thing. When Danny returned from the bar a minute later with two beer cans in her hand, she wished she'd asked for water instead. "No glasses?"

"What?" Danny looked at the beer she held outstretched. "Oh. Yeah, no glasses. I could ask for a mug, but don't make me. I have a reputation to protect."

A reputation for drinking beer straight out of the can. Now that was worth protecting. Ellen couldn't deny she'd had a very different kind of evening in mind. Maybe a martini or two, or a bottle of wine, shared in a nice club with soft music, maybe even a live band, playing in the background. Kicking it over a couple of cans of beer wasn't the kind of date she'd ever imagined.

Probably for the best. Business. Business. I'm here to talk business. She silently repeated the mantra, while Danny found them a booth. As they worked their way through the happy hour crowd, every other person they met clapped Danny on the shoulder, offering "How's it goings?" and "What're you up tos?" She watched, admiring the easy way Danny interacted with everyone she met. Admiring her legs and her butt in those jeans. Business? Who was she kidding? She could've told Danny what she'd learned over the phone. No, she was here because of the spark between them and her own hopes that a business drink might lead to a casual evening.

As they slid into their booth, Danny focused her attention on her. "Are you hungry? They have great burgers here."

"I had a really big salad at lunch. Still full." Ellen bit her tongue before she could say another word. The woman offers up a burger and you say salad? Key that up as the stupidest thing you could've said. I may as well hang a sign on my head that says, "I'm so not into you."

Except that would be a lie. A big one. She scrambled to recover. "I'll have to come back when I'm hungry and try one. A burger."

"Do I make you nervous? You seemed so put together at your office. Unflappable."

Had she? She hadn't been trying, but she supposed she had felt more comfortable at her own office instead of here, on what was clearly Danny's turf. Danny, who'd seemed rattled at the office, appeared perfectly at ease in this dive. She struggled for an answer that wouldn't make her seem like a freak. "Not nervous, but I am anxious. I found some information you might be interested in."

Danny raised her eyebrows and Ellen plunged in. "After you left, I went through the files. Do you remember hearing about Joyce Barr? She died earlier this year. Not from natural causes. The police determined it was a suicide, but her family was never convinced. There was a small article in the paper at the time."

"And how do you know her family?" Danny's tone was even, and Ellen had a hard time gauging her interest level.

"Well, that's the point. Joyce Barr is, or was, an Alpha Nu alum. She graduated from a different university than Marty, but don't you think that's odd? Two Alpha Nu alumnae died under suspicious circumstances within a few months of each other?"

"How many Alpha Nu alumnae are there?"

Ellen stared down at her beer, suddenly feeling very foolish. The alumnae association had thousands of members, not including the graduates who'd never bothered to sign up with an alumnae chapter. Danny had a good point. "Tons. Look, I just thought maybe Joyce's death might be like Marty's. That maybe there is a connection." She waited, but Danny only shook her head. Realizing she'd been off base, she said, "I get your point. People die every day. Don't worry, I'm not a conspiracy theorist or anything." She half stood and shoved an envelope into Danny's hand. "Here's the information I have on Joyce. Use it or not. You said to call if I thought of anything. Sorry I bothered you."

Danny reached out a hand to stop her departure. "Hey, don't go. I did ask you to call. It's just that in my line of work, I have to be able to separate coincidences from significant facts. If I don't, some defense attorney will do it for me and make me look bad."

"I bet that's hard."

"What?"

"Making you look bad."

Danny blushed ever so slightly and Ellen wondered what had gotten into her. Despite her earlier touch of nerves, now her confidence level was off the charts. She'd usually never make such bold statements, but even Danny's brush-off about the "evidence" she'd discovered didn't deter her from flirting. She hoped her actions came across as flirting. It'd been so long since she'd engaged in the behavior. She wasn't entirely sure she knew what she was doing or even wanted to take the risk.

What's the worst thing that could happen? Danny could be all business? Well, then they'd just be back to how they started. She pushed the point by parroting back Danny's earlier words. "Do I make you nervous? You seemed so unflappable just a minute ago."

"Is that so? A large part of being a trial lawyer is maintaining a poker face. Can't blame me if it slips every now and then."

"Maybe I'm hoping I'm the reason." Ellen reached for the can in front of her, and drowned the bare truth of her statement in a big gulp of now warm beer.

"You might be. As I recall, I was a bit of a mess when we met this afternoon."

"Were you?"

Danny grinned. "Like you couldn't tell. I swear I'm usually much better at playing the part of the badass."

"Badass, huh?" Ellen cocked her head. "Yeah, I can see that. I suppose you're used to getting whatever you want." Danny shifted in her seat. Had she touched a nerve? Maybe she wasn't used to women calling her out on her flirty ways. Ellen switched subjects to ease the tension. "How long have you worked with the DA's office?"

"Just over seven years."

"And you find it fulfilling?"

"Fulfilling? Yes, definitely. Plenty of attorneys work for the DA's office just to gain trial experience, but I'm in it for the long haul. I get a lot of personal satisfaction knowing that what I do helps in some small way to keep our community safe. How about your work? Is working for a sorority fulfilling?"

"Do I detect a hint of sarcasm?"

Danny shook her head. "No, really, I was serious."

"I'm pretty sure I don't do anything to keep our streets safe, but sororities definitely provide a sense of community to women during college and after. Active alumnae like Marty help dozens of young women make connections with former graduates who can serve as mentors and help them find jobs."

Danny reached across the table and curled her fingers into Ellen's. "You sound very passionate about what you do."

"My mother says I'm a passionate person, but she doesn't mean it as a compliment." The minute the words fell from her lips, she longed to bite them back. Distracted by the heat of their touch, she'd veered into unplanned territory. Danny's next question doomed further conversation.

"Do your parents live in Dallas?"

Ellen grabbed her beer and murmured an unintelligible answer as she took a healthy draught. Stupid. Stupid. Stupid. Her fantasy of a few drinks followed by whatever fun Danny was up for didn't include getting personal. She scrambled for a change of subject that would keep things light and keep her private life private. What's your favorite color? Favorite food? Favorite car? Desperate, she blurted, "You and Detective Ramirez seem to work well together." There. An observation. Rhetorical. At most, Danny would talk about work and work talk was safe talk.

"Did you have another reason you wanted to meet?"

She hadn't anticipated the non sequitur. "You mean besides to tell you about Joyce?" Ellen stalled. She knew what Danny was asking, but her confidence crumbled in the face of a direct question. "I guess I... Well, I hoped..."

The sharp ring of the phone on the table saved her rambling. Both of them glanced down at the display and Danny muttered, "Damn it." She reached for the phone and swiped the answer key. "Soto. Whatcha got?"

A couple of brief words later, she ended the call. "I have to go."

"Hot date?"

"He's hot, but he's not a date." She stood and tossed a ten on the table. "Have another beer on me. Sorry I have to run."

"No problem. I understand."

Danny started toward the door, but came back, leaned down, and whispered in Ellen's ear. "Next time maybe I can stay longer and you can tell me what you really wanted."

Ellen waited until Danny was completely out of sight before she climbed out of the booth. She set the ten-dollar bill on the tray of a passing waitress and left the bar. Danny's words echoed and the tickle of her breath lingered.

Next time. She hoped there was a next time.

❖

Danny cleared the door of the bar and sprinted toward her truck. She hadn't expected another call so soon. The timing sucked, but when she considered that George had his life interrupted on a regular basis, she resolved it was a small price to pay to be involved in a big case. And this was shaping up to be a whopper. George had been brisk on the phone: "We've got another one." He'd given her the address and hung up. She knew the neighborhood and accelerated toward it while thinking about the woman she'd left behind.

It was clear Adair's wasn't Ellen's kind of place. Danny had her pegged as a cosmos and couches, not cans and hardback booths kind of woman, but Ellen had taken the dive in stride. One check in the plus column. And she was attractive and quick-witted. Checks two and three. The attraction between them was palpable, and she suspected Ellen's motive for meeting in person to share her nugget of information was a smokescreen. Perfectly fine by her since she was already plotting an opportunity to see Ellen again. She glanced at the envelope Ellen had given her and vowed to follow up.

A few minutes later, Danny pulled up in front of the address, but she had to circle the block to find a parking space. Patrol officers, detectives, and a crime scene unit took up the area in front of the house. She pushed her way through the crowd of gawking neighbors and flashed her district attorney badge to the young cop who stood guard at the edge of the yard. She found George deep in conversation with the medical examiner, and interrupted them. "Seriously, George, we have to stop meeting like this. I was about to have dinner with a hot date."

She watched as he tried to hide a shocked expression. Only took a few seconds before he quipped, "And miss the fun? Be glad you didn't eat dinner. I had a rack of ribs and potato salad before I got the call. The perfect food for a bloody crime scene."

"Ick. Maybe if you'd stop talking about it, you'd feel better. Besides, you should be used to this stuff since you see it all the time."

George shook his head. "You never get used to it."

Danny figured that was probably true. Hard to believe less than an hour ago, she'd been in the presence of a beautiful woman and now she was in the presence of evil. Rita Randolf, spread-eagle on her bedroom floor, noose around her neck. Dead. Just like the others. "This is number four. He's escalating."

"You sound like that hot chick from *Criminal Minds*."

"Which one? And does your wife know you fantasize about other women?"

"I think she counts on it."

"Seriously, Alvarez and the Chief are about to go crazy trying to keep a lid on this before it gets out that we have a serial killer on our hands. Shit, it's only been a little more than a week since the last one. He could strike again at any time."

"You're so cheery. Why don't you wait outside while I talk to the crime scene folks? I'll be right out."

Danny wanted to stick around, but she knew she was mostly in the way. If George wasn't around to run interference, the rest of the law enforcement crowd combing the house would have run her out a while ago. True, they were all on the same side, but she knew they viewed her as an overseer, sent to make sure they knew how to do their jobs.

They were partly right. Alvarez wanted to make sure that if these murders did turn into a high profile case, his office was involved from the beginning, and every aspect of the investigation would stand up under intense press and public scrutiny. She went out front and scanned the crowd while she waited for George. Maybe the killer was lurking among the neighbors, watching the police pick apart his handiwork. They usually did on TV. If she was a character on *Criminal Minds*, she'd probably know what she was looking for, but she didn't have a clue what a person who could do the damage she'd just seen would look like.

"Danny, come in here. I want to show you something."

She turned at the sound of George's voice and followed him back into Randolf's bedroom. Danny noticed the medical examiner, Dr. Winter, in the corner of the room, dictating notes into a digital recorder.

"What's up?" Danny asked.

George pointed to the body. "There are a couple of differences here."

"You think we have a different killer?"

"Hard to tell," he said. "Everything else is the same, but there are additional markings on the body. If we had a copycat, I'd expect to see details missing, not added. We've managed to keep a lid on the specifics. Would be pretty unusual if a copycat added their own touches."

"Show me."

George walked her over, using a path he and the others had taken to minimize their presence in the room. "Doc, can you point out to Soto what you found?"

Danny knew Dr. Olivia Winter well. She'd used her as a witness in numerous trials and was impressed by how well she performed on the stand, even under the most intense cross-examination. She squatted next to the sturdy, practical doctor and followed along as she pointed out her findings.

"See these marks on her thighs? These weren't present on the other bodies. They almost look like the killer was trying to draw a picture. Small arrows or spikes of some kind. Why do you think the killer went in for these extras?"

Danny shook her head. She didn't have a clue, but she knew it was significant. A defense attorney would have a field day pointing out the differences at trial. If she couldn't offer a plausible explanation, then she would have delivered a big load of reasonable doubt to the other side. Unacceptable. "George, let's talk, but first make sure the CSU techs get every angle of these markings. And have them get me copies by tomorrow." She walked away before Winter or George could continue the conversation with her. She wanted to speculate, but not here, where everyone involved in the investigation could listen in.

Twenty minutes later, George walked out front and joined her in the yard. Hands crossed over his chest, he gazed at the now dwindling crowd.

"See the killer?" she asked.

"Maybe."

"How do you know what you're looking for?"

"They look all different kinds of ways. Mostly, I'm seeing who gives me a creepy feeling. I trust my gut way more than I trust my eyes."

She could relate. During trial, she had to rely on instinct. Strike this juror or that one? Ask one more question, or save it for argument? Her gut rarely let her down. "Are you done here?"

"Yes. I've got a few officers canvassing the neighborhood, and I've got to write up my report. Let's get the same warrants that we got for Lawson."

"Yep. Something's off, but there's definitely a connection between this murder and the others. Alvarez's going to want a report tonight. He's not going to be happy."

"I hear that. You going to call him now?"

"Night's already shot. May as well get this over with."

"Sorry you had to bail on your date. Anyone I'll ever get to meet?"

Danny started to say, actually, you already know her, but she bit her tongue. George and her family hadn't tried to hide their concern after her last breakup, and she knew they would all be relieved to hear she was wading back into the dating pool. But she wasn't ready to answer a ton of questions about a new woman in her life, especially not one that they'd just questioned in a case. "Maybe. Someday." She fiddled with her badge while she spoke the words to keep him from reading anything into her expression.

He clapped her on the shoulder. "I won't bug you about it. You should date up a storm. Give all us married Joes something to dream about."

Danny faked a smile. A dating machine, that was her. Yeah, right. "Frankly, right now I'd rather go on a dozen bad blind dates then have to tell Alvarez what's going on."

She made the call on her way home and, as she anticipated, Alvarez grilled her on the details and told her he wanted full reports by noon the next day. She sent a text to George, letting him know she'd need to be fully briefed before then and then rummaged in her bare kitchen for something to eat. *I should've had a burger at Adair's.* Crime scene or not, at least a few bites would've staved off the intense hunger she felt now.

Had Ellen stuck around to eat? Doubtful. Maybe she should've suggested somewhere with a little more swank. She stopped mid thought as self-doubt crept in. She wouldn't be suggesting anywhere else because Ellen had called her about a case, and there was nothing else to discuss. Besides, she didn't need to try to impress a woman like Ellen with fancy places that weren't normally on her budget. Her modest county income was comfortable, but not lavish. Beer and burgers fit nicely in her budget, and besides, she liked simplicity. No need to get mixed up with someone whose tastes didn't mesh with hers. No need to get mixed up with anyone at all.

But she did owe Ellen an apology for rushing out. She pulled out her cell phone. Damn. She only had an office number. If she tried hard enough—maybe called George—she might be able to come up with a home number, but then he would ask questions and Ellen might think she was a bit of a stalker. She'd call Ellen in the morning. On her office line. Like a professional.

Right. Because her desire to see that smile, hear that laugh, and admire those legs again was purely professional.

Whatever.

Chapter Six

Ellen pulled into the parking garage the next morning, tired and grumpy. She'd gone by Cedar Acres after she'd left Adair's, hoping to salvage the evening by doing something productive, but her visit had been anything but. Her mother was stuck on whatever was bothering her before, insistent that she speak to her husband, certain that it had to be right away. There was no consoling her, no breaking through. It was as if she wasn't even there.

When she'd gotten home after seeing her mother, Ellen had called her father, but he wasn't in or didn't care to answer. She left a scathing message, not worried about running him off with her anger. Not like he could get any farther away. She didn't feel any better for the venting. A glass of wine later, she fell asleep in her clothes on the couch, waking up this morning to the sound of a text on her phone from Jill, letting her know she had a visitor at the office.

She consulted her calendar before taking a quick shower. She didn't have any appointments scheduled. Jill usually ran off solicitors, so whoever was waiting must be important or persuasive enough to merit a pass from the gatekeeper. She'd sent a text asking the identity of her early morning visitor, but Jill's response—*you won't regret coming in early*—had been vague at best. Forgoing her usual coffee, she had dressed and sped to the office, hoping her blouse matched her suit.

Her phone rang while she was waiting for the elevator. Assuming it was Jill to ask where the hell she was, she answered without glancing at the number displayed on the screen. "I'll be right there."

"Ellen?"

"Dad?" She hadn't expected a call back, and she certainly hadn't expected a tentative voice on the other end of the line. "This isn't a great time. I'm running late." For what, she didn't know, but anything was better than having this conversation in the lobby of her building.

"I know you're angry with me."

No defensiveness, just the simple statement. It was hard to keep her anger going when she heard the pain in his voice. "Angry isn't the word. Frustrated. Disappointed. You can change all that. It's an easy fix."

"Not for me it isn't. I don't expect you to understand."

"Do it for me." She hated herself for the pleading tone of her voice. If she thought anything else would work, she would've tried it first. Her fear was that even her most pathetic plea wouldn't move him.

Her fear was well-founded.

"I'll think about it."

Death knell. She'd heard it enough when she was younger. "I'll think about it," "maybe," "we'll see." All half promises she heard countless times, only her adult self wasn't about to give her usual tacit response. "Well, you better think about it soon. You may not care about her anymore, but I'm still your daughter and you can't go to court to get rid of our connection. I need you, Dad. I wouldn't ask if I didn't."

She clicked off the line before he could respond, unable to stand any empty platitudes. He'd show up or not, but she wasn't going to hold her breath waiting to see which.

When she finally reached her office, she heard voices and remembered Jill's urgent message. She wasn't in the mood for an unexpected visitor, but Jill popped out, cheery and exuberant. "Hey, Ellen. Danielle Soto's in your office." In response to her look of surprise, Jill added, "She made me promise not to tell you she was the early morning visitor. I'd get you coffee, but I think she brought you some." Without another word, she took off down the hall and Ellen stood fixed in place. Danny was the surprise visitor? With coffee?

She walked into her office and found Danny sitting on her couch. Comfortable, beautiful, and with coffee. Two cups. She cleared her throat to announce her presence.

"Did we have an appointment?"

Danny stood up. "No. I wanted to apologize in person for my hasty departure last night." She reached down and lifted a cup off the table. "And bring you a drink you might like better than the one I offered at the bar."

Ellen instantly felt like a jerk for her brash welcome, and she smiled to soften her words. "I'll give you my right arm if there's coffee in that cup."

"Prepare to lose an arm." Danny handed Ellen the cup. "It's a mocha. I imagine the whipped cream has probably melted by now, but there might still be sprinkles."

"If I'd known you were coming, and bearing coffee, I would have been on time." Hell, she would have been early. And she would've worn her favorite suit. "Do you deliver coffee to all the women you interview about a case?"

"Not all of them."

"Cagey answer, Ms. Soto."

"Actually, I have a couple of follow-up questions."

"Oh." Ellen bemoaned her inability to mask her disappointment. Of course Danny was here on business. She was working on a case to which she was tangentially connected. "Why don't you have a seat? I'll help however I can."

"I can't stay and it'll only take a minute. Will you have dinner with me?"

"What?"

"Dinner? With me? Tonight?"

"Are those your 'few' questions?"

"Well, that's really only one. The others were something along the lines of 'should I pick you up' and 'what kind of food do you like' since clearly burgers and beer aren't your thing."

"That's a lot of questions."

"Are you stalling so you can figure out a way to say no?"

"Maybe I'm stalling so you don't rush off."

Danny walked toward the door. "I wish I didn't have to, but I have to be somewhere"—she glanced at her watch—"about twenty minutes ago. You have my number. Give me a call if you make up your mind."

"I don't need to. Yes and yes. Italian. Do you need my address?"

"If I told you I already have it would you think I'm a stalker?"

"I'd think you were resourceful."

"Keep thinking that. I'll see you at seven."

Ellen watched Danny leave her office, her eyes firmly fixed on her nice ass. Seven o'clock couldn't come soon enough.

❖

When Danny reached the courthouse, she made a quick stop to talk to the investigator assigned to her court. She handed him the information she'd gotten from Ellen and asked him to find out what he could about Joyce Barr's death. She didn't think whatever he learned would amount to anything, and she didn't see any point stirring up shit until she found out more. With that task out of the way, she rushed through the doors of her boss's office suite twenty minutes late. Any reprimand would be totally worth it. Ellen was cute in the morning, when her sophisticated self gave way to a sleepy and slightly rumpled version. Coffee had been the perfect touch.

Danny studiously ignored the glare of her boss's secretary and when she wasn't looking, punched George on the arm for his not very well hidden smirk. Seconds later, Frank Alvarez appeared in the doorway and ushered them into his office, where the chief of police was waiting.

"Have a seat," Frank said. Danny and George settled into the two remaining chairs and waited for one of their bosses to start. Larry Dunbar, the chief of police, went first.

"This situation is already out of control. I'm getting pressure from the press and we're not going to be able to keep a lid on this much longer. Frank and I have placed a call to the Behavioral Analysis Unit of the FBI. They're sending two of their best out here first thing in the morning. They'll work with us, but for now, we retain control of this investigation." He paused and then added. "But one more dead body and I'm afraid we'll get shut out. That would be unacceptable. This is a Dallas case and it needs to be closed by the servants of this city. Are we clear?"

Danny nodded because it was expected, but she knew this was only a prelude to chaos. Once the feds arrived on the scene, the local U.S. Attorney would make a play for the case. She and George needed to huddle with their team and get a handle on the evidence they had so far.

"We're clear."

While George gave a rundown of the evidence they had so far, Danny realized her prospect for a date tonight was dwindling. They'd have to work round the clock, and even then it was unlikely they'd solve anything by morning. She'd leave here and head directly to the autopsy of the killer's latest victim, then meet with the crime scene folks to review the evidence they'd processed from the scene. This was the first time she'd been involved in an investigation this early on. Challenging, but definitely demanding. Not like her work was ever conducive to a personal life, and the last time she'd put a woman ahead of her work, she'd been burned. But she'd been looking forward to an evening with Ellen, more than she was looking forward to working on the case. As soon as the meeting was over, she pulled George aside and told him, "I need to make a call before we head over to the ME's office."

"No problem. I'll drive so you can talk."

"Well, uh…" She scrambled for a way to tell George she needed privacy without resorting to a lie. She gave up. "It's kinda private. Only take a sec."

"Girl?"

She nodded.

"I get it. Take your time. I'll head on down to the garage and pick you up out front."

Girl? Hardly. Ellen Davenport was full on woman, and she hated canceling their dinner. She called and practiced what she'd say through the rings.

"Hello?"

"Ellen, it's Danny."

"Are you standing outside with another cup of coffee?"

Danny blushed at her teasing tone. "I wish. I mean, no. I mean, I'm glad you enjoyed it. The coffee." She plowed ahead to cover her awkward opening. "Look, I'm sorry to do this, but something came up and—"

"Work something or personal something?"

"Work. Definitely work."

"You'll be late?"

"Too late for dinner."

"It's never too late for dinner if you're hungry."

Danny melted into the flirtatious direction this conversation was taking. "I'm pretty hungry."

"Well then, later tonight I expect you'll be starving."

"I imagine so."

"Why don't you come by when you're finished working and I'll feed you."

"It might be late."

"I'll be waiting."

"Okay, great. I'll text you when I'm on my way. Thanks for being such a good sport. I can't wait to see you." She hung up before the last bit of cool she possessed puddled on the floor. Ellen had flirted shamelessly and her best reply was "thanks for being such a good sport" and a giddy "I can't wait to see you"? What was it about this woman that made her stumble all over herself? She had no business getting so swept up into Ellen's charms. Thank goodness George wasn't standing there listening.

She made her way down the steps of the courthouse and climbed into George's waiting car. She'd never attended an autopsy before and she wasn't looking forward to seeing a dead body again. She glanced over at George and plotted a way to ask questions about how the autopsy would go down without losing his respect.

Either he was genius at reading her mind, or he just assumed no one knew as much as he did. "The first time is weird. We won't get there in time for rounds, but they actually do rounds—like you see on one of those shows, like *ER* or *Grey's Anatomy*. Of course they aren't trying to diagnose so they can make the person feel better, they are just trying to figure out what happened to cause their death. By the time we get there, the body will be in a room on a big silver table, with drains. There'll be scales and specimen bottles. It smells, although this one won't be too bad 'cause it wasn't like they fished her out of a lake or she laid around in the woods for days before we got to her."

"Anyone ever tell you you're gross?"

"All the time. Seriously, wouldn't you rather be prepared?"

As if anything could prepare her for the continued aftereffects of these vicious murders.

A few minutes later, they pulled up to the beautiful and fairly new offices of the Dallas County Medical Examiner. George led the way to Dr. Winter's office and they were promptly ushered in. Winter looked surprised to see Danny. "Olivia, my turn to watch you at work. Alvarez's orders. Hope you don't mind."

"Frank wants a set of eyeballs in the room? I understand. I've reviewed the file so far on this case. Like I said at the scene, it looks like there are some differences between this case and the others."

"I'm hoping you can clear that up for us. Do the differences indicate a copycat or is the killer escalating into more violent behavior?"

"Let's go find out." She led the way to the floors where the autopsies took place, narrating the features of the new complex as they walked. "In our old space, we were only able to do six autopsies at a time. Now we can do sixteen. We even have a special bay that will fit a car, so if the people on the scene aren't able to extract the body, we can look at it while it's still in the car." She spoke the final three words with such enthusiasm, Danny almost expected her to fist pump the air. As a fellow county employee used to dealing with mismatched furniture and scarce resources, she appreciated the doctor's excitement.

After they suited up in scrubs and booties, Danny and George followed Dr. Winter into her shiny, sterile showplace. Rita Randolf was already on the table in the center of the room. Naked. Before she could dwell on how sad Randolf appeared, Dr. Winter introduced her to a resident who would assist with the autopsy, Dr. Sebert. At Winter's direction, the younger doctor explained the preparation he had already done, including a summary of his external exam.

"Here"—he pointed to the abdomen—"you can see these markings are the same as the ones on the two prior victims. But, then look here." He directed their attention to the inner thigh. "See these? Like he was carving, or trying to draw a picture of something, but I have no idea what. Maybe he started to write a message, but was interrupted by something."

Danny forced her senses to stay in check and she stared again at the spiked marks she'd witnessed at the crime scene. Something about them signaled a memory, but she couldn't place it. "You have plenty of photos of these?"

"From every angle. They'll be compiled with the report, but I can e-mail them to you beforehand if you like."

George interjected. "We like. Anything you can get us on a preliminary basis would be most appreciated. We have lots of people breathing down our necks for information on this case."

Winter nodded. "I understand. Shall we begin?"

Rhetorical question. She had a scalpel in her hand and was ready to get to work. She placed the scalpel on the skin near Randolf's right shoulder, bowed her head, and held it there for a silent moment. Danny flicked a look at Sebert. He had his head bowed as well. Interesting. She would've thought the doctors would be more practical about their approach, but she appreciated their respect for the life they were about to examine. The life that wasn't, anymore.

At the first cut, Danny forced down rising bile, but didn't look away. Transfixed by the Y incision and the pulled back flesh, she shivered. Exposed, vulnerable. A ruthless killer had already violated this woman once. Now, they had to violate her again in order to catch him. Totally unfair, but totally necessary. For the next few hours, she watched as Winter and Sebert cut skin, sawed bone, and examined organs. Initial conclusion: elderly woman died of a gunshot wound. The tightening of the noose and the cuts had been inflicted postmortem. No overt sexual contact. Lab tests would be done to see if she'd been drugged, but nothing the medical professionals had learned today or would learn in the coming weeks would answer the one question that plagued Danny. The one question that would lead to the apprehension and conviction of the killer: Why?

Seven minutes until ten o'clock. Seven minutes until hot Danny Soto rang the bell. Ellen rearranged the pillows on the couch for the hundredth time, switched the lamp on the end table on and off and back on again, and straightened the painting on the wall. She studied her outfit, shook her head, and changed into a different sweater. One that hugged her breasts, showed a little cleavage. She hadn't planned the delay in their evening plans, but she couldn't be happier. A romantic dinner meant talking, sharing. Here, she had more control over the agenda and the only thing she planned to share was a healthy desire to fool around.

She had carefully hidden anything personal. Pictures, notes, even the mail. Since she'd moved her mother into Cedar Acres, she'd given up her apartment and moved back into her childhood home. Vivian had insisted she keep the place, and it was easier to stay here than it was to keep up with two homes. She'd gotten used to living in the home she'd grown up in, and had taken for granted how many memories permeated the many rooms, but tonight she didn't want any conversation starters about her personal life to derail her plans to get Danny undressed.

Now, it was only five minutes to ten.

She started to open a bottle of wine, but wondered if Danny might like something stronger. Lord knows she could use a stiff drink. She wasn't sure she remembered how to seduce a woman. Hard to believe she was even going to try. She paced her living room to work out her nerves.

Maybe Danny would be early. Maybe she wouldn't show at all. She could get a call with a legal emergency, whatever that meant. Maybe she would confiscate her phone the moment she came in the door. Danny wouldn't need a phone, or car keys, or anything other than her body for what Ellen had planned.

She jumped at the sound of the doorbell. Two minutes to ten. It had to be her. She swung the door wide and feigned a relaxed pose. "Come in."

"That was quick. Were you standing right by the door?" Danny checked her watch. "I'm one minute early."

Two, but who's counting. Ellen offered a nervous giggle and ushered Danny into her home. "Can I get you something to drink? Wine or something else?"

Danny's eyes twinkled. "No beer in cans?"

"I'm fresh out."

"I'll have whatever you're having."

"Whisky or wine. Your choice."

"It's been a whisky kind of day. Thanks."

The twinkle was gone and Ellen desperately wanted it back. She pulled two chunky crystal glasses from a cabinet in her dining room and rummaged in the back for the bottle she knew was there even though she'd never opened it. The thirty-year-old Scotch had been a gift, and she'd been saving it for a special occasion. A prelude to getting laid for the first time in a year seemed like a special enough occasion. She poured them both a healthy dose of the amber liquid and handed one glass to Danny who took a sip. Her eyes rolled back in her head and she said, "I'm not sure I should drink this."

"I'm sorry. I've never tried it. No good?"

"Exactly the opposite. Too good to get used to." Danny set the glass on the coffee table and stretched her arms over her head. "But exactly what I needed."

Ellen matched Danny's smile. "It was a gift."

"Better than I've ever tasted. Whoever gave you the gift obviously cared about you very much."

Ellen searched her memory. Isabella. She'd gone on three dates with her a few years ago. They didn't click and Ellen knew it on the first date, but she accepted the second and third because her mother had always told her she was too picky, that she should give people and opportunities a chance. Isabella had definitely been what her mother would have considered an opportunity—rich, good-looking, and clever. Ellen doubted she had given a second thought to the cost of the Scotch. To her it was a trifle.

She sensed Danny would think less of her for dating someone like Isabella, so she offered a slight untruth. "An alumna sent it to the office as a gift. I wound up with it." Partly true. Isabella was an alumna and she had picked her up at work that night, likely assuming Ellen would open the bottle and they'd wind up naked on her couch. Maybe the spirit would lead to nakedness tonight.

"Can't say I'm sorry you did."

"Would you like something to eat?" That's right. Fortify your date before you take advantage of her.

"I don't want to put you out."

Ellen pointed to the glasses of Scotch. "Grab those and follow me." She led the way to the kitchen. "Snacks okay? I have some antipasto and a few things I picked up from The Festive Kitchen in Snider Plaza. You know the place?"

"Can't say I do."

"Try this." Ellen picked up a bite and held it up to Danny's mouth. After a slight pause, Danny parted her lips and accepted the offering. Within seconds, she was groaning.

"You like?"

"I have no idea what that was, but it was amazing."

"Bacon apricot zinger."

"Zinger, eh? I still have no idea what that was, but my last meal was a slice of cold, greasy pizza about six hours ago. You could feed me pretty much anything and I'd wolf it down."

Ellen resisted the urge to reply with a salacious remark. Not yet. She lifted the tray and said, "Follow me." She led Danny into the living room and back into less suggestive conversation. "Hard day?"

"Definitely."

"Do you have a trial going on right now?"

"No, I've got other stuff going on."

She motioned for Danny to have a seat on the couch, as she set the tray of snacks on the coffee table. She smiled when Danny dug into the food. "Let me guess. You're still working on Marty's murder."

Danny coughed and set down the cracker she'd been chomping on. "Well, uh, yes. Kind of." She reached for her drink and took a healthy draught.

Cagey response. Maybe Danny didn't want to talk about work. Of course. She'd spent the entire day there, worked late, and the first thing Ellen did was ask her to relive it. She changed the subject.

"Tell me about you. Did you grow up in Dallas? Do you have family here?"

"Oak Cliff, born and bred. Went to Bishop Dunne High School. My parents still live in the house we grew up in, and my five brothers and sisters all live and work in Dallas. How about you?"

She'd been stupid to bring up family when it was the last thing she wanted to talk about. For the second time that evening, she offered a half-truth. "I grew up here too. Only child. Parents are still around." She moved quickly to change the subject to keep from having to lie anymore; although why she cared she couldn't really say. Maybe it was just that she didn't really want to be talking at all. She wanted to be doing. Doing Danny. She changed the subject to bide her time until

Danny had enough food and liquor to consider other comforts. "Do you like being a lawyer?"

"I do, especially being a prosecutor. I get to speak for the weak and vulnerable, or, in the case of people like Marty, for those who can no longer speak for themselves."

"Comforting to know you're on the case."

"It's a team effort. I just do my part."

Time to move things along. Ellen placed a hand on Danny's. "Are you modest about everything or just your work?"

Danny turned her palm up and curled her fingers into Ellen's grasp. "I don't think I've ever been called modest before. In fact, I answer freely to 'shark' and 'tiger.'"

"Only in the courtroom?" She could hear Danny's breath quicken and she took it as a signal to move closer. "Or are you a tiger everywhere?"

"I guess you'll have to let me know." Danny leaned back and tried to hide a yawn. "I'm sorry I got here so late. What do you say we make another date and try this all over again? I promise the restaurant I had picked out would make a much better start to the evening than me showing up late and tired on your doorstep."

Another date? Ellen couldn't think about another date when this one wasn't going anywhere, or at least not where she wanted. She wasn't interested in a romantic dinner, or romance in any form. She was interested in immediate gratification. Danny had struck her as the same. Had she misjudged? Only one way to find out. She closed the distance between them and slid a hand around Danny's waist, pulling her close. She grazed her lips against Danny's neck and whispered in her ear. "Are you too tired to enjoy the date you're on? Because I don't need dinner first, if you get my meaning."

She felt Danny sway, then turn her head. Their lips almost touched, the heat between them fused them both in place. She didn't move for fear of breaking the spell. She'd made the first move. Danny would have to make the second.

One beat passed. Then two. She couldn't take it any longer. She ran her hand up Danny's thigh as she leaned into her lips. For a split second, the surge of heat threatened to explode.

And then Danny made her move. Jerking back. Out of reach. The trance was broken, and it wasn't about fatigue. No, something else entirely made Danny withdraw. Ellen scrambled to pull her back. "Too quick? We can take our time. Another drink?"

Danny stood. "No, thanks. I need to go. I think we had different ideas about what this"—she waved her hand between them—"is about. Don't worry. I'm sure you can find plenty of others to enjoy your expensive Scotch."

She was out the door before Ellen could come up with a response. What the hell had just happened? She'd come on to a beautiful woman who'd asked her on a date, not the other way around. Was she that rusty that she didn't recognize an invitation when she got one? Well, there were plenty of other women in the world besides Danny Soto.

CHAPTER SEVEN

The drive home was long and Danny mentally kicked herself the entire way. A beautiful woman had served her expensive whisky, fancy food, and had started to feel her up, and she practically ran out the door. Now she was headed home alone and hungry in more ways than one. Ellen's closeness had definitely caused her to crave something, but it wasn't a one-night stand, and that was clearly all Ellen wanted.

It's what she should have wanted too. A good round of meaningless rolls in the hay might cure the loneliness she'd felt since Maria left. But she sensed meaningless sex might leave her lonelier than ever. She could almost see her mother wagging her finger, warning her she'd grow old alone. She'd finally met a woman she wanted to get to know, and the woman turned out to be a Casanova. Ironic didn't begin to describe the situation.

It would be so much easier to be the one on the other end. The one who didn't get caught up in feelings other than the immediate need to feel good. She'd assumed Ellen wouldn't be like that, but she wasn't sure why. Good little rich girl? No, it was something else. Classy. Interesting.

She washed away the evening with a long, hot shower. As she was toweling off, her phone rang and she rushed to answer, thinking maybe…

The number on the display was disappointing, but she answered anyway. "Hey, Ma."

"What are you doing? You sound out of breath."

Danny rolled her eyes. "I was taking a shower. You know, so I can be clean before I go to bed. I thought you'd be proud."

"Then why are you answering the phone? Go, bathe, be a good girl."

She knew better. "It's okay, Ma. I was done. What do you need?"

The sigh on the other end was heavy and long. "The list is long, but I didn't call to bother you with my troubles."

Then why did you call? Danny prayed for patience and tried another tack. Mama Soto would not be rushed. "Did you have a good day?"

"It started good, but then the toilet in the guest bathroom overflowed. I told your father to stay out of there to keep it nice, but he doesn't listen to me. And then when the plumber finally came, he said…"

Danny listened to her mother rail about the troubles of her day and sympathized with her father who had to endure her endless diatribes on a daily basis. The day could've been perfect by anyone else's standards, but Mama Soto would find something to complain about. She loved her mother, but then she didn't have to live with her.

She tucked the phone between her chin and shoulder and went in search of clothes, murmuring an occasional "oh" and "I can't believe that" in response to whatever new subject her mother addressed at the moment.

Dressed in boxers and tank and ready for bed, she finally cut to the chase by yawning audibly. Only took a moment for the expected response.

"It's late, dear. You should go to bed."

"Good idea, Ma. You sure there's nothing I can do for you?"

"No, dear. Get a good night's sleep."

"I will. Good night." Danny started to hang up, but a bellow from the other end of the line stopped her.

"Oh, wait!"

"Yes?"

"I remember what I called you about. Come to dinner Saturday night. For Joe's birthday. I'm making his favorites."

Of course you are. Danny's brothers were spoiled rotten. Joe may be forty years old, married, with kids, but on his birthday, his mommy treated him like a boy prince. Whatever she thought were his favorites were likely to have changed long ago, but he'd ooh and aah over his mother's creations like the proud son he was. For her birthday, Danny got to help cook like the little lady her mother wished she was.

"You can bring a date."

Danny sighed at her mother's hopeful tone. "Thanks, Ma, but it'll be just me."

When she was finally able to hang up, she was no longer tired. Restless, mind and body, she prowled her apartment, looking for something to occupy her thoughts. Did Ellen have a mother who nagged her to be more of a lady? Doubtful. She was the model woman— fashionable, pretty, and a gracious hostess. If the roles had been reversed and Danny had invited Ellen to her place, not that that would happen, then she would only have light beer in cans and questionably fresh potato chips to offer. Maybe she should've listened to her mother, learned more social skills, been more of a lady.

Right. She'd spent her life making her own way, breaking down barriers. She wasn't about to conform to the roles her mother and her mother's mother expected from her. The irony struck her hard again. She'd missed out tonight because she hadn't been willing to do what was expected of her. Ellen had wanted sex and she'd expected Danny to deliver. Why shouldn't she? People had a right to their expectations. Who was she to defy them?

Tomorrow. Tomorrow she'd call Ellen. See if she'd agree to another date, or whatever she wanted to call it. Like it would kill her to have a good time. If Ellen didn't mind being a temporary stop, then why should she care? She crawled into bed and closed her eyes. She still wasn't tired, but now at least she had a plan to take care of her restlessness.

❖

"Jill, do you know where the invite to the mixer at The Joule is? I swear it was sitting right here." Ellen pawed the contents of her desk, without success. Seconds later, Jill strolled into her office with the invite in her hand.

"I thought you wanted me to decline."

"I changed my mind."

"I'll RSVP for you. Are you bringing a date?"

"Hardly." If last night's disaster was any indication, her small foray back into the dating scene was a misstep on the road to what she really wanted. Release. Clearly, she'd sent Danny the wrong signals. Or maybe Danny just wasn't into her. She'd spent the morning torn between whether she should give her a call or just move on. Maybe all she needed was a night in a bar with drinks, lowered inhibitions, and an opportunity to get laid without having to exchange a bunch of personal information first.

"You work too much." Jill sat down across from her desk, her gaze was full of concern.

"I work just enough. I just haven't allowed myself a personal life in a while."

"Why not?"

"Oh, no particular reason." Ellen cursed inwardly at her over share. No way was she going to start a personal discussion with her assistant about the personal life she worked so hard to compartmentalize. Where would she start anyway? With her mother who was tucked away in a home and only remembered who she was half the time? Or her father who moved across the country to hide from a life he could no longer handle? Her present life dictated her future. Relationships didn't work.

Maybe she was going about this in the wrong way. She shouldn't have made a date. She hadn't dated in a while, but she still remembered that the process was about getting to know someone, and as much as she wanted to get to know Danny, she had no desire for Danny to get to know her. She'd decided to settle for sex, but she'd forgotten to send Danny the memo, and now she was pissed at her heavy-handed attempt to circumvent the whole getting-to-know-you process. She should've been honest about wanting to hook up. Who knows, Danny might have been relieved to know she didn't have to work hard to get between the sheets.

She should call. Apologize at least. She owed Danny an explanation. Or maybe she just didn't want Danny to think she was a slut. If only she could figure out a way to offer an explanation without Danny realizing she had kind of assumed she was a slut as well. It wasn't a crime to want to sleep with a woman, was it? She'd meant it as a compliment. Really.

Jill stood up and Ellen realized she'd drifted off. She laughed off her mental struggle. "Maybe I'll find a date at the mixer. If I brought a date, I wouldn't be able to look around."

"Kind of looked like that attorney was checking you out. Maybe you should see if she's free."

"Really, you thought she was checking me out?"

"Uh, yeah. And she brought you coffee. First thing in the morning. Definitely not one of her regular duties. Pretty sure she's into you. Maybe you should ask her out. Besides, have you been to one of these mixers in a while?"

Instant guilt. She really should attend these events since they were part of the coordinated networking efforts of her office, but her desire to avoid social situations combined with dealing with her mother's affairs meant she'd sent Jill and other staff members in her place to these after-hours events. "No, why?"

"They tend to be heavy on the cougar and less on eligible bachelorette set. Maybe cougar's what you're looking for, but I don't really see you hooking up with someone old enough to be your mother."

Ellen winced at the unintentional reference to her mother even as she tried to picture Vivian Davenport at a hip and trendy bar. Did not compute. Looked like she'd better find another source for the no strings hook-up. "Fine, I guess I won't be trolling for women at the mixer, but I should go. I've shoved a lot of these evening events on you and the rest of the staff. It's time I got more involved."

"I don't mind. Besides, it seems like you've had a lot going on. Anything you want to talk about?"

She did and she didn't. Her mother's admonitions echoed. Ladies, if they feel they must have a career, should not discuss their personal lives in the workplace. Her mother wasn't old enough to be that stodgy, but her own upbringing as a socialite had skewed her view of the world. Vivian's old-fashioned ways hadn't rubbed off on her, but Ellen stubbornly clung to her desire to keep up appearances. Maybe she wasn't that much different from her mother after all.

But then she remembered her behavior from the night before. Plying a date with alcohol, trying to get into her pants within minutes after inviting her in under other pretenses. No, she was vastly different from her dear old mother.

❖

Danny plucked the cup of coffee from George's grasp. "Did you bring lunch? Or do I have to survive on caffeine alone?"

He produced a bag from behind his back. "Only enough for us. No handouts for the feds in this bag."

She grabbed the bag of Dickey's barbecue out of his hand and prowled through the contents. She'd spent the entire morning at police headquarters and, since she'd skipped breakfast, she was starving. The closest restaurant was a place called Chicken and Things and she hadn't thought she was hungry enough to try any "things," but today she might be. She wolfed down half a chopped beef sandwich. "Are they here yet?"

"Just saw them with the chief. I expect they'll be throwing their weight around any minute. Although I suspect you might enjoy it, at least when it comes to one of them."

Danny swallowed her gulp of coffee, but before she could ask George what he meant, they were interrupted by the booming voice of Chief Larry Dunbar. "Soto, Ramirez, meet Special Agents Sarah Flores and Peter Buckner."

Danny wiped her mouth, fixed her face into a fake smile, and turned around to meet her nemesis.

A nemesis wasn't supposed to look this good. Agent Flores was tall, dark, and handsome. Dressed in a sharply tailored navy blue suit, she was every bit the cliché of an FBI agent. Her deep chocolate eyes were steady and commanding, but looking closer, Danny caught a hint of a grin in her eyes, the only crack in her G-woman façade. She reached out a hand.

It hung in the air. Guess the feds are too good to shake hands with us local folks. Whatever. Wasn't like Dallas was some Podunk town. The Dallas police were better equipped to handle a murder investigation than the feds who only caught these kind of cases if they were lucky.

"Are you offering that to me? The way you were chomping on it earlier, I'm a little scared to take it from you."

"What?" Danny frowned and looked down at her lonely hand. She still held half her sandwich, sauce dripping on the floor. She met Sarah's eyes. They were full on laughing now and she recognized the twitch of her face as a choked back smile. She smiled big. "You were wrong not to take it when you had the chance."

"I'll remember that when, or if, you ever offer me anything again."

Her voice dropped low as she delivered the last few words, leaving Danny no doubt that she wasn't talking about a sandwich. She'd been solid about hating these folks before they arrived, but now…Well, now Sarah Flores was striking and quick and she liked barbecue. What wasn't to like?

"This is Peter. He and I are part of the Bureau's Behavioral Analysis Unit."

Danny stuck her free hand Peter's way and he met it with a firm grasp, which surprised her because he looked like someone who regularly got his butt kicked in high school. In fact, he looked like he was still in high school. He murmured a greeting and, despite the strong handshake he'd offered, she quickly decided Flores was in charge. "ADA Danielle Soto." She started to say "call me Danny" but decided the familiarity might scare him.

Flores held up an iPad. "We've reviewed everything you sent yesterday. Anything new to report?"

George cracked a smile. "No new deaths. Other than that, you are up to date. The tox screen and any DNA analysis is going to take a while. In the meantime, we figured you'd want to go over the patterns we've been able to determine so far."

"Assuming they are different from what we've already discovered, sure."

Danny could practically see the smoke coming out George's ears after Flores' know-it-all response, so she took the lead and directed them to the conference room they'd designated as their war room for the cases. The walls were covered with photos of the dead women, the crime scenes, and all the forensic information they had so far. In addition, George had a group of cops in the room, partly for help and partly for show.

Danny took a seat in the back of the room. This was a law enforcement show. She was here to monitor, offer suggestions, and facilitate gathering of evidence. Sarah and George could arm wrestle over who was the best dick in the room. George started to call the meeting to order, but a uniformed officer appeared at the door and waved him out of the room. Danny took the short break as an opportunity to review her notes. She didn't get far before a shadow fell over the page in her hand.

"Mind if I sit here?" Sarah didn't wait for an answer before sliding in the seat next to her.

"I don't mind. Although you strike me as a front of the room kind of gal."

"You learn more by observing than you do with bluster."

"I'll make a note." Danny kept her head down, hoping Sarah would get the hint and leave her alone.

"I thought you were a cop."

"I'm not."

"Clearly."

Danny heard the slight and couldn't resist hitting back. "You, on the other hand, ooze cop from your pores."

"I'm going to take that as a compliment."

Of course she did. "Your choice."

"Do you always give such curt answers?"

"Are you always so inquisitive?"

"It's my job. Besides," Sarah lowered her voice to a soft whisper. "You make me very curious. Are you busy later?"

The tone of her voice signaled she was asking about personal busy, not work busy. Danny flashed back to an image of Ellen coming on to her last night. A much more engaging prospect than the dominating cop pursuing her now, but somehow the same. Later, she planned to call Ellen, make nice, and make a date for whatever Ellen wanted. Sarah would have to find some other way to entertain herself while she was in town. "Very."

"Too bad. Working a case gets me all keyed up. I'm always looking for some release."

Danny ignored the invitation. Sarah Flores was trouble. Granted, she might be a lot of fun, but if she was going to fuck around, she wanted Ellen. And who knows? Maybe if Ellen got to know her, she might want more. Hell, she sounded like a little girl. A pathetic little girl.

But she resolved to call anyway. First break she got.

George cleared his throat and Danny turned her focus to the front of the room for his presentation.

"We have four victims. All between the ages of fifty-five and sixty. Three white, one African-American. Each kill occurred at the victim's home, and we believe the killer entered under the guise of a flower delivery man based on the presence of fresh flowers, still in wax paper. That is the only detail we've released to the press in an effort to warn the public to be cautious. The flowers were white roses. No one outside of this room except the Chief and the DA know that particular detail."

"And the cause of death in each case?" Sarah tossed out the question while looking at her iPad. She probably knew the answer already, which left Danny wondering why she bothered to ask. She shot a glance at George. He nodded and she answered the question herself.

"Gunshot wound to the chest. The other injuries, including the skin carvings, were inflicted postmortem. The noose was only there for show."

"Connections between the women?" Sarah was no longer looking at George as she asked her questions. Instead, she was firmly focused on Danny.

Danny shook her head, and deferred to George who answered, "We're working on that, so far we don't know of anything else that connects all of them. Plus, as I'm sure you know, it's highly unusual for a serial killer to perform cross racial killings."

Peter Buckner piped in. "Unusual, but not unheard of. Why are you certain you have a serial killer? Isn't it true that the last kill contained different modalities than the first three?"

Modalities? Seriously, who was this guy? Danny couldn't resist cutting in. "The 'modalities,' and I hope you don't talk like that when you're on the witness stand, weren't different; there were just more of them. Looks to me like the killer's getting angrier."

"Looks to me like he's taking them more personally," Sarah interjected. "And you can be sure we know what we're doing. Here and in the courtroom."

Again with the smoky look, implying a level of familiarity Danny wanted to avoid. She started to tell Sarah to back off, but stopped when a uniformed officer stuck his head in the door and waved George over. The rest of the personnel in the room took the moment to talk among themselves, but she walked to George's side and snuck a look at the papers the officer had handed him.

"Anything good?"

"Not sure yet." He handed her an envelope. "This one has your name on it. You expecting something?"

She shook her head before she remembered it might be the information she'd asked her court investigator to look up about Joyce Barr. Not ready to share what might turn out to be nothing, she tucked the envelope under her arm and said, "Probably just some court filings."

He handed over half of his stack of paper. "These are more statements from the patrol officers who canvassed the neighborhoods. You go through this and I'll go through the rest. We can use one of the witness rooms down the hall. "

"Gladly. I'd like nothing more than to catch a break before these know-it-alls pretend they solved the case all on their own."

George told the rest of the group they were taking a short break and he ducked out of the room. Danny started to follow him, but Sarah tapped her on the shoulder.

"You mind sharing whatever it is you've got there?"

Danny looked down at the papers in her hand. "Oh, this? Just some legal mumbo jumbo. Probably wouldn't interest you." She started to walk away, but Sarah stopped her.

"I think the Chief might be interested. At the very least, he'd want to know why you didn't feel the need to share."

"I don't work for the police department."

"So? When we work with the United States attorney, we have a very close relationship."

"Well, I'm not an AUSA. And I'm not into relationships." Danny delivered the lie easily, but Sarah Flores wasn't easily deterred.

"Exactly as I'd hoped. How about we grab a drink later? Have a little non-relationship after-hours fraternizing?"

Apparently, she'd become a magnet for one-night stand seekers. Was it a sign? Stronger than her mother's warnings, her friend's teasing? Should she go with it?

"Danny, you coming?"

She murmured a silent thanks to George, took his interruption as a sign to go with her gut, and left the room without a second glance at Sarah.

CHAPTER EIGHT

D anny tried to focus on the stack of papers in front of her, but George wanted to veer off topic.

"She giving you grief?"

She didn't have to ask who he was talking about. "Not the kind of grief you're talking about."

"Oh." George made kissing noises. "She's pretty hot. Maybe you should take one for the team. You keep her distracted while I solve this case."

"Get some other chick to do your dirty work."

"Oh, that's right. You're dating someone. Is it serious? Are you going to bring her to Joe's birthday dinner? Mama said you might bring a date."

"Mama's delusional."

"She just wants you to be happy."

"I'm happy."

"Okay." Long pause. "So, is it serious?"

"We just met."

"I'm not talking about Sarah."

"I'm not either."

"Back to my original question."

"No, it's not serious. I'm definitely attracted and she seemed like a real together type. You know the kind you could get serious about, but…"

"But?"

"She's way out of my league and she's only interested in one thing."

His look changed from teasing to concerned. "Might not be a bad way for you to get back in the swing of things."

"Maybe. I guess I just wasn't ready for the first woman I date in forever to want in my pants five minutes into the first date."

"Damn, you have it rough."

"Don't be an ass. You guys are always telling me to get a personal life. Now I finally try to have one and you tease me when the woman turns into a whoredog."

"Whoredog, huh?"

"Whatever. She isn't what I thought, but maybe that's okay. Maybe I'll just have a little fun with her and move on."

"Could be just what you need."

"Is this more envy for my singlehood?"

"Grass always looks greener, but I like married life just fine."

"Sure. Remind me of that next time Anita makes you sleep on the couch because you spent your anniversary at a crime scene." Danny pointed at the pile of papers in his hand. "Anything good in there?"

"Bunch of crap. These women banked at different banks, ate at different restaurants, shopped at different stores. So far, no connections. I can feel this case slipping right into the hands of the BAU."

"Hang on, Mr. Doom. I have a little bit more to wade through." She handed him part of the rest of her stack. "Here, help me out since your little interrogation into my personal life put me behind."

They spent the next couple of minutes in silence before Danny's cell phone rang. She glanced at the number and sighed. "I'm going to step outside and take this."

"Breaking case or mystery woman?"

She shoved the rest of the papers into his hand and moved to the door. "Be right back." Once outside the office, she strode down the hallway, took a deep breath, and answered the call. "Soto, here."

"Hi, Danny. It's Ellen."

Warmth flooded through her at the sound of Ellen's voice. "Hey, you. I was going to call you later."

"Is this a bad time?"

Ellen's tentative tone melted any residual frustration Danny felt about their date. "Actually, I'm in the middle of something, but I was just thinking about you. You must have read my mind."

"I think I owe you an apology. Last night, well, I didn't mean to chase you off. To be perfectly frank—"

"Don't worry about it." Danny saw George emerge from the office, and she rushed the conversation along. "It was me, not you. You were perfect. I've been working too hard lately. Makes me unable to recognize a good thing when it's right in front of me. Give me another chance?"

"Absolutely."

"I have no idea how today is going to go. How about I call you later and we can pick up where we left off? Only this time I'll stick around for the good parts. Deal?"

"Deal."

Danny shut her phone, relieved at their easy interaction. She'd call Ellen later and make a date. One like Ellen had expected the first time. One that would leave them both wanting more, but without any desire to do something crazy, like set up house together.

"Danny, you ready?"

She turned to George and smiled. "Oh yeah, I'm ready."

"Whoa, girl, I was talking about the case." He punched her lightly in the ribs. "Come on, I think I've found something."

Excitement about a potential break in the case and her upcoming date with Ellen put her in a much better mood. "Excellent. Best news I've heard all day."

Back in the war room, Danny was relieved to see Sarah sandwiched between her sidekick, Buckner, and a DPD detective who only had eyes for her chest. Sarah shot her a look that said save me, but Danny just smiled back. Save yourself, Hotshot.

She settled in across the room from Sarah and her fan club while George called everyone back into the room. As he reviewed some of the points he'd made earlier, she casually opened the envelope she'd received from the DA's investigator and glanced at the contents. Just as she'd thought, it contained a full report on the death of Joyce Barr, age fifty-eight. Principal of an exclusive private school. Health history unremarkable. Death ruled a suicide. She turned pages until she found the cause of death. Cardiac arrest. She kept reading to figure out what had caused the heart attack. Two more pages and she found the photographs. First the body. Dark marks around her neck. She kept turning pages until she saw what she already knew was there. A photo of a noose. A coarse, rough rope hangman's noose.

She didn't have to be a fancy FBI profiler to know that suicide by hanging was pretty common. Danny recalled reading somewhere it was the second most common method of self-inflicted deaths among women. Mostly because it was fairly easy. Tie something around your neck and use some leverage to choke yourself to death. You'd lose consciousness, stop breathing, and eventually have a heart attack. If you were able to make a long drop after you had the makeshift noose around your neck, you might be lucky enough to sever your spinal cord and die more quickly.

But the noose in the picture wasn't makeshift. It was professional. A classic hangman's noose. The kind you see in old westerns. Tied with the perfect knot, it required forethought and skill.

And it looked exactly like the ones they'd found at every murder scene they'd investigated over the last month.

She heard her name and turned the autopsy report face down. Everyone in the room was staring at her. Had she said something?

George saved her. "I was just telling the group that we'd already been to visit the sorority's executive director. She didn't mention any of these other victims, but then again she may not know about the circumstances of their deaths. What's your take on it?"

She had no idea what he was talking about. Unless he somehow knew about the file she'd just reviewed. Knew that Joyce Barr was an alumna of Alpha Nu. Knew that she had spoken with Ellen after they'd both met with her.

No, the envelope had been sealed. She'd just missed something he'd said while she looked through it. Better to confess she hadn't been paying attention and get it over with. "Sorry, George. I missed what you said about the sorority."

He shot her a curious look and then held up some papers. "I was telling the group that I've just learned that all of these women have a direct connection to Alpha Nu. Three of them were members, and one pledged, but dropped out shortly after. That last one may be why Davenport didn't make the connection. If Sally Jones didn't stick around long, the sorority may not have any records on her."

The killer wanted Alpha Nu members dead? The realization rocked Danny. Did Ellen just work for the sorority or had she been a member herself? The potential danger fueled her anxiety. She needed to call Ellen, warn her.

But wait. Ellen already knew something. She'd been the one to give her the information on Joyce Barr. Information Danny knew she had to share, although she wasn't at all sure she had a good explanation for why she had the information in the first place. She swallowed her fear and spoke. "There's something else." She rushed through the details in Barr's file and then circulated the photo of the noose, while waiting for the inevitable question.

It came from Sarah. "Where did you get this?"

"I requested the file from University Park PD, but Ellen Davenport told me about the death. Said Barr's family never believed it was a suicide."

"How did she know about the noose?"

"She didn't. At least I don't think she did. She just thought the connection was the sorority. Frankly, I blew her off at first."

"I guess that wasn't the brightest detective work you've ever done. Oh, wait, you're not a detective at all."

"Guess I'm detective enough to follow up on a lead."

George broke in. "Cool it. Danny's right. We need to follow up on this. Flores, go see Davenport and get her to give up all their records. We need to know about *any* deaths among their members. Period. There's bound to be more connections here. Check for links between the vics and their other members. Danny, work with Flores on this since you apparently already have a relationship with Davenport. I'd like to see if we can get what we want from her without a subpoena. Also, I want some assurance she's not jacking with us and that what she told you is all she knows."

While George barked orders to the rest of the room, Sarah shot her a snarky look that she ignored. She was too focused on George's words. Relationship. Ha. She'd resigned herself to a relationship with Ellen that consisted of nothing more than fooling around, but now it looked like she wouldn't even get that.

❖

Ellen spent the afternoon shoving paper around her desk, while she replayed her earlier conversation with Danny. Maybe she'd misread the signs the night before. Danny was working on a big case. Of course she was tired. She'd promised her a meal, but instead she tried to climb in her lap. She should've been more subtle, worked her way in. She so wasn't used to this. She should buy a new vibrator and call it quits. Or she could give it another try and do it right this time. First step, focus on something else until Danny called.

She cleaned her desk, organized her files, and made calls to a dozen well-heeled alumnae about their annual giving. When five o'clock finally rolled around, she felt justified in calling it a day. Better to spend her time waiting for Danny's call with a glass of wine and a hot bath than pretending to work. Driving on autopilot with the sound of steady rain outside her windows, she almost didn't hear her cell phone ringing. When she finally clicked to the fact she had an incoming call, she scrambled around in her purse but didn't catch it before the caller rang off the line. In less than a minute, it dinged, telling her she had a voice message.

"Ms. Davenport, this is Dorothy Patterson with Cedar Acres. Please give me a call as soon as you get this message. We have a situation and I need to talk to you. It's urgent."

Peeved that the message didn't contain any details, Ellen chucked the phone on the seat and made an illegal U-turn. If she hurried, she could make it to Cedar Acres in twenty minutes.

During the frantic drive, the rain began falling in torrents, pounding out her ability to see. Any thoughts she'd had about calling Patterson back faded, as she needed both hands on the wheel to keep the buffeting winds from pushing her out of her lane. When she finally pulled up under the portico, she was tense from sharing the road with several semi trucks who left a wall of water in their wake and she was anxious about the reason for Patterson's call. Surely if her mother had a medical emergency, they would have said so. Unless it was too late. Maybe they hadn't wanted to break very bad news in a voice message. She jumped out of the car and tossed her keys to the valet before he had a chance to put his hand on the door handle. Once inside, she ran to the front desk and barked at the receptionist to page Mrs. Patterson.

A hand on her shoulder had her almost jumping out of her skin. Mrs. Patterson's demeanor was calm, but her face expressed concern. "Why don't you come with me?"

Ellen followed her over to the same couch where they'd had their last conversation about her mother. Perplexed by the seeming lack of urgency, Ellen asked, "Don't sugarcoat it. Is she dead?"

"What?" Patterson shook her head. "Your mother? No, no, she's fine." She motioned for Ellen to take a seat. "I'm so sorry you drove all the way here with that image in your head. If you'd called, I would have set your mind at ease. Please accept my apologies."

"What in the hell did your message mean then?" She took a deep breath and focused on tamping down her anger. "Sounded pretty ominous for someone who is 'fine.'"

"She's fine now, but she had an episode today and it was pretty severe. Somehow she found out about Marty Lawson. She got violent. Started talking about how she knew it would happen and that she would be next. I thought you should know that she's aware of Marty's death and that it has had a profound effect upon her."

"What in the world did she mean by that? And I thought you said we'd deal with it when she found out. Doesn't sound like it was dealt with very well."

"She was lucid right before, but the news apparently caused her to regress. Honestly, I don't know how she found out. Could be another resident heard it on the news, read it in the paper and then discussed it. She's very social, you know."

Ellen shook her head. Her mother had been the ultimate socialite in her circle, but here? With all these strangers? Difficult to believe. "I'm sure she tries to make the best of it. She's big on keeping up appearances."

"Would you like to see her in action?"

"Uh, sure." She followed Patterson to the dining hall. Her stomach growled as they approached. Thank goodness this place had decent food. Maybe she could grab a bite before she braved the storm for the ride back to Dallas. Her thoughts stopped cold when she spotted her mother, laughing like a schoolgirl, seated with a group of men at least ten years her senior. What in the world was going on? She wouldn't have been surprised to see Vivian with a group of women, sharing sedate, civilized conversation, but the way she preened and giggled, it almost looked like she was flirting.

"Who are those men?"

"They're other residents."

"And you let them leer at my mother? She's a married woman. She doesn't know what she's doing."

"Neither do they."

Ellen heard the slight reproach and backed down. Of course. No one here knew what they were doing. That's why they were here. "I'm sorry. It's just…" She tried to nail down what was really bothering her. "I've never seen her like this. Is she always this way?"

Patterson shook her head. "Never. Not until this evening. Her episode this afternoon, after learning about Marty's death, seems to have triggered this behavior. I apologize again for upsetting you, but I thought perhaps you might have some insight."

Ellen, glued to the sight of her mother, the flirt, barely registered Patterson's words. "Insight?"

"Clues as to why news of Marty's death may have brought on this behavior. If we know more details, it can help us work with her on her memories. Processing them can lead to increased recall."

"I don't have a clue, but she sure seems happy."

"She does. Do you want to visit with her?"

"I don't want to interrupt."

"She'll be done soon. Have some food and then you can have some time with her." Patterson frowned, "She hasn't been with us since she heard the news, so I can't guarantee she'll—"

"I get it. She's not going to know it's me."

"Highly doubtful."

"It's okay. I think I should spend some time with her, anyway. Besides, I'm starving and I have no desire to go back out into that storm."

Ellen settled in across the room with a steaming chicken pot pie. Cedar Acres may be an institution in name, but every aspect of the place spoke home. With food that ranged from comfort to gourmet, rooms furnished according to individual taste, and common areas lined with plants and recognizable art prints, this "institution" felt more like home than the stiff, formal house she'd grown up in. Maybe it was time to change some things at home. Make it more her own. She considered discussing it with her father, but then her own memory kicked in and she realized he wouldn't care. Her mother, her mother's house, everything about her mother was her problem, her burden. Bill Davenport had moved on, and no way was she going to beg him for help anymore. She'd have to start spending more time here, making sure her mother got the care she needed.

She glanced at her cell phone, which she'd placed on the table in case Danny called. Days like these were exactly why relationships were out of the question. What if she'd been with Danny, naked and willing, when the call had come? Would she have even answered the phone? Doubtful. Still, she was entitled to a little fun, wasn't she? Late at night when her mother was dreaming sweet dreams about the past, the only thing she ever seemed to remember—surely then she was allowed a respite.

When Danny called tonight, she'd invite her over, and, if she was willing, indulge in a bout of passion and relief. But if Danny wanted more, she'd have to cut it off. More wasn't possible, advisable, or attainable.

The chicken pot pie was rich and she managed to eat only half. She gave her tray to a passing employee and looked up just in time to see her mother walk out of the dining hall with her entourage of elderly men. She practically ran across the room, dodging waiters and residents, and then skidded to a halt as she watched her mother give each one of her escorts a peck on the cheek.

She waited, off to the side, secretly hoping her mother would head off to her room and they could have a quiet moment, even if she wasn't lucid. She was totally unprepared for what happened next.

"Marty Lawson! I can't believe you've come to visit. I was just talking about you."

Vivian rushed toward Ellen, and Ellen turned to look behind her. It wasn't until she was swept up in a tight hug that she realized what was going on.

"Mother?"

"Don't yank my chain. It's me, Vivian. I'm so excited to see you. We have a lot to talk about." Vivian's voice dropped to a whisper. "I think you might be in trouble again."

"Trouble?" Desperate to cut through the mystery of her mother's words, Ellen played along.

"You know what I mean." Vivian play slapped her shoulder. "Don't be an imp." She grabbed Ellen's arm. "Come along. We can talk in my room."

Ellen, arm linked with her mother's, followed her to her private room. As they entered, she noticed the Grisham book lying on the dresser. The one Vivian had insisted had been stolen. Everything else was in perfect order. Bed made, every framed photo perfectly in line, not a thing out of place. Vivian hopped on the four-poster bed and patted the space beside her. "Sit; we need to catch up. Where have you been?"

Ellen sat down slowly, using the time to come up with an appropriate response. Her mother thought she was Marty and she wanted to talk to her as Marty. Dispelling that notion seemed like a bad idea. Besides, she was curious about the trouble she'd referred to. Did it have something to do with Marty's death? She decided to play along.

"I've been around. What have I missed?"

"Don't be coy. You know."

Marty might, but Ellen didn't. She considered ways to keep the conversation going. "I do, but I didn't think it would cause trouble. Is everything okay?"

"You've got to keep a better eye on the pledges. I know you're not in charge of them, but you're the responsible one. She's a rule breaker, that one."

She who? Only one way to find out. "She?"

"You picked her. You should handle it."

Was Vivian talking about a pledge or a sorority sister? And what did she mean? What did she think wouldn't "cause trouble"? As she struggled to frame a question, she saw the curtain fall. Vivian was fading. Any minute now and she wouldn't remember who she was, where she was, or anything about this conversation. No time to be subtle. "Who did I pick? What should I handle?"

"Please bring me some new towels. I'd like to take a bath before bed."

Just like that. Ellen wasn't Ellen or Marty. She was a servant. She tried one more time. "Mother, let's talk about Marty."

A blank look told her all she needed to know. The conversation was over and her mother might never bring it up again. She left to get the towels, and then she read the Grisham novel until her mother fell asleep.

Several hours later, at home reading in her own bed, loneliness swept over her. Her mother was in another world, and her father, several states away, may as well have fallen off the face of the earth. And her phone was silent. Almost midnight and no message from Danny. Not a text. Nothing.

She's busy. She said she was working late, big case, lots to do. Ellen hated to admit how much she'd counted on her call, another date, and another opportunity to try again.

Probably for the best. No matter what Danny said, she wasn't convinced they wanted the same things. If Danny was up for a one-night stand, fooling around, no strings, then she wouldn't have taken off the other night. She would've stuck around, taken what Ellen was ready and willing to offer. But it wasn't what she wanted, so why bother calling?

Ellen sighed and snuggled into the covers. Funny, she was the one who didn't want any strings, but here she was obsessing about why Danny hadn't called. The irony brought to mind the picture of her mother, the uppity socialite, prim and proper, yucking it up with a crowd of older men. As her head hit the pillow, all Ellen could think about was how nothing was what she expected.

Chapter Nine

The next morning, Danny sat in her office with the door shut, staring at her phone. She hadn't called Ellen last night, but she could still remedy the situation. Call her now, at least warn her that she and Flores were on their way to disrupt her world.

Sarah had tried to reach Ellen yesterday, but she'd already left the office. Sarah had tried to reach her on her cell, but she hadn't answered and she didn't want to leave a message that might have her rounding up the sorority's lawyers. Danny knew she should've called herself, that Ellen would've answered her call, but she would've answered expecting something else. Something Danny knew she couldn't give, no matter what she'd told herself.

She started dialing Ellen's number, but halfway through she stopped. What was the point? Professionally, a heads up was the wrong thing to do. Personally, she shouldn't care. They didn't really even know each other. Why couldn't she stop thinking about her?

"You ready to go?"

She looked up into Sarah's icy eyes. "I told you I'd meet you out front."

"Didn't feel like driving around in a circle until you showed up. Besides, I figured I could see where the JV squad works."

Danny resisted rising to the bait. Sarah had been full of digs over the course of the last twenty-four hours. No reason to expect she was going to change anytime soon. She grabbed her briefcase. "Come on, let's go."

On the ride to Ellen's office, Sarah pumped her for information. "What's this Davenport like? Stuffy old bitch or girly young amateur?"

"Neither."

"Okay, then what's she like?"

"How would I know?" Danny hated the direction of the conversation. "You're going to take the lead on this, right?"

"What's the matter? I thought you were all cozy with her? Scared she'll tell you no?"

"You're the cop. I'm just along to make sure you get what we need without violating anyone's rights."

"And here I thought you were here because you wanted to catch a killer."

"Are you always this abrasive? Does it get you far?"

"Usually does the trick." Sarah pointed. "That the building?"

"Yes." George shouldn't have offered her up for this interview or should've let her handle it on her own. She knew that last wasn't possible. If Ellen turned out to be a witness at trial, it would be important that someone other than the trial attorney handled her initial interviews. But she couldn't stomach the idea of Flores roughing her up. She'd dealt with federal agents before and was all too familiar with their hardball interview techniques. After going back on her promise to call last night, she owed Ellen the courtesy of a gentle approach. "And I'll take the lead. Your demeanor is going to shut these people down."

"Whatever. I've got a gun and a badge. I don't need to wave them around to feel like I'm in charge."

While they were waiting for the elevator, Danny tapped Sarah on the shoulder. When Sarah turned to face her, she said, "Make no mistake. You're not in charge. This is our investigation. Nothing federal about it. You're here to offer your 'expertise.'" She couldn't resist delivering finger quotes. "And when you've offered all you have to give, you'll be leaving. I'll be prosecuting this case with one of my colleagues. At the Dallas County courthouse."

"Whatever you say, Soto." Sarah motioned to the opening elevator doors. "After you, Miss In-Charge."

Danny strode into the lobby, instantly recognizing Ellen's assistant. She put on her most engaging smile. "Excuse me, I'm, I mean, we're looking for Ellen."

The young woman grabbed her hand. "You're the attorney, right? I'm Jill, Ms. Davenport's assistant. Where's the handsome detective you brought last time?"

Danny laughed as she felt Sarah bristle beside her. "Good to see you again." She waved at Flores. "This is Special Agent Sarah Flores. We'd like to see Ms. Davenport. It's important."

"I understand. She's in. I'll let her know you're here."

A moment later, they followed Jill into Ellen's office. Ellen didn't stand to meet them. In fact, she barely looked up from her desk. Danny didn't need to see her eyes to know she was pissed. Pissed and beautiful. Stunning really. Not calling her last night had been a mistake.

The last thing Ellen had expected when Jill buzzed her was a visit from Danny. The second to last thing she hadn't expected was for Danny to show up with another beautiful woman. Like salt in her wound. What had Jill said, Special Agent Flores? Apparently, this was not a social call. She kept her head down for a minute, pretending to read the junk mail on her desk, while she gathered her thoughts. When the silence became uncomfortable, she faced the women seated across from her desk. "What can I do for you?"

Danny spoke first. "Hi, Ellen, we need to ask you a few questions related to Marty Lawson."

Sarah shot Danny a surprised look, and Ellen wondered about the dynamic between them. Had they known each other long? Had Sarah replaced George on the case? Didn't matter. All that mattered was that Danny was here for business and no other reason. Well, she could be all business too. "Whatever you need. Tell me what you want to know."

"We need access to all your files, especially alumnae records. And we need it fast."

Ellen focused on Sarah who had made the request. "When I said whatever you need, I didn't expect you to ask for that."

"We can get a subpoena." Again Sarah, but this time Danny placed a hand on her arm and shook her head. Sarah softened her insistent tone and smiled brightly. "Sorry, we're working really hard to catch a killer, and it's important we explore all avenues."

Ellen flashed to last night's conversation with her mother. "Do you have some reason to believe one of our alumnae might be involved in Marty's death?"

Danny answered this time. "To be perfectly honest, we don't know. At the very least we'd like to see what connections we can find between Ms. Lawson and your current members."

"Is this because Joyce's case is related after all?"

Again meaningful looks passed between Sarah and Danny. Danny cleared her throat. "It's not public information yet, but there has been more than one death that we are reasonably sure is related."

"A serial killer?"

Flores leaned forward, again with the bright and shiny smile. "Nothing for you to worry about, except to the extent you can help us catch him."

This woman gave her the creeps. Did she think she was stupid? Like she was going to hand over all their files without a good reason why? Plus she'd just tripped over her own request. "Him? Well, that wouldn't be one of our members. Why don't you tell me what you're looking for and I'll search the records? That would probably be more palatable to my board."

"You shouldn't discuss this with your board. Or with anyone." Sarah delivered the warning in a stern voice.

"I understand your need to keep a lid on this, but I have an obligation to keep my board informed about anything that affects the sorority, its members, or its reputation. If you can't tell me more, then I'm afraid you're going to have to talk to our lawyers." Ellen shot a pointed look at Danny, ready to hear her take on the subject. Was she going to let this Flores dictate the tone of this meeting, because if she was, then why was Danny even here?

Danny didn't disappoint. "Agent Flores, I need a moment alone with Ms. Davenport. Please step outside."

"You're kidding, right?"

"I need you to step outside."

Flores stood and looked between Ellen and Danny, shaking her head. She left the room grumbling about amateurs, her complaints punctuated by the slamming of Ellen's office door. Danny waited until the door stopped shaking before leaning forward. "I'm sorry."

Loaded words. Ellen wanted to ask if her apology included walking out the other night and not calling last night. Or was Danny's regret confined to showing up here, unannounced, seeking nothing more than business?

Better not to get into all that. "Okay."

"Pretty sure she's used to bullying people to get her way."

"And how do you get your way?" Oops. That one had been hard to resist. "Look, I'm sorry too. We obviously got off on the wrong foot. You're here on business. We're both professionals. Tell me what you really need, and I'll do my best to help."

Danny glanced back at the door. "I can't tell you much. There's no evidence to suggest that Joyce Barr's death was anything but a suicide. However, our investigation has led us to believe that the sorority might be a common thread among several recent murders."

"Several? Exactly how many are we talking about?"

"You've heard the recent news stories, warning folks about opening their doors for unexpected deliverymen? Reports of assault?"

"Sure."

"Those assaults were actually murders."

"And you've been hiding that little detail from the press? How many?"

"Four that we know of."

"Oh my God! And you think they are connected to the sorority?"

"We know that at least three of the women were Alpha Nu members. Another pledged, but then dropped out. May be a total coincidence, but we don't have any other viable leads, so we're looking at everything."

"If I give you access to our files, can you at least tell me what you're looking for and what you'll do with the information you find?"

"I can't tell you exactly what we're looking for because I don't know. Something, anything, that connects our victims to each other. Any kind of pattern that will hopefully give us a clue to the killer's identity."

Ellen pointed at her closed office door. "And if I don't cooperate, you'll sic her on me?"

"Not my call, but yes, I think she'll wind up getting a grand jury subpoena or a search warrant if you won't work with us voluntarily. You'll have to get your lawyers involved, and if the judge orders you to turn over the records, then you won't have much control over who sees them after that. If you share them with us on your own, then I guarantee you, I'll guard the privacy of your members."

Could Danny keep such a promise or was she just trying to get Ellen to trust her? Should she trust her? Danny had thrown Flores out of the room for this little chat. She wanted to trust her, but she had to know something first. "Why didn't you call? Last night. I mean I get it if you changed your mind about seeing me, but you could've called. I don't want to sound like I'm looking for something here." She took a deep breath and pushed on. "I'm not, I mean I wasn't really interested in anything more than a casual date. Fun, you know, with no obligations. But still…"

Danny's face flushed and she cleared her throat a few times. "Like I said, I'm sorry. I can't mix work and fun. We discovered this possible connection yesterday and Flores called here, but you were already gone. She tried to reach you on your cell, but you didn't answer. By the time we finished up work, it was too late to swing by your house."

No, it wasn't. Late last night, she could've used a visitor to help her forget the odd visit she'd had with her mother. Remembering the visit gave her pause. What had her mother said about Marty's death? *I knew it would happen and I would be next.* That's what she'd told the staff at Cedar Acres. And she'd said to her: *Keep a better eye on the pledges. She's a rule breaker, that one.* Beyond odd. Almost as if her mother was connecting Marty's death with the sorority. Or not. More likely her statements weren't connected to each other at all. There wasn't much rhyme or reason to her mother's ramblings. No need to send Danny chasing leads that didn't exist. Besides, as far as she knew, her mother didn't know any of the other women who'd been killed, and the last thing she wanted to do was interfere with what little peace her mother had by sending the cops her way. She'd give them only what they asked for.

"I'll give you access to the files, but I need your word that they will remain private."

"I can guarantee that right now, but if we turn up a solid lead, I may not be able to keep that promise."

"I understand. I just need to be able to assure my board that any release of information was absolutely necessary. I don't want any individual's private information exposed unless it's essential."

"Got it. I can make you that promise."

No matter what Danny promised and no matter how much she wanted to believe her, she needed to take care of something before she gave her access to the files. "I need a few hours to pull together the data." She looked at her watch. "Why don't you come back after lunch, say around two?"

"Perfect."

A few beats of awkward silence passed. Business was over, and Ellen figured neither of them wanted to dip back into anything personal. Except she did. Badly. But Danny had made it clear she wasn't interested and no way was she going to push the point.

"You want to bring the wolf back in?"

"Wolf?"

"Special Agent Pushy. The way she stares at me, I can't tell if she wants to tear me apart or eat me alive."

"Ha. Probably both."

Danny left the room and Ellen heard her whispering to Flores. She sat at her desk and waited. She couldn't help but wish Danny looked at her the way Sarah did.

❖

Danny herded the protesting Flores to the elevator.

"She could do anything with those records while we're gone. I can't believe you agreed to wait to see them. What's your thing with her?"

Danny placed a finger over her mouth and waited until they were alone in the elevator car. "Is this how you guys usually conduct an investigation? Boy, do I feel sorry for the prosecutors who have to work with you on a regular basis." Sarah opened her mouth to speak and Danny hushed her again. "Look, whatever evidence you get will wind up on my desk for me or some other lawyer to use at trial. I'm involved at this point for a reason and that's to make sure you do things the right way. We don't have a subpoena. You pressure her too much and you'll have a fleet of lawyers in court arguing to the judge that you're not entitled to these records. If you have to get a subpoena, I'll have to explain to the judge why we want these records, and right now, I'm not convinced I've got enough to show a connection to the murders. The fact that these victims belonged to a sorority once upon a time probably won't cut it. Chicken, egg. We need the records to prove a connection, but we need to show a connection to get the records. The judge will tell me we're on a fishing expedition and he'll quash the subpoena. That could take days. So you can wait a few hours or a few days. You decide."

Sarah, mouth open, stared at her.

"What?"

"You're kinda hot when you're all riled up."

"Back off, Flores."

"Guess you're all business all the time."

The echo of the words she'd spoken to Ellen burned. "Whatever."

"Except when it comes to a certain Ms. Davenport. Seems like you were real anxious to get me out of the room so you two could have a little alone time."

Leave it to Miss Behavioral Analysis not to miss a thing. She'd have to be more careful. Good thing she'd made it clear to Ellen work trumped attraction. "I threw you out of the room to keep the witness from clamming up in the face of your overly aggressive tactics. For someone trained in behavioral analysis, I thought you would be better at handling a witness interview." Would this woman ever stop getting under her skin?

"You haven't even begun to see my skills in action."

"Don't even."

"Don't worry. Your all business self is safe with me. And I'm okay with waiting a little while to see those records, but I have to say it'll be hard not to see the lovely Ms. Davenport again until this afternoon."

Danny refrained from punching her, but not out of fear of the consequences of assaulting a federal agent. No, her primary concern was keeping her desire for Ellen Davenport a secret. A change of subject was in order. "Why don't you take me back to the courthouse so I can get my car? I'll meet you back here at two."

Sarah's stare was penetrating, but Danny didn't wince. She wanted to ditch her to check in with George, see if there were any new developments, and she didn't want to share. Besides, if they were going to spend the next few days working together, she needed time alone to steel herself. The only bright side to this particular project was Ellen Davenport. She pushed the thought away. Ellen was a distraction and one that she couldn't afford if she was going to do her part to keep this case.

Chapter Ten

Danny grabbed a grilled cheese from the cafe in the basement of the courthouse and took it to her office on the eleventh floor. She dialed George's cell, and then scarfed down a few bites before the call connected.

"Ramirez."

"Anything new?"

"Nice to talk to you, too, Soto. Shouldn't I be asking you that question?"

She swallowed and took a big drink of iced tea. "Good news. We get access to the files this afternoon."

"That is good news. I can assemble a team and have a room ready. Just give me a shout when you get here."

"Hold up. By we, I mean Flores and me. Ellen agreed to give us access without involving their lawyers or us having to get a subpoena if we would look at them at her office." She left out the part about how they'd agreed to keep the information confidential.

"Okay, just make sure you cover all the bases and that she'll keep the access open. We're bound to get a break soon. What time are you headed back over there? I'm about to e-mail you Winter's report on the latest victim."

"Two. I've got time. Send it my way. Anything interesting?"

"Not necessarily, but take a look and see what you think. There are some good shots of the new wounds. If this guy's escalating, I think these are the key."

"Send it. I'm eating so you have perfect timing."

"Bon appetite."

Danny opened her e-mail account and waited for the report. They already had the preliminary report from Dr. Winter, but this was the final, official version. Toxicology results didn't show anything of note. Cause of death was the gunshot wound. Same as the others. She flipped through to the photos. They brought back the memory of standing in the autopsy room, bracing against the onslaught of senses. She could almost smell the raw, aching smell of death, and she tossed the rest of her sandwich in the trash.

First the noose. Around Randolf's neck. The more she examined it, the more convinced she was that Joyce Barr's death was related to the current murders. What were the chances Barr had committed suicide with exactly the same type of noose that had been found around the neck of each of the recent victims? They needed to have the rope analyzed. She consulted the file on Barr. Luckily, the ME who'd pronounced Barr's death a suicide had logged the noose into evidence. Hopefully, it hadn't been destroyed yet. If they could compare it to the same ones they were accumulating on this case, maybe there was a connection. Problem was, the lab Dallas County sent all its forensic evidence to was backed up beyond belief. It had taken Winter herself standing over them to get the toxicology report back in record time.

The FBI lab, on the other hand, had a reputation for quick and efficient work. And their database of information was crazy big. She'd have to ask Flores, though, if she wanted their help, and the request would give the feds another inroad to taking over. Maybe she should get George to ask the brainiac Flores had brought with her. Buckner. He didn't strike her as a power hungry type. She sent George a quick text asking him to give it a go. Time to go meet Ellen. And Sarah.

Sarah was waiting for her in the lobby to Ellen's office. Sleek and powerfully pretty, she lounged on the sofa while still giving off the impression she was ready for anything. If they'd met under other circumstances, Danny might have asked her out. They were in the same line of work, and as much as she hated to admit it, Sarah was sexy. Too sexy. Wham, bam, thank you, ma'am. That one wasn't going to stick around for a picket fence and kids.

She shook away the thoughts. Relationships were all she seemed to think about lately. Her mother was to blame. Begging her to get back out there, find a mate, and settle down. Now she evaluated every woman she met as the future Mrs. Soto. Crazy really, since her first foray back into the game had imploded.

Even as she wrote off Flores as potential date material, she resolved to establish a rapport, but only because they had to work together. That woman was trouble.

"Hey."

"Hey. Jill said Ellen would be ready in a minute. They're setting up a conference room for us."

"Great. How do you want to do this?" Danny had a plan in mind, but she figured it wouldn't hurt to get Sarah's perspective.

"I figured you'd charge in, throw me out, and then spend the afternoon looking at files about old biddies with pretty girl in there."

"Don't be an ass. I'm trying to be nice, you know, include you. Act like you're an adult and answer the question before I change my mind."

Sarah held up both hands. "Truce. I guess it depends on what kind of information they keep. We should definitely gather everything we can find on any alumnae in the same age group as the victims."

"And the same graduation years."

"Good point. Some of the graduates could have been older students who started college late. Although it's not common for older students to rush."

"And you know this because?"

"Because I was a Chi Omega. Still am last time I checked."

"You're fucking kidding." Danny was so surprised she didn't hear Ellen approach.

"I'm going to assume that wasn't an insult."

"So am I. Although Chi-Os aren't Alpha Nus, that's for sure."

Danny and Sarah both turned to face Ellen. She sounded amused, but her expression was hard to read. Sarah sprang out of her chair and shook Ellen's hand.

"And that's a bad thing?" Sarah said, "I don't think so."

"You wouldn't, of course."

Danny glanced back and forth between them, unable to process what had just happened. Had Ellen and Sarah just bonded about their Greek sisterhood? Unbelievable. She'd never have pegged Sarah as a sorority girl, but it was more than that. Jealousy grabbed her gut. In the span of a few moments, Sarah had gone from wolf to sister, and she didn't like it.

She interrupted their friendly rivalry. "Shouldn't we get started?"

"Absolutely. Follow me." Ellen led the way, and Sarah made a big show of waving Danny ahead of her. She should have been happy to spend the afternoon with Ellen, but all she could think about was having to spend the next few hours listening to Ellen and Sarah reminisce about their college Greek experience. Making up with Sarah had been premature. Right now, she hated her guts.

❖

Ellen ushered them into the room. Weird. Danny was obviously angry about something and Sarah was suddenly super nice. Maybe they'd exchanged personalities before they arrived. "Would either of you like something to drink?"

Danny spoke first. "Not me. I'm ready to get to work."

"I'd love a Diet Coke if you have one." Sarah apparently wasn't as focused.

Ellen handed her a can from the small refrigerator in the corner of the room and grabbed a couple of bottles of water. She placed one in front of Danny. "In case you change your mind."

Danny grunted a reply.

"I've placed a copy of all the alumnae files on this laptop." She pointed to a stack of papers beside it. "These are new files that haven't been input in the system yet."

"I don't understand. Wouldn't you have a file set up if they were already members when they were students?"

"Not necessarily. We keep the information in separate databases, and besides, some graduates elect not to join the alumnae organization. Some wait a number of years to join, especially if they aren't making much money after college."

"You allow poor kids to be part of your exclusive club?" Danny asked.

Ellen chose to ignore the derisive tone. "We have a diverse membership and programs set up to allow for sliding scale membership dues for our student members. The alumnae dues are fixed, though, and not everyone chooses to pay them right out of school. We often have members who wait a few years, until they are established, before they sign up for the alumnae organization. If you're interested in graduates who haven't joined the alumnae group, you'll have to check a different database. If you want, I can get you access to it as well."

Danny didn't respond, but Sarah was eager with questions. "If we identify the range of women we're looking for, can you just run a cross search on the other database to keep us from having to review both? We may eventually have to look at both databases, but for now, it seems like that might be more efficient."

"I can do that." She'd do just about anything they wanted to keep control of the computer information. In the few hours while they were gone, she'd made a couple of changes to the database. Her mother's name was now Vivian Donnelly and her address was in Chicago. Not entirely dishonest. Vivian's maiden name was Donnelly and the address in Chicago belonged to her husband. Her dad was still married to her mother, after all. She hoped the distance would make it less likely they'd try to contact Vivian, and the name change...well, no doubt Danny would think it odd that she hadn't mentioned her mother was an alumnae and the same age as Marty Lawson. Bringing it up now would seem odd, and there was no way she was going to expose her mother to police questioning. Besides, Vivian was using her maiden name while at Cedar Acres. She'd insisted on it to maintain privacy. Only two other people knew where Vivian was. Her dad and...make that one. Marty Lawson was dead. Anyway, she promised to keep her mother's secret and, while she couldn't make her father stick around, keeping quiet about where she was and why was just one small thing she could do. As long as no one knew where Vivian was, she was safe from any harm. "Tell me what you're looking for and I'll start running searches."

Sarah pulled her chair over and huddled close. "Let's start with an age range. Fifty-five to sixty." She glanced at Danny. "Sound right to you?"

"Sure, whatever."

Something was up. Ellen couldn't tell if the something was between her and Danny or Sarah and Danny, but the tension in the room was palpable. She turned the laptop toward Danny. "You want to drive?"

Danny's frown dissipated. "Yeah, that would be great," Danny said as she scrunched closer, her arm nudging Ellen's as she took over control. Ellen knew she should move over, give her room to work, but she liked being close. She liked the spark that passed between them. Her mind wandered to the kiss they'd almost shared, and seconds later, she found herself staring at Danny's lips instead of the computer screen. She looked over at Sarah to see if she noticed her trance. Sarah had moved away a bit to give them room, but kept a hand on the arm of her chair. *I'm like a law and order sandwich.*

She spent the next few minutes showing Danny how to formulate searches on the database. When she had the hang of it, she stood up. "Guess I'll leave you to it. If you need something, you can get Jill on the phone by pressing the first extension."

"Wait." Sarah, not Danny. "I have a few questions about how your organization runs. Maybe you could answer those. Of course, we don't want to keep you from your work."

"My work will keep. This is important and I want to do whatever I can to help." She looked at Danny whose fingers typed furiously. She hadn't raised her head and didn't appear to be listening or even care about her discussion with Sarah. "Ask away."

"How did you know Joyce Barr had died?"

Not exactly a question about the organization. "We often get notice from friends or family about a death of one of our alums. We publish a monthly newsletter that includes memorials for members who've died."

"So, if I give you a list of names, you can tell us how you heard about their deaths?"

"Sure. If they were recent, I'll probably even remember off the top of my head."

"You understand you can't share this information with anyone."

Danny jerked out of her computer trance long enough to say, "She gets it, Flores. She said she wouldn't tell. Give it a rest."

"Easy, Soto. I hear you. I trust Ellen gets it." She flashed a big smile and handed Ellen a note card with four names. Marty Lawson, Joan Gibson, Rita Randolf, and Sally Jones. "Heard of these women?"

"Well, Marty, of course. She's who Danny and Detective Ramirez came to see me about last week. The other women don't ring a bell."

"Can you run their names for us? We have reason to believe they are connected to the sorority in some way."

Ellen looked at Danny who pushed the laptop her way. She typed in a few searches. "Gibson is here." She pointed at the screen, "but Rita Randolf and Sally Jones aren't coming up in this database."

"Does that mean for sure they aren't alumnae?"

"Not necessarily. They might be in the other database, the one for former students. I'll have to go to my office to check."

Sarah stood. "I'll come with you."

"Okay. Danny?"

"I'm good. I'll keep working here." Danny's response was clipped and she didn't raise her head. She'd obviously meant what she said about keeping things purely professional between them. Fine. Now that she was poking around in the sorority's files, it was probably best to keep her at arm's length.

Danny looked up as the conference room door closed. She could barely stand being in the room with Ellen, but the minute she left, she realized she couldn't stand being away from her either. This was ridiculous. No reason she should spend so much energy thinking about Ellen, when it was obvious Ellen wasn't giving her a second thought. Ellen and Sarah were probably enjoying each other's company, bonding over sisterhood, girl power, and all that. Pretty clear she wasn't part of their little clique. If being close to Ellen didn't drive her crazy enough, seeing Sarah fawn all over her was going to push her over the edge.

She did her best to focus on the database. The number of registered alumnae was staggering, even after she narrowed the search by age. And these women were located all over the country. Hard to believe that if the sorority was the common thread, that the kills would be confined to the Dallas area. Either there were similar murders scattered throughout the country or geography was just as important a factor as membership in the sorority. She had a feeling her searches were going to turn up unsolved crimes in other jurisdictions that would only complicate matters. Once Dallas was no longer the only jurisdiction where the murders took place, the feds would have a legitimate reason to take over the case.

She saved several search results onto the desktop of the computer, and then fished a flash drive from her pocket and downloaded the results. She tucked the drive away just as the conference door opened and Sarah and Ellen came back in.

Boy, did they look chummy. Sarah slid a sheet of paper across the table. "Take a look at this."

Danny studied the paper. "What am I looking for?"

"Randolf and Gibson were members of the same chapter as Lawson, Jones, and Barr. For whatever reason, they never registered as alumnae, but they attended school at the same time as the others, so they must have known each other. There's our connection." Sarah pounded a hand on the table. Danny could tell she wanted to say more, but wouldn't with a civilian in the room. Maybe they'd prematurely decided the murders had been committed by a man. All signs were pointing to a strong connection within the sorority. Could another member have committed these vicious crimes?

She turned their attention to the list she'd compiled. "Here's the list of women who fit within the search parameters. Ellen, can you check your records to see if you have any reports regarding deaths of anyone on this list? Just a yes or no, will do and we'll follow up about the cause. Also, I'm curious, do you have any idea why so many of these women wound up in the Dallas area?" Danny asked.

Ellen studied the chart of search results. "Looks like a lot of them attended Richards University. Alpha Nu has always had a strong presence on that campus. Not that unusual for women to stick around the area."

She was right. It wasn't that unusual. The thought gave her hope that the murders were all confined to this area, that she could hold on to the cases and personally take care of delivering justice for the victims and their families. "How soon can you get us the information about who on this list is deceased?"

Ellen looked at her watch. "I have a function tonight, but I could look into it first thing in the morning. Does that work?"

Sarah interjected. "A sorority function? What kind?"

Danny was annoyed at the interruption. Why should Sarah care about Ellen's personal life? Wasn't like they'd actually attended the same school, belonged to the same sorority. Anger bubbled up as she considered that Sarah might have turned her outrageous flirting in Ellen's direction. She had no business getting involved with a witness.

"It's an alumnae mixer. We have them once a quarter. I've been letting my assistant handle them, but I really need to make an appearance. Otherwise I'd stay in and work on this list."

"No, this is perfect. I'm coming with you. Are you going home first? What should I wear? I can pick you up."

Danny's head spun at the string of jumbled questions and comments and Ellen's expression said she was confused as well. Danny cut to the chase. "Flores, no parties for you. We have work to do."

"Don't you get it? If someone is singling out sorority alums, what better place to find them than at an event designed to bring them all to one place?" She turned to Ellen. "I'll need a cover. Do you have an RSVP list? Maybe we can pick a college that's not represented and you can say I graduated from there. What do you say?"

Danny held her breath while she waited for Ellen's answer. Sarah was right. It was a great idea, but she didn't want to acknowledge that Ellen might be caught in the middle of a manhunt. Here in her office, surrounded by paper and computer files, she was safe. At an event, surrounded by potential victims, she could quickly become collateral damage. Sarah was reckless not to consider the danger. She opened her mouth to say so, but Ellen beat her to the punch.

"Great idea. I'll go home to change. Why don't you pick me up there? Say six thirty? Let your hair down a little, but what you're wearing is fine."

"Perfect. I'll see you then."

Just like that, Sarah and Ellen had a date. Before she could process what had just happened, Danny was on the elevator with Sarah who couldn't stop talking about the prospect of spotting the "UNSUB" lurking around the bar, hunting down middle-aged women. As if it would be that easy. This guy had committed at least four murders and gone completely undetected. He wasn't stupid and he wasn't careless. But he was dangerous.

Danny decided she should tell Sarah that this wasn't such a good idea after all, that she should leave Ellen out of it. When Sarah finally stopped chattering about her plans, she spoke, but the words that came tumbling out weren't at all what she'd planned.

"I'm coming with you. We should have two cars in case you need to follow someone, and you should ride alone since that's going to fall on you. I'll pick Ellen up and meet you at the bar."

The elevator doors opened and she rushed out before either one of them could change their minds.

Chapter Eleven

Danny stood on Ellen's doorstep. She never should've knocked Sarah out of this duty, and she didn't have a clue what she'd tell Ellen when she opened the door and found out the woman she was expecting wasn't there. She should've let Sarah pick her up and sent some other female cop to cover the mixer. She should've had Ellen come down to the station and talk to George when she'd first called about Barr's death. She should've completely eliminated the sorority connection before she ever made a date with a potential witness. The list of things she should've done was long, but she couldn't help adding to it that she should've kissed Ellen when she'd had the chance.

She rang the bell and paced the porch while she waited for Ellen to answer. She'd gone home and changed into black slacks, and the emerald green shirt everyone always said she looked good in. She was about to ring the bell again when the door opened, and she froze. A minute ago she'd been confident, but now she felt like a slob compared to Ellen who wore an indigo blue sweater and a short black skirt that hugged her like a second skin. Danger, hell. Looking like that, Ellen would be surrounded by too many women for the killer to get close.

If he even showed up. Danny doubted he would risk it. This guy wasn't randomly choosing these women. There was a deeper connection. She felt it in her gut.

"Is Sarah waiting in the car?"

Danny noticed Ellen straining to see around her. She didn't look surprised or disappointed to see Danny, but it was clear she was missing her new pal. "Just me. She'll meet us at the club."

"Okay."

"Are you ready?"

"Almost. Why don't you come in and wait while I finish up?"

Danny glanced back at her car. She knew what she should do. Go to the car, send Sarah a text with their ETA, and wait patiently while Ellen did whatever last minute prep she needed to do. She shrugged off the should haves and walked into Ellen's house. At least she was consistent.

She lingered in the foyer and watched Ellen trail off to the back of the house. Her bedroom no doubt. She couldn't imagine what else Ellen needed to do to get ready. She looked amazing. Maybe she'd gone in search of some secret device to help her walk in the super high heels she sported. Or she wanted to add just another small dab of the amazing cologne she wore to keep everyone in her path mesmerized.

"Would you like something to drink?" Ellen called out.

Golden layers of way too rich Scotch called out, but drinking wasn't on the agenda tonight. She'd need to stay sharp, more to keep from crossing the line with Ellen than protecting her. Sarah was there to protect her. Her own presence was completely unnecessary and motivated only by a jealous desire not to see Sarah end up with every prize in this investigation. "No, thanks. I'm good."

Danny wandered into the living room. Pacing again to pass the time. She hadn't noticed much about the furnishings the last time she was here. Too focused on the occupant. The interior style didn't seem to fit. Ellen's office was ultra modern and sleek. This house was full of heavy antiques, elaborate paintings, and velvet curtains. Rich, but definitely dated.

"I've been meaning to redecorate."

She turned at the sound of Ellen's voice and stifled a gasp. Ellen had changed out of the sweater she'd been wearing earlier and now she wore a different top with a plunging neckline. Talk about dressing to impress. Danny cleared her throat to disguise her initial reaction. "Everything is beautiful." She hoped Ellen thought she was talking about the decor, but she knew her eyes were fixed on Ellen's chest and the full display of cleavage.

Ellen followed her gaze and blushed. "Too much?"

Danny looked away. "Maybe."

Ellen reached out and grasped her hand. "I feel like we got off on the wrong foot. Can we start over?"

Start over? Danny wanted to start something all right, but it didn't involve going back to the beginning. All she wanted was to lean forward and place her lips against the creamy white skin that so captivated her attention. Not gonna happen. And just to make sure, they needed to get out of this house and go somewhere public. With lots of people around. The mixer would be perfect. Lots of other women to distract her. "I think we should go."

They barely spoke on the ride to the downtown hotel where the event was being held. Ellen offered short fragments of conversation to which Danny responded with grunts designed to signal she didn't want to engage. "Turn here." "Nice night." "Should be crowded." "Club is comping valet."

Danny ignored Ellen's comment about the valet and found a spot on the street, close to the hotel. No doubt Sarah would leave her car where she could get to it quickly, and while she may not be a cop, ready to give chase at the first sign of danger, she didn't feel like being boxed in with a bunch of overgrown, dolled-up sorority sisters while Sarah sped away to be the hero.

Stupid thoughts. Highly unlikely there would be any action at this event. She knew in her gut the killer was connected to the sorority somehow, but he was a careful guy. Hell, he'd eluded them for weeks, killing four women, maybe more. Chances were good, even if he was here, they would never know it.

She fed the meter and opened Ellen's door. Ellen climbed out and stepped up to the curb, but one foot didn't move and she pitched forward into Danny's arms. Danny grabbed tight and helped her get steady on the sidewalk. "What the hell?"

"Sorry." Ellen pointed at the grate on the ground by the car door. "Heel caught." While Danny stared at her tall heels, and slim ankles, and toned calf, Ellen said, "And that is why I use the valet. I swear I wasn't throwing myself at you. In fact, I think I'm done doing that." She marched off toward the hotel. Danny stood still for a few minutes while she tried to process this new irritated, angry Ellen. She was doing her level best to stay professional and she'd blown it by leering at their one helpful witness's legs. She needed to focus. On the job, on the case, on the reason they were even at this club tonight or she was going to be in trouble.

But they were damn fine legs.

❖

Heels or no heels, Ellen sped to the club like she was running from a fire. And she was.

She hadn't wanted to attend this event in the first place. Now, not only was she going to have to glad-hand a bunch of senior sisters, she'd have to spend the evening knowing Danny was watching her every step. Biggest challenge? Not letting Danny see that she was watching her too. That would be hard since she hadn't been able to take her eyes off Danny from the moment she saw her standing on her doorstep. The way that green shirt hugged her torso left no doubt that a beautiful body lay beneath. She'd wanted to fall into her arms and skip this event entirely.

Instead she'd rummaged through her closet to find the sexiest top she owned. She'd bought it a year ago on a whim, but she hadn't ever worn it. The plunging neckline wasn't quite office attire, and no date she'd had in the last year merited the show. If Jill was right and the crowd tonight was mostly the older alums, there'd certainly be talk tomorrow about how their national director had acted in a manner unbecoming of a lady. Her mother would die. But it had been worth it, if only to see the expression on Danny's face. She may act like she wasn't interested, but she wasn't made of stone.

"Ellen!"

Sarah stood by the valet stand with open arms. She smiled, unsure how she was supposed to play this. Sarah embraced her in a big hug and saved her with a few whispered words. "Act like we're long lost friends that haven't seen each other in forever. I'll handle the rest."

Sarah's embrace lasted past the words, and it wasn't until Ellen felt a tap on her shoulder that she decided to pull back. She turned and faced Danny who stared between them with a frown on her face. She didn't know what her problem was, but she didn't have to spend her evening trying to sort out the moods of Danny Soto. She grabbed Sarah's hand and pulled her into the hotel. As they entered the elevator, she saw Sarah flash Danny a smug grin. Looked like even these two strong, powerful women were capable of a little girl drama. This night might be doomed, but she was determined to make the most of it. She looked at Sarah's hand in hers. Sarah Flores was a gorgeous woman. Yes, they were only playing roles, but there was no reason not to enjoy the attention.

The elevator stopped at the roof and they stepped out into a perfect Dallas evening. Slight breeze, mid-sixties. The sun was just setting against the backdrop of a cluster of beautiful buildings. The pool was lit with floating candles and colorful Gerbera flowers. Flanked by two gorgeous women, she couldn't ask for a better setting for a date. Too bad this was the furthest thing from it.

She turned to Sarah. "Would you like a drink? We're a little early. We may as well take advantage before I have to be the hostess."

"I'd love one. Maybe Danny can get them for us and we can talk about how you should introduce me around."

Didn't take a rocket scientist to tell Danny was seething, but she took their orders and stalked off to the bar. Ellen took advantage of her absence to pry. "Is she mad at you or is she mad at me?"

Sarah leaned back and stared at her face as if she were studying an insect. "You're kidding, right?"

"Not a bit. I think I may have done something to make her mad. We seemed to get along really well, and then all of the sudden…" She trailed off, mentally trying to pinpoint the change in Danny's behavior. If anything, she should be the one slighted. Wasn't like she was the one who'd shut things down when they'd started to heat up. Maybe that was the problem. Danny thought she was shallow and didn't want to have anything to do with her. No, that couldn't be it. She had called back after that first botched encounter, even said she was interested in trying again. While she tried to figure out the source, Danny returned with their drinks.

"What are y'all talking about?"

Ellen rushed to answer. "Nothing." She took a big gulp of her martini.

Danny looked suspicious, but Sarah spoke up. "Ellen was telling me how these things work. Why don't you fill her in?"

Whew. Why couldn't she think of a good save on her own? Probably for the same reason she couldn't string two thoughts together when Danny stood close. "Women will start arriving in a few minutes. They sign in over there." She pointed to a woman seated at a table full of name tags. "That's Angela. She's an intern, a student Alpha Nu member, interested in working in our office when she graduates. She's got the list of RSVPs and she'll make sure everyone gets a name tag and drink tickets."

Danny interjected. "We'll want a copy of that list."

"Of course. Anything else you want me to know before the crowds start to arrive? I'll be pretty busy, shaking hands, introducing newcomers, and I have a few announcements to make about upcoming events."

Sarah spoke first. "I think you should introduce me as a newbie. It'll give me a chance to meet these women without appearing to be a stalker."

"And what am I supposed to do?" Danny asked.

Ellen turned toward Danny. "I don't know. For some reason, I thought you two would've worked that out."

Danny flashed an annoyed look at Sarah who merely shrugged. "Fine. I'll figure something out on my own." Danny started to walk off, but Ellen grabbed her arm.

"Wait a minute." Danny looked at her with those big brown eyes, and her earlier frustration faded as a not very well thought out idea popped into her head. She didn't take the time to process it because her instinct told her it wouldn't stand up to scrutiny. "You can be my date."

Sarah's mouth fell open and Danny sputtered. "That's a stupid idea."

"That you'd be my date or that anyone would believe it?"

Sarah picked her mouth up off the floor and chimed in. "Actually, it's a great idea. One newcomer that can't possibly have connections to the rest of the group is interesting. Two is odd. Besides, I'm trained in undercover operations. Better you stick to a role that might actually suit you."

"What's that supposed to mean?"

Sarah shot her a wicked smile. "You figure it out. I'm going to go get my name tag and leave you two lovebirds alone."

Ellen stared at Sarah as she left, uncomfortably conscious of Danny's growing anxiety. Introducing Danny as her date was definitely a stupid idea, if only because Danny looked liked she'd rather be anywhere but by her side. She cast about for a harmless topic of conversation. "What are you drinking?" Lame.

"Soda with lime. I had them put my vodka in your drink." A hint of a smile.

She gave Danny a playful shove. "Trying to get me drunk?"

"I should go."

"Is that what you want?"

"No."

"Why did you come? I mean, it's not like you're a cop. Would you really be able to do anything if the killer popped out of the corner?" As she spoke, she saw Danny start to bow up. She couldn't really blame her. "Look, I'm not trying to make you mad; I just want to know why you're here when you so clearly don't want to be."

Danny's shoulders sagged. "That's not true."

"You sure about that?"

"This is not Sarah's case."

"And in the whole city of Dallas, there were no female cops who could've shown up to make sure this social gathering didn't turn into a bloodbath?"

Danny shrugged. "I'm here. Let's make the best of it."

"Fine." Ellen looked around and noticed women were starting to arrive. "Come on, I'll introduce you around. Try and act like dating me isn't the most painful thing you've ever endured." She stalked away, half hoping Danny wouldn't follow. She had a bug up her butt about something and Ellen was tired of trying to figure out what made Danny Soto tick.

❖

The room was full of older women. If she didn't know better, Danny would've thought she'd stumbled into a cougarfest.

As she followed Ellen around the room, she did her best to memorize the names of the women Ellen introduced her to, trying to match them against the searches she'd performed earlier that day. She hoped Sarah was doing the same thing, but from across the room it looked like she was too busy flirting to do any meaningful investigation. And Ellen thought Sarah was better equipped to deal with anything that might happen. Whatever. This evening was an exercise in futility. The women were nice enough, although some raised their eyebrows when Ellen introduced her as her friend, without reference to a graduation year or chapter affiliation. She couldn't really blame them since this wasn't exactly a bring-a-date kind of occasion. After three of these encounters, she excused herself to the restroom.

The room was empty so she took a moment to check the mirror. Every hair was in place, but her expression—was that really her frowning? She practiced a smile or two. She should at least pretend she was having a good time rather than give either Ellen or Sarah the satisfaction of thinking they had any control over her moods. She settled into a semi-happy expression, and then ducked into a booth. Seconds later she heard the door open and a woman whispering. She held perfectly still and strained to hear the conversation, only half embarrassed to be eavesdropping on an obviously private conversation.

"Mostly old hags here tonight. Pretty much the usual crowd." Giggle, but no response to her question. Danny realized the woman was talking on a cell phone.

"No, I haven't seen her, but it's been a long time since she's been around. The other one's here, though. Why do you care, anyway? The others are more important and I promise I can get all the information we need. You just have to be patient."

Danny listened carefully through the next few beats of silence, wishing she could hear the voice on the other end of the phone. She strained to see through the tiny space between the stalls, but she could barely make out the figure talking mere feet from her. Medium height, long blond hair, skinny.

"I'll bring the list by later. Not sure when I'll get out of here." A creaking noise sounded from across the room. "Someone's coming. I gotta go."

Danny heard a faucet running followed by footsteps. She counted to ten, flushed the toilet, and then walked out of the booth. A gray haired woman she recognized from the mixer stood at the mirror, reapplying her lipstick. She washed and dried her hands, then pretended to find a compact on the floor. "I think that woman who was just here left this. I don't recall her name, do you?"

"Angela Perkins. She's working the registration table. You should be able to find her there."

Danny flashed one of the smiles she'd been practicing. "Thanks. Have a great evening." She walked back into the reception and rolled her mind around the conversation she'd just heard. No mistaking, it was odd. Angela was talking to someone about the sorority's alumnae, but it was totally unclear who she was talking to. Another sorority sister? Wouldn't be out of the realm of possibility for the students to poke fun at their aging counterparts, but calling them "old hags" was pretty harsh. And what had she said—"isn't that what you like?" No telling what that meant, but it didn't sound right. And who were they looking for that hadn't shown up tonight or for a while? And why?

Only one way to get the answers to her questions. Danny scanned the room until she found Ellen escorting Sarah around the room. Chummy. Too chummy. She pasted on her most dazzling smile and strode over to break them up.

Sarah saw her first. She dropped the hand of the woman she was talking to and swept Danny into a tight embrace. "Danielle Soto! Is that you? I was hoping I would see you here." She turned back to the woman she'd abandoned and said, "I'm so sorry. I'd love to hear more about the foundation's work, but I absolutely have to catch this woman before she gets away. I'll call you next week for lunch." The woman beamed, and Sarah dragged Danny halfway across the room, away from the crowd.

"I swear, I've never been hit up for money so much in my entire life."

"Maybe you should tell them you make a lowly government salary."

"Not a chance. I'm an oil tycoon."

"Really? What kind of cover is that?"

"Go big or go home."

"Your big ego is going to get you in trouble."

"Did you haul me off the job to lecture me or did you have something important to say?"

"Don't look, but you know the girl who's working the registration table? Angela?"

"She's too young for you, but if you want help finding a date, I'm sure we can find some better prospects. You might have to come up with a donation. Besides, aren't you supposed to be here with Ellen?"

"Shut up. That's a cover and it's about as believable as you posing as an oil baron."

Sarah shook her head. "You keep telling yourself that. And it's baroness."

"Can you focus for a minute? Angela. Blonde. Registration."

"The intern. What about her?"

"She was just in the restroom, having a strange conversation with someone on the phone."

"She's what, twenty years old? All her conversations are strange."

"Not like that. She and whoever she was talking to were discussing the women here at the mixer. Who was here, who wasn't. Their potential. She promised whoever it was on the other end of the line that she would bring the list of attendees over when she was done here."

"That could be anything."

"Seriously, I think she's up to something."

"All college students are up to something. Maybe she's planning some dumb initiation for the pledges that involves prank calling alumnae."

Danny pulled out her cell phone and pulled up the Internet browser. "Fine. You're not interested in following up on a lead. I'll see what I can find out on my own."

Sarah grabbed her arm. "I think I have a better lead. Don't look now, but there's a guy over at the bar. He arrived shortly after we did. You think he would've figured out by now that there's a private party going on."

Danny waited a few seconds, then did a subtle turn to catch a glimpse of the man at the bar. Turning back to Sarah, she said, "So, what are you going to do about it?"

"Do about what?"

Danny and Sarah both turned to find Ellen standing behind them with her hands on her hips. "You two mind explaining what you're up to? My date"—she pointed at Danny—"has spent the evening looking like she'd rather chew glass than hang out with me, and my long lost sorority sister"—chin jerk at Sarah—"would rather exchange whispers with my date than meet a bunch of influential women who might be able to help her with her oil business."

"I'm not your date."

"Good thing, because you suck at it."

"Well, I wonder why. I mean—" Danny stopped when Sarah squeezed her arm.

"Ellen, wait a few seconds and then look over at the bar. There's a guy over there, talking to one of the bartenders. Do you know him?"

She made a show of scanning the crowd as if she was looking for someone specific, without lingering on the bar. "Never seen him before. Why?"

Sarah shook her head. "Probably nothing. Just looks a little out of place."

Danny stared the guy down. As a lawyer she was as much a trained observer as any cop. He wore a wool overcoat, definitely out of place on a mild spring night. Could be he was an out of towner, staying at the hotel, who'd put the coat on before checking the weather. Or he could be the killer, stalking his next victim. She didn't want to alarm Ellen, but she did want to protect her. She held up her phone. "Sarah, a text came in from George. He wants us to call him. Now." She walked a few steps away and motioned for Sarah to follow.

Sarah was annoyed. "I want to check that guy out."

"Yeah, well I want you to too, but I don't want to spook these women or place any preconceived notions in their heads."

"Got it. Why don't you keep Ellen occupied while I check him out?"

"I'm not so good at this."

"I think you'd be great at it if you'd relax and enjoy it. It's not like you don't really want to be her date."

Danny struggled not to react. "You don't know what you're talking about."

"I do this for a living. Everything about you screams that you're attracted to her. Can't say I blame you. If she felt about me like she feels about you, I'd nudge you out of the running."

"You should stick to analyzing criminals. When it comes to real folks, you don't know what the hell you're talking about. Go check out that guy. Like you said, you do this for a living. Maybe it's time you earned your keep." Danny stalked back to Ellen's side before Sarah could prod further.

Ellen's stare was intense. "What's up with you two?"

"Nothing." She glanced over her shoulder. Sarah was walking toward the man at the bar. Time to distract Ellen. She pointed across the room. "I don't think I've met that group of women. Introduce me?"

"Okay. Sure you don't want to wait for Sarah?"

"Positive. Lead the way."

Danny followed Ellen across the room, grateful she didn't have to hide her face since she was sure her expression was a jumble of emotions. Annoyance at Sarah. Arousal for Ellen. Aggravation that this investigation kept her from trying another date.

Ellen slowed her pace until Danny was beside her. "What did Detective Ramirez want?"

"What?"

"You said he sent a text, asked you to call?"

Damn. She forgot she'd used that as an excuse to talk to Sarah alone. "He didn't answer."

"It's okay, you know."

"What's okay?"

"I don't expect you to share details. I get that I'm only around to give you what you need."

Danny stiffened. "Give me what I need?" Ellen didn't have a clue what she needed.

"You know, for the investigation."

"Oh." Ellen's smile told her that her face had betrayed her. "We're not using you. If you don't want to help, you don't have to. Flores is a bully, but I can get her to back off. You can call your lawyers, let them run interference." She shouldn't be making this offer, but a selfish desire for some professional distance drove her. "In fact, I can get Sarah and we can leave right now."

Ellen answer's was to slide an arm through hers and playfully bump her hip. "You don't get off that easy. This is the first time I've brought a date to one of these events in I don't know when. Let's go show these women what a fine catch I can make when I'm really trying."

Danny resigned herself to playing the role. For a little bit longer, anyway. Not like it was such a hardship. Ellen walked close, their hips touching, arms linked. Her hair smelled like lavender and her breath was warm and sweet as she whispered the names of the women they were about to meet. For a moment, Danny forgot why she was here, what she was doing, who Ellen really was. The buzz of her phone jerked her out of her trance. As she read the text from Sarah, she struggled to remain calm. *Guy's leaving. I'm going to follow. Keep everyone here until I make sure he's not up to anything. Will text when it's clear.*

Danny looked back at Ellen and shook her head in response to the questioning look she gave. She held up a finger and considered her options. One was to tell table monitor Angela that she should keep the guests on scene, but no matter how little credence Sarah gave to her suspicions, she didn't trust the girl. No, she'd better bring Ellen in on the plan. She'd know what to do.

Chapter Twelve

Ellen stared at Danny huddled over her phone. Again. No matter how much she pretended, Danny wasn't really her date. Good thing since she'd spent the entire evening either avoiding her or engaged in whispered arguments with Sarah who had played the role of a female J.R. Ewing to a tee.

After a few awkward moments spent staring at Danny and Sarah, she strode toward the women she'd planned to introduce Danny to, resolving to forget about the investigation and Danny Soto. Her original design on this mixer was to meet new people. So what if most of the women here were her mother's age? She had to start putting herself out there if she wanted to connect, and since a connection with Danny was out of the question, she may as well focus her energy elsewhere. Maybe one of the older alumnae had a nice daughter interested in a casual affair.

She zeroed in on the local alumnae chapter president. "Sophia, so nice to see you. Have you had a good time?"

"Ellen, dear, it's been too long."

Sophia Falco delivered the greeting with a crushing embrace. Ellen extracted herself and answered with a smile, "I know, I know. I've let Jill have all the fun, but I decided it was time I get out of the office and see what you all were up to." She shook hands with the rest of the group, determined to ward off any other big hugs. This was the in-crowd. She'd tried to get younger women more involved in the local alumnae chapter, but she could see why candidates might find this power trio intimidating. Sophia ran a successful real estate empire, and although the other two specialized in running their own households, their successful marriages meant the budgets they worked with were larger than that of most small businesses. Younger alumnae tended to focus on their careers, marriages, and children, and were less likely to forge relationships with the graduates who'd gone before.

Sophia took the lead. "We're all great. I went to the doctor this week and he says I'll live forever." She stage whispered, "Unless I meet an untimely death like Martha. Horrible. Simply horrible."

She should have anticipated the topic, but it still took her by surprise. Ellen felt her face flush and she glanced over her shoulder to where Danny and Sarah were presumably discussing the case as well. "Terrible indeed."

"You wrote such a nice piece in the newsletter. Made her seem like an absolute saint."

Ellen pushed past the slight edge in Sophia's tone. "I had good material to work with."

"You're just too young to know better. You should ask your mother for some stories. How is your mother, by the way? I haven't seen her in ages."

Damn, she'd walked over here to suck up a little, keep the power people happy. She hadn't expected every topic raised to make her want to flee. She started to give her well-practiced response, but was saved from lying when Danny appeared at her side.

"Hi, honey, care to introduce me to your friends?"

Sophia's eyebrows shot up and she turned her laser focus onto Danny. "I'm Sophia Falco, and you are?"

"Danielle Soto." She extended a hand. "Nice to meet you. I've heard so much about these events that I insisted Ellen bring me along so I could meet the women she works so hard to please."

"Well, aren't you charming? Are you the reason Ellen has been staying away?" Sophia introduced Danny to the rest of her little group.

Danny answered with a knowing smile she hadn't earned, and then flirted shamelessly with the older women while she peppered them with questions. They practically giggled at her attention and Ellen watched, speechless. Tempted as she was to break up the lovefest, she found that she too was entranced by Danny's charms. More than she should be.

She spent the next several minutes half-listening to Danny entertain the power trio while she scanned the room for a worthy distraction. She'd been silly to think this event might be a hunting ground for future dates. Jill was right; most of the women had aged out of her dating pool. Danny and Sarah were the most worthy potential date material and both were off-limits. Danny had made it clear she wasn't interested in a fling, especially not now that she was working a case in which Ellen was involved, even if "involved" was a strong word to describe her situation. And Sarah, well, she was a shameless flirt, but all business as well.

Probably for the best. Until her mother settled into more of a routine at Cedar Acres, she should focus on her work and her mother's care. Why she'd thought she could have a personal life of her own she had no idea. She was definitely not her father's daughter, able to easily cut ties and act as if his family meant nothing to him. His call the other day made it clear that no matter how much guilt he might feel about abandoning his family, the connection wasn't a strong enough motivation to bring him back, to keep him involved, to offer anything concrete. It was all on her. All the more reason she should stay focused.

Danny gently squeezed her arm, rousting her from her reverie. Sophia was looking at her, as if waiting for her to answer a question she'd obviously not heard. "I'm sorry, what?"

"I asked about your mother. I haven't seen her in a while. Is she doing well?"

"Great. She's great. She's been traveling. You know how she likes to travel." Not a complete lie. When she was well, her mother indulged her penchant for first class flights, luxury cruises, and five-star hotels.

"Your father spoils her. Give them my best." Sophia gathered her group and then delivered fierce hugs to both her and Danny. "And don't hide this one anymore. She's a catch." Seconds later, she was gone, leaving Ellen alone with Danny in an awkward silence.

Danny spoke first. "Do you think she's leaving or just finding someone else to charm?"

"Charm? That's what you call it?" Ellen watched Sophia and her posse stride across the room and descend upon another group. "I have no doubt she's about to ask those women for a favor. She won't leave until she gets it. Sophia Falco always gets what she wants." She felt the blush before she realized what she'd said. Danny had the good grace not to remind her that Sophia had just said she wanted Ellen to keep her around.

"Good. It's important that no one leave right now. Can you do something to keep them all here?"

"Like what? I already did the announcements, thanked our sponsors." *Which you'd know if you'd paid any attention to me earlier.*

"I don't know." Danny kept checking over her shoulder as if she expected someone to materialize. "Tell them the bar's having a special on white wine or something."

"You're funny. Guess you didn't notice Sophia was drinking bourbon. Neat. Knowing her, it was the most expensive pour at the bar. No way am I blowing our budget on free liquor for this crowd."

"What?" Danny murmured the question, but she wasn't paying attention to anything Ellen said, and her attention was focused on the registration table. Ellen waved her hand in front of Danny's face. "Over here. Me. The person who's talking to you. What's going on?"

"Uh, nothing. I just promised Sarah I would keep everyone in the room for a minute while she checked something out. It's probably nothing."

"Are you sure?" Ellen looked around the room, trying to discern what had Sarah worried enough to contain them. "Did she get a lead? Is there something I should know about?"

Danny reached for her arm. "Quit looking like a fire's about to break out and you're scoping out exits. You're going to start a panic."

"It would help if you would just tell me what's going on."

"I can't."

"Won't"

"What?"

"You won't. You won't tell me anything and you won't have anything to do with me, and don't tell me it's just about work. You've acted like I'm a disease you were trying hard not to catch ever since…" She let the words trail off as she flashed back to Danny, in her living room, on her couch, lips parted and ready for the kiss Ellen was all too willing to give.

Danny's breath hitched and her lips parted as if ghosting the original moment. Ellen drew back. The intensity was too much. She didn't need to put herself back in this position, especially since it was doomed to follow the same path as before. As she pulled away, Danny said, "I'm sorry. I never should've put you in that position."

"You didn't put me anywhere I didn't want to be." Ellen didn't bother trying to hide her anger. "And I don't need you to take responsibility for my decisions." She lowered her voice to a whisper. "If I want to kiss someone, that's on me. If they don't want to kiss me back, well, I'll live."

The sound of a new text from Danny's phone saved them both from having to say more. Danny stared at her phone and then thumbed a reply.

"Hot date?"

"Hardly. It's okay for folks to leave now." Her eyes were sad and pleading, but all she said was, "Let me know when you're ready to go." And just like that, Danny walked away, over to the registration table. Ellen watched her go. She should've been surprised at the abrupt departure, but she wasn't. Everything and nothing about Danny surprised her.

❖

Danny couldn't get away from Ellen fast enough. She'd almost kissed her, right here in the middle of this crowd of aging sorority girls, without regard to the audience, her job, or anything else. Sarah's text couldn't have come at a better time. *all ok. mt me @ station later.*

Vague, but comforting. Except for the part about meeting later. Sarah must have found out something or she could wait to talk until tomorrow. Aggravating that she couldn't just stick around and fill her in. And drive Ellen home, since Danny was now dreading that particular task. The good news was that whatever Sarah had found must not involve any of the women here in the room since she was cutting them loose.

"Are you leaving?"

She looked up to see Angela, the intern, staring at her. "Soon." She glanced at the table where Angela had packed the unclaimed nametags into a carrying case and placed a rubber band around the markers. "Packing up for the night?"

"I can't leave until Ms. Davenport is ready to go, but I'm ready for anything else the night may hold." Her words dripped suggestion and her leering eyes left no doubt. Disturbing, but Danny decided to use the opening to explore her hunch that this young woman wasn't what she appeared to be.

"I doubt many of these women are up for an after party, right?"

"I doubt many of these women are up past eight on a normal night."

"Ouch. Aren't they supposed to be your sisters for life, or something like that?"

"You know what they say about family—just because you're stuck with them, doesn't mean you have to like them."

"Does that go for El—I mean, Ms. Davenport too?"

Angela cocked her head. "You're her date, right? Are you trying to get me in trouble?"

"No." Let the kid figure out which question she was answering. "Just curious about how all of this works. I was never in a sorority."

"Why not?"

"No particular reason." Not true. Sororities cost money and time, two things she hadn't had while putting herself through college. Besides that, they were frivolous. Why should she pretend a bunch of women she'd didn't know were her "sisters" when the only thing they had in common was time to waste on parties and silly rituals? She'd entered college with a goal of finishing fast and getting into law school early, and she'd let nothing distract her. The only all-girl gatherings she took part in were Sunday afternoons at the local lesbian bar.

"You're smart."

"Huh?"

"You're smart for not getting involved. I'm a legacy and I didn't really have a choice. My mother practically made it a condition of my tuition."

"So there's nothing you like about it?"

"I hear lots of good gossip at these things."

Danny could tell she was waiting for her to ask, dying to tell her some secret she'd learned. Angela was going to have to make the first move. "I bet you do."

"Maybe I could tell you about it sometime."

"Are you flirting with me?"

"Didn't mean to. I have a boyfriend. Besides, not a good idea to make a play for the boss's girlfriend."

"She's not my—" Danny stopped, unsure what to say. "We're not exclusive."

"Tell her that. The way she stares at you across the room." She jerked her head. "I don't think she has eyes for anyone else."

Unable to help it, Danny let her gaze follow Angela's and she caught Ellen staring. Hard. But her expression wasn't adoring. She looked pissed off. She smiled and turned back to Angela. "Maybe you could tell me about what goes on here, someday. Give me your number."

Angela reached over and tugged at Danny's pocket, and then she pulled out her phone. She scrolled through the screens and then started tapping on the screen. Seconds later, she slid the phone back into Danny's pocket and let her hand linger on her jacket. When her fingers started to stroke her hip, Danny placed her hands on Angela's. She wanted to pump Angela for information, but keep from crossing a boundary at the same time. "I thought you had a boyfriend."

"He's flexible."

"I'm not."

"Well, when you live in a house with a ton of girls, you get used to trading roses."

Had she just said roses? And used the phrase as a euphemism? She mentally reviewed the crime scene photos, each set displaying green paper wrapped white roses at different angles, and more than a dozen photos of the single stem sitting next to the body. "What did you say?"

"I keep forgetting, you're not a sister." She reached into the bag under the table and pulled out a long-stemmed silk white rose and handed it to Danny. "I usually remember to set this out on the table with the name tags. It's the official flower of Alpha Nu."

Danny held the rose in her hand like it was a bug she was about to destroy. It looked so real, she was tempted to smell it. Instead, she held it away from her body.

"What are you doing?"

The sharp voice from over her shoulder almost caused her to drop the rose. Danny looked back at Ellen, an explanation on her lips, but then she caught that Ellen wasn't talking to her. Angela struck a defiant pose and answered, "I'm keeping your girlfriend company. Looked like you were pretty busy working the room."

"Working the room is my job. Do you need help packing up?"

"No, I'm good. If you want, I can take all this stuff back to the office tonight."

Ellen reached into her purse and handed Angela a key. "That would be great. Just leave the key with security and I'll get it from them in the morning."

Danny watched the entire exchange, acutely aware she was standing right next to these two women, holding a long-stemmed white rose. Ellen finally addressed her. "You going to keep that?"

"I, uh, well…" She had planned to keep it. It was a clue. A big one, but it wasn't like she needed this silk version of the flower that had appeared at the crime scene to let the rest of the team know about this new connection to the sorority. Still, her find would have more impact with the symbol. Angela's and Ellen's eyes were on her, waiting. Reluctantly, she thrust the rose toward Angela, but Angela waved her off.

"Keep it. I've got more." She practically leered at Danny. "Besides, it's an insult to return a rose."

Danny nodded, scared to look over at Ellen and witness her response to this suggestive exchange, but Ellen made it clear how she felt. "I'll leave you two alone. Meet you at the car." And she was gone.

True to her word, Ellen was waiting beside Danny's locked car. "Not the best neighborhood to be standing by yourself in the dark," Danny said.

"I'm perfectly capable of taking care of myself. Besides, looks like we have a police escort."

Danny followed the direction of Ellen's finger and saw a nondescript, but very familiar, car. George. She waved and he got out and walked over.

"How's it going, ladies? Did you have a good time?"

Danny willed him to read her mind. "It was okay. I guess Sarah called you?"

Ellen broke in before he could respond. "Detective Ramirez, if something is going on with my sorority, I think I have a right to know. And don't tell me you just showed up here because you like the ambiance of downtown. Agent Flores took off without a word, I was told to keep everyone in the room while we waited for an all clear, and now you're here. Something's going on, and before you get another ounce of cooperation from me, you're going to fill me in."

Danny looked at George who seemed stymied by Ellen's outburst. She shrugged. Time for him to step up and deal with the reluctant witness.

"Ms. Davenport, you have our sincere apologies. We didn't mean to hijack your event. Agent Flores was only being thorough when she confined you all to the premises while she checked out a lead. I hope no one was overly inconvenienced."

Danny watched the expression on Ellen's face morph from indignant anger to humble contrition. "I'm sorry. I know you're only doing your job. I just feel helpless and frustrated not knowing what's really going on."

"I understand. Where are you two headed?"

"I'm taking her home," Danny answered.

"How about I ride with you and we can talk on the way? Danny, you'll have to come back by here anyway, right?"

"I can get a cab home," Ellen said. "I don't want to inconvenience either one of you."

Danny opened her mouth to say that was a great idea. She was dying to talk to George about the rose and her gut instinct that Angela the intern was up to no good, but George beat her to the punch.

"Nonsense. Danny won't mind. Her mother brought her up to have better manners than that."

With a sigh, she said, "Both of you—get in the car." What else was she going to say?

George sat in the back seat, leaning forward into the space between her and Ellen. She hadn't wanted to be alone with Ellen, but having someone else there to witness their stony silence was somehow worse. After several conversation nonstarters, George caught her with an open-ended question.

"What did your mom ask you to bring Saturday night?"

As she tried to figure out a way to steer him clear of the personal conversation, she noticed Ellen sit up straighter in her seat. She wished she could make George vanish. The last thing she wanted to talk to Ellen about was the surge of attraction between them. The second to last thing was her family.

"She didn't."

"Damn. I've been craving some of that special queso. You know, the one with all the different cheeses. If you don't bring it, I think the entire night will be a disaster."

"It might be one anyway if you and Joe drink as much as you did last time."

"Family gathering?" Ellen asked.

Not answering would be rude. "George and my brother go way back. It's Joe's birthday tomorrow night, and my mother spoils him rotten."

George laughed. "She spoils him just right. You have any siblings, Ellen?"

"No, just me."

"Your folks live here in Dallas?"

"Not anymore."

Ellen shifted in her seat, and Danny could tell she was uncomfortable with the questions. Maybe her parents were dead. No, she'd been talking about her parents with Sophia Falco and her groupies. Chances were she just didn't feel like getting personal. Made sense since she'd made it clear she wasn't up for anything other than surface level fun. "Save the personal questions for suspects, Ramirez. I'm sure Ellen's had enough for tonight. Give her a break."

"I'm fine. No need to go easy on me, Detective." Ellen's words were directed at George, but her intense look was focused on Danny. She took advantage of the fact they were stopped at a light to return the stare, unable to read beneath the gaze. When the light turned green, she was the first to break the connection, both glad and sad to have to look away.

In the rearview mirror she could see George looking between them, his expression curious. After a few seconds, he caught her eyes on him, and he grinned like he knew all her secrets.

"You bringing someone to your brother's party?"

If she weren't driving, she would've punched him. He thought he was so clever. "Why are married people so interested in making sure single people get coupled up?"

"We want you to share in our bliss."

"Oh yeah, because you always seem so blissful." Danny cut her eyes at Ellen, wondering if she was buying her cavalier attitude. "How about you, Ellen? Are your married friends always trying to set you up?"

"I have my share of meddling friends. I spend a lot of time begging off, but the old 'I have to wash my hair tonight' excuse only goes so far."

Danny's mind raced with questions she wouldn't say out loud. Do you ever give in? Try one of your friend's setups? What if the perfect woman is out there, but you're so interested in a one-night stand, that you miss something deeper? No point in asking any of these. She already knew Ellen wasn't interested in her that way. But Sarah's words echoed. *It's not like you don't really want to be her date.* Whatever. What she wanted was no more distractions. She had no business letting a woman get her flustered, especially when nothing would come of it. She had a job to do, and the minute she dropped Ellen off, she planned to turn her entire focus to her work. She'd get Sarah to convince Ellen to copy the computer files so she could continue her review of them at her office, not Ellen's. No more mixers, no more hanging out at Ellen's office, no more wanting something she couldn't have.

The rest of the ride was quiet and Danny sighed with relief when she finally pulled up in front of Ellen's house. George mouthed a big "oh my God," and she almost laughed. It was a pretty huge place for a single woman. Hell, it was a pretty big place for a family of ten. Ellen touched her on the arm. "Thanks for the ride. I hope it wasn't too boring for you. I actually had fun for the first time in a while." She was out of the car and heading up the walk before Danny could respond.

George climbed out and looked between her and Ellen. He leaned into the car and whispered, "Hey, rude ass, you going to walk her to the door or should I?"

She hesitated a moment. She'd stood at that door before. Ringing the bell. Excited about the prospect of a new beginning. Appropriate to end it there as well. She climbed out of the car and hurried up the walk. Ellen turned and smiled. "I guess you're not tired of playing the role of date, after all."

"No one's around. No need to play roles anymore. I'm just being polite. My mother taught me well."

"Your mother sounds like a good woman."

"She's something. More like a meddler. But I love her anyway."

"Your family sounds nice."

"Nice is one word for it. They have no boundaries and they all think they know what's best for me."

"And what do they think is best for you?"

"They think I work too hard. They think I should find a nice girl, settle down, and raise a family of my own."

"And what do you think?"

"I think they should mind their own business."

"So are you bringing someone?"

"What?"

"To your mother's? Are you bringing a date?"

"Uh, no. I may not even go. I may be busy working." She wouldn't be working. Her mother would have her hide if she didn't show up, but the lie saved her from answering other questions.

"So they're right about you working too hard."

"I work hard enough."

Ellen placed a hand on her chest. Warm heat poured from her touch, burning quickly into intense attraction. "I hope it wasn't too hard for you to play the part of my date tonight. You were perfect, and I'm pretty sure Sophia and her friends are telling everyone I had the catch of the night."

The blush burned Danny's cheeks. The pleasure had been all hers, but she couldn't resist the question on the tip of her tongue. "Want to repay the favor?"

CHAPTER THIRTEEN

Ellen threw another discarded outfit on the bed. Danny had said dress casual, but the range of casual defied her. Picnic casual, go to the mall casual, business casual? She laughed. Her mother didn't believe in casual. Vivian's range of clothing went from dressy to dressier, and she believed that every time a lady left the house was an occasion and she should dress as if she might run into the president or a foreign dignitary while out and about.

She finally settled on tan slacks, a light blue sweater, and flats. A couple of modest pieces of jewelry to finish out the look. A little preppy, but casual and put together. Should work no matter what Danny's family had in mind. Not that she gave a rip what her family thought. She was dressing to impress Danny. She had to do something to keep her interest since it was pretty clear Danny had written her off. Hell, she'd practically tricked Danny into inviting her to this event, and she was both nervous and excited. Family wasn't her thing. Not her own anyway, but other people's families usually embraced her, possibly because they sensed she had no real family of her own.

The doorbell signaled Danny's arrival. Ellen grabbed her purse and practically ran to the door. A polite hostess would invite Danny in, offer her a drink, but she wanted this date to actually happen, and following convention hadn't worked out so far. She swung open the door and stepped out. "Look at you, exactly on time."

Look at her indeed. Danny was dressed in another pair of snug-fitting jeans, a crisp black cotton shirt, and black loafers. Dark and dangerous, exactly the opposite of the approachable look Ellen had been going for. And totally hot. "You look fantastic." She'd resolved to keep things as casual as she could, but she couldn't help the arousal that seeped into her tone. She looked down at her own outfit. "Do I look all right?"

Danny smiled. "You look great. Mama will say you look like spring." She glanced at her watch. "We don't have to leave right now if you don't want to."

Ellen cocked her head, trying to read the hesitation. "Having second thoughts about taking me to meet your family?" Probably not a bad assessment. How would Danny introduce her? Here's the woman I told you about, you know, the one that invited me over for dinner, but tried to get in my pants instead. Or better yet, here's the woman I'm only interacting with because she has information about a case I'm working.

Danny shook her head. "I'm not having second thoughts about inviting you out. It's the meeting my family part."

"I get it. Maybe you should just go on your own." She pulled her keys back out of her purse and reached to unlock the door, but Danny's hand on hers stopped the action.

"I hate going over there alone."

The whispered confession sounded painful. Ellen looked into Danny's eyes, trying hard to read the message behind the words. "Detective Ramirez made it sound like your family is a big ball of love."

"If you're going with me, you better start calling him George. And they are. Too big. If you show up with me, my mother's going to start planning our wedding. I should've thought of that before I asked you."

Or did you and you just conveniently forgot to mention it? Ellen tried not to over think Danny's invite. She'd known when she accepted an invitation to a family gathering that no matter how casual the event may be, the invite wasn't. But she'd accepted anyway. She had to because she couldn't deny the attraction she felt between them. The entire night of the mixer, she'd been distracted, wondering where Danny was, who she was talking to. And then the flirty intern Angela, handing her a white rose. She imagined the roses signified what they always had. The official flower of Alpha Nu had turned into a calling card, an invitation. Sorority members handed them out at the end of a function to whoever they wanted to sneak up to their rooms, whether it was a guy from one of the fraternities or, in her case, a fellow Greek from a rival sorority.

But that was in college. She'd outgrown silly gestures like white roses, but she wished she hadn't. Waving a flower would be so much easier than putting words to whatever this was she was feeling. For now, she'd settle for playing the part of date. She put her keys in her purse and led Danny down the walk to her truck. As Danny helped her climb in, she said, "I'll call Detective Ramirez, George. As for the wedding plans, you're going to have to wear the white dress. White washes me out."

"I doubt anything could make you look bad."

The blush warmed her. "You shouldn't say things like that."

"Why not? If you're going to pretend to be my date, you should try on the part before we get there."

Ellen took the out. "Fine then. I suppose I should know a little more about you as well."

"My favorite color is blue. Indigo. I hate long walks in the rain. Never have understood why anyone thinks that would be romantic."

"So you like romance?"

It was Danny's turn to blush and Ellen enjoyed watching her fumble for an answer. "No one's ever accused me of that."

"It was a question, not an accusation. Come on, Counselor, don't you know the difference?"

"I may not be as good at reading situations as some might think."

Ellen couldn't ignore the implication, but she didn't have to rise to it either. Their easy levity fell away and the rest of the ride passed in silence. Ellen spent the time staring out the window, watching the neighborhoods change as they drove across town. Soon they were in a neighborhood in Garland quite unlike her mother's. Instead of custom homes, the streets were crowded with single-story brick look-alikes. Kids played basketball in the street, and driveways were littered with hastily thrown down bicycles. When they pulled up in front of a small but well-trimmed lawn, the silence between them was so stark she could hear Danny's breath hitch. Out of the corner of her eye, she watched her staring at the house, her face impassive, but Ellen sensed she was girding herself for whatever she would encounter inside. A family who loved her so much they wanted her to be happy? Relatives who'd tease her about her relationships? On a purely intellectual level, Ellen understood how Danny might be annoyed at the unwanted attention to her personal life, but she couldn't help but wish for an ounce of the attention Danny professed to dislike. For one night, she could pretend her life was something other than what it was. She reached over and grasped Danny's hand. "Let's go inside and show them what a great couple we are."

❖

Danny grunted as her mother's hug threatened to crush her ribs. "Ma, you're going to make me drop the bowl." When sufficient injury had been inflicted, Mama took the covered bowl out of her hands and inspected her date.

"She's beautiful, but skinny."

Danny rolled her eyes. "This is my friend, Ellen Davenport." She had practiced the introduction several times that afternoon, worried any hesitation on her part would leave an opening for too many questions. As it was, Mama Soto was certain to assume Ellen was a serious girlfriend since the last woman she'd brought to a family gathering had been Maria. For the fortieth time that day, she questioned her judgment in bringing Ellen here.

"Ellen, welcome to our home." Mama Soto gently pushed Danny aside and led Ellen toward the kitchen. "We have chips and guacamole, and if my daughter knows what's good for her, this bowl is full of queso."

Danny laughed at the worried look on Ellen's face, unable to tell if it was the food or the fact she'd been kidnapped that had her stressed. She started toward the kitchen to run interference, but was stopped by a hand on her arm.

"Hey there, pal, you have some explaining to do."

Danny faced George's questioning stare, daring him to ask what she knew he was dying to. After a few beats of silence, he must have decided she wasn't going to volunteer any information on her own.

"Pretty sure that was Ellen Davenport your mother just abducted and is probably putting into a food coma as we speak."

"Yep."

"The same Ellen Davenport who runs the sorority that is definitely connected to each of our victims?"

"Yep."

"You want to tell me anything?"

Danny squared for a fight, but then decided there might be a way to avoid the battle. "Actually, I want to ask you something. Any more news on the guy from the mixer?"

"You know what I know. Sarah and a few of our guys have him under surveillance. They've been watching him since he left the bar at the hotel."

She already knew the rest. Sarah had run his plates and found his car was registered to a Ron Keck. A team had followed him home and then followed his every move. While they watched, Sarah had determined Keck was an employee of a mail service business located near the hotel and he had a rap sheet, although it contained mostly minor offenses, one of which was public lewdness. A misdemeanor and it had occurred in an adult theater, not a public park, so generally harmless. In the meantime, Danny had spent the day before going through the sorority's files, which she'd convinced Ellen to let her take offsite. No other suspicious deaths, but she'd put together a list of women whose ages fit the killer's profile and handed it over to Sarah to run through her magical FBI databases. Hopefully, it would all be for nothing. "You think he's involved in these murders?"

George shrugged. "Hard to tell. Flores and Buckner say Keck fits the profile. Middle-aged bachelor, lives alone, small crimes in the past as if he was testing the waters. But I asked you about Davenport. Why are you changing the subject?"

"I'm not. It's just that it doesn't seem like you're focused on sorority members as part of your investigation."

"No, besides the fact the killer is targeting them, I haven't seen anything to make me think the good girls of Alpha Nu are killing their own. What's your point?"

"My point is if she's not a potential suspect, what's the harm in having her over to dinner?"

"Danny, is this the woman you've been dating?"

"Well, we haven't really even made it that far, but I like her so I asked her to join me. Thought I'd try something different and bring potential dates to a family gathering first and weed out the ones who can't handle the onslaught." When she'd finally exposed Maria to her family, it only took a few minutes for her to realize they didn't like her, but by then they were already living together.

"Did you even prepare her?"

"Mildly."

"What if info breaks that points in a different direction, like back at the sorority?"

"Is it dumb to say I'll deal with that when or if it happens?" She knew the answer, but she also knew George would have her back even if she chose to pursue a woman she shouldn't. And she was right.

"Maybe, but it won't be the first time someone's acted dumb about a beautiful woman."

"Well, we haven't even made it through a meal together yet. If she can make it through a night full of Sotos, then she can handle anything."

"That's for sure."

"What's for sure?" Ellen looked between them with a beer in one hand and a bottle of water in the other.

Danny took the beer Ellen offered. "You escaped."

"Only long enough to bring you a beer. If you're going to stay here chatting, I'm heading back to the kitchen and the queso. It's going fast."

George nodded at Ellen. "If you don't go with her, I will. That queso is the only reason I'm here."

"Listen to the man."

Danny looked between them. "Come on, you two, let's go."

Their arrival in the kitchen was met with shouts of greeting. Danny hugged her brother, Joe, and his wife, Pam, and introduced Ellen. But this time the "friend" reference didn't go unnoticed.

"Right, sis. You bring a woman home for the first time in I don't remember how long and she's just a 'friend'? Give me a break." Joe took Ellen's hand and made a show of inspecting her fingers. "Where's the ring?"

Just as she was about to melt into the floor, Ellen saved her. "I'm not big into rings. I was thinking about a car instead." She cocked her head and looked into Danny's eyes with a dreamy expression. "What do you think, honey? Maybe something big enough for kids?"

"Uh…" She'd stopped digesting coherent sentences after "honey." Seconds later, Joe, Pam, and Ellen burst into laughter, but it wasn't until Joe punched her on the arm that she realized they didn't take Ellen seriously. "She's a funny one. You should keep her around. Ellen, can I get you a margarita?"

Danny watched while her older brother, who usually let everyone else wait on him, fixed a perfect drink for perfect Ellen Davenport. Ellen laughed at his antics and charmed everyone in the room. She was a perfect catch, but she was playing a part of the girlfriend, and Danny needed to remember playing didn't make it real.

❖

They'd been sitting in front of her house for several silent seconds when Ellen pulled Danny's hand into her lap and said, "I had a good time tonight."

She wasn't lying. The crushing embrace of Danny's family had been more comforting than claustrophobic and she'd enjoyed the role as center of attention. Danny, on the other hand, was hard to read. Something about the evening had caused her to draw into herself, become distant.

"They really like you."

"You say that like it's a bad thing."

"It would be a great thing, if…"

"If?"

"Never mind."

Ellen squeezed the hand in her lap. "No, not fair. What's on your mind? Spill."

"I really should go."

Ellen locked her fingers with Danny's. "But I have you prisoner. Seriously, why don't you come inside and tell me what's going on in that beautiful head of yours?"

"I'm not sure I'd know where to begin."

It wasn't a no. Ellen took the slight opening and pushed a little harder. "I don't want to end the night like this. I feel like something's unresolved between us. I won't be able to sleep. Come in. We'll talk, just talk. I promise."

Danny squeezed her hand and nodded.

When they entered the house, Ellen motioned Danny to the living room. "I'm dying for water after those amazing margaritas. What can I get you?"

"Water's good."

"Wait here. I'll be right back."

Ellen stood in front of the refrigerator with the door open, hoping the cool air would give her an idea of what to say when she returned to the living room. All evening long, she'd sensed both attraction and resistance from Danny. Did Danny feel like she couldn't date her because of the murder cases she was helping investigate? If that were true, why did she keep coming back? From the first night at Adair's to becoming her personal escort to the mixer, to inviting her to a close family gathering, Danny was sending signals of attraction. But when she got close, especially physically, Danny pulled away, mixing up the message. She wanted to ask her what was going on, but she didn't know how to approach the subject without spooking her.

Maybe spooking her was the only way.

When she returned to the living room, Danny was standing in front of the fireplace, staring at the mantel. "Hey, you want to have a seat?"

Danny shook her head. "I'm good." She accepted a water bottle and downed half the contents. "Joe's margaritas are definitely salty." She drank some more, and then pointed at the mantel. "The mantel at my mother's house is covered with family pictures."

Ellen sat on the couch and looked up at the mantel. An expensive crystal vase and an antique clock were the only features. She had a feeling she knew where Danny was going with this, but she decided to wait it out. "Your mom's house is a very welcoming place. What's your place like?"

Another long drink of water and the bottle was empty. Ellen watched Danny look around for somewhere to set it down, but she could tell she was stymied by the formality of the room. She walked over, took the bottle, and with her free hand, led Danny to the couch. She pointed at the cushion. "You sit there and I'll sit over here," she pointed to the adjoining chair. "Tell me about your place."

"Not much to tell."

"Do you live near your parents?"

"I have an apartment not far from them. One bedroom. It's small." She waved her hand. "Way smaller than this house. Of course, everything is way smaller than this house."

Ellen started to say "it's not my house," but she bit her tongue. Instead, she said, "It's pretty crazy. Way too big."

"Why don't you have any pictures around?"

"What?"

"Pictures, you know, photographs? Framed memories of people you love, people who love you? Even in my tiny apartment, I have personal stuff out. Nothing about this place is personal. Is that because you don't believe in personal?"

Danny's tone was calm, but her words signaled anger, and Ellen was stung by the unexpected emotion. She started to tell Danny that how she chose to decorate her house was none of her business, but she had a feeling Danny's anger wasn't about the house. Something deeper was going on here, and as much as she didn't want to get involved, she wanted to erase the pain from Danny's face. She abandoned her promise about staying put in the chair and joined Danny on the couch. "I have pictures, but I have reasons why I choose not to display them. Maybe when we know each other better, I'll tell you those reasons, but for now, why don't you tell me what's got you all twisted up?"

"Nothing."

"It's not nothing."

"It's nothing to you if it doesn't involve having a good time."

"Ouch, that's harsh."

"Those were your words, not mine. You should find someone else to have a good time with. Clearly, I'm not that person."

Ellen bristled. "If it were so clear, you wouldn't be here. You're the one who asked me to go with you tonight. You're the one who showed up to take me to the mixer. You're the one who brought coffee to my office. If you weren't interested in having a quote unquote good time with me, then you sure are sending the wrong signals."

Danny stood up. "Look, I'm sorry, I should leave. I had no business doing any of those things."

Ellen looked up into her eyes. Hurt, confusion, regret—she couldn't distinguish the emotions, but none of them were happiness, pleasure. What had happened? The night had started well. She'd enjoyed meeting Danny's family, being with Danny, and getting to see her off the job. She imagined the evening's end way differently. A kiss at the door, a gentle tug inside. Maybe another drink, more kissing, and whatever else that might lead to. But Danny clearly had had something else in mind. She flashed back to the awkward conversation Danny had with her brother after he'd teased her a little too much about her date. She'd give anything to know what had been going on there, but bottom line, if Danny wasn't interested, why did she keep coming back for more?

Because she wants more. The thought hit her like a Mack truck. If she wasn't already home, she would've run for the door.

But she didn't want to run. This was Danny, sweet, gentle, coffee bringing Danny. Danny with the nice family. Gorgeous Danny. Could they find a middle ground? She could give a little more. Surely it wouldn't kill her to give a little more? "Don't go."

"I really should."

"I really don't want you to." She patted the seat beside her. "Please? I promise, we don't have to do anything you don't want to do. We can talk, hang out, get to know each other." She heard her own offer, powerless to stop the tumble of words. Getting Danny to stay seemed more important than guarding her privacy. Almost. She offered up a tiny disclosure in the interest of compromise. "The stuff on the mantel *is* personal. The vase was a gift to my mother from the president of Richards University for charitable work she did on one of his favorite causes. The clock's been in our family forever. My dad likes to tell some story about how it was smuggled out of Germany by relatives during World War II. I don't know if that's true, but we let him believe that we believe him." She started to say more, but the intense focus of Danny's gaze stopped her cold. She wasn't making this stuff up, but she hadn't meant to get caught up in sharing, especially not such personal, painful memories. Right now, all she wanted to do was reel her words back in and burrow back into the cocoon she'd made for herself since her mother had gotten sick and her father cut ties.

"Are you trying to tell me you live with your parents? That would help explain why you have such palatial digs. And it would make me feel a little better about taking you to my tiny place someday."

"I'd love to see your place sometime," Ellen said, thinking this entire conversation would be much easier if they were at Danny's home, surrounded by mementos of Danny's life instead of hers. "They used to live here, but they travel most of the time and they have a second home. They didn't want to let this place go, so I agreed to move in and keep it up. Frankly, I'd rather have a tiny place. I feel lost in this much space."

"Grass is always greener, I guess."

"If I were at your place, what would I see?"

"No crystal vases or antique clocks. I have loads of personal stuff, but most of it's in boxes."

There was a story there, but Ellen could tell if she wanted to hear it, she'd have to tread lightly. "Did you move in recently?"

Danny made a face. "About a year ago."

"So, either you're slow to settle in or you have some other reason you don't feel like unpacking those boxes."

"Is there a reason you're curious about my living space?"

"I think you got us on this subject."

"True, but some things are better left boxed up."

Amen. But as much as Ellen shared the sentiment, she wanted more. Whatever Danny had boxed up carried pain. She could relate, and she wanted to ease her suffering, or at least not contribute to it. Mostly what she wanted was inside, but Danny wasn't going to cough up what was wrong. She'd have to guess, and she thought she had an idea. "What's her name?"

CHAPTER FOURTEEN

Pow. Ellen's question slammed hard, and Danny's first instinct was to run. From her house, from her prying questions, from her magnetic beauty. She pushed off the cushion of the couch, but Ellen's hand on her chest stilled her retreat. She didn't want to talk about Maria. Not here, not now. Not ever. But after badgering Ellen to share more about her personal life, she'd be a jerk not to do the same. Being a jerk would be easier.

Ellen watched her face, and Danny wondered if she could see the parade of emotions. After a few minutes of silence, Ellen was the first to speak. "I'm sorry. Guess I got a little too personal. It's just that I can see you're hurt, and maybe even a little angry. If I contributed to any of that, I'm very sorry."

"No, no." Danny pulled Ellen close and whispered into her hair. "It's not you." The words weren't enough to push past the barrier she'd erected between them. While she contemplated whether she wanted to share more, Ellen traced her hand with delicate fingers. Light touches that left a deep impression. This woman hadn't hurt her. She'd imposed the pain Maria had inflicted on her experience with Ellen, and it wasn't fair. She should give this, whatever it was, a chance, past the taint of what had gone before.

"Her name was, is, Maria. She's a lawyer, a prosecutor. Just like me."

"Here in Dallas?"

"Yes."

"How long did you date?"

"Date? Funny, we didn't really date at all. We met at the office, worked on a couple of big cases together, and suddenly we were living together. I was her first 'true love.' The first woman she'd ever been with. She was so excited to have discovered passion, intensity, and all that. Her excitement was intoxicating." She didn't try to hide the bitter edge to her voice. Anything else would be insincere.

"She hurt you."

"My own fault. I had every opportunity to see the signs that she would never be satisfied with only me, but I spent two years deluding myself. I honestly believed she was the one."

"She cheated."

"Understatement. The courthouse is big in size only. Didn't take long before I started hearing about her antics. She fooled around with anyone who would have her. I lost sleep; I started fucking up at work. When I finally got the nerve to confront her, she insisted she loved me, but really what did I expect? I was only the first woman she'd been with. Did I really think she wouldn't want to explore the wide world of women she'd never before realized were there for the taking?"

"What did you say?"

"There was nothing left to say. She made it clear playing the field was way more important than the commitment we'd made. I was devastated. I wound up spending less and less time at the office to keep from facing her, facing the rumors about her. I know for a fact I was passed over for a couple of promotions during my mourning period.

"Joe and George helped me move out. I took only what I'd brought to the relationship—didn't want anything that represented whatever it was we'd had. Not like it meant anything anyway. A week after I moved, I found several boxes on my doorstep. Guess she didn't want the memories either."

"Ouch. Do you two still work together?"

"No, she took a job at the DA's office in Fort Worth a few months ago. Can't say I wasn't glad to see her go."

"But the pain, that's not gone."

"I thought it was." The last thing Danny wanted to do was scare Ellen away. Even if Ellen wasn't looking for something serious, that didn't mean she would leave a trail of hurt. If she was at all interested in seeing Ellen again, she needed to toughen up and test the waters. "That first night here, when you made it clear you only wanted one thing, well, I have to admit I had a tiny case of PTSD."

Ellen's smile was kind and gentle. "I bet. Totally my fault. I never should have assumed late dinner was code for anything other than food. Forgive me?"

"Nothing to forgive. Besides, it feels kind of weird to say, 'hey, wish you hadn't wanted to get in my pants.'"

Ellen nodded. "I see what you mean. Should we just call it an unfortunate miscommunication and let it go?"

Loaded question. Danny contemplated her responses. The smart thing to do would be to accept Ellen's gracious apology, shake hands, and leave. She'd see her now and then as they worked on the case, but all these unresolved feelings, this pent up arousal would linger. She could avoid Ellen. Sarah or someone else on the team could interact with her. All she had to do was say the word to George and he would make it happen. With any luck, she wouldn't have to see Ellen again unless or until they went to trial.

Would not seeing Ellen again really be lucky? Wasn't the real luck running into Ellen in the first place? Right now Ellen may only want a fling, but what if they had a chance to get to know each other? As potential date material, she had more pros than cons. She'd been great at the family dinner, interacting easily with her brothers and their wives. She'd treated her parents' home with respect, asking Mama Soto where she'd purchased her drapes as if she intended to buy a set herself. She was beautiful, smart, and successful. And her lips, smiling, poised in thought, or about to kiss—didn't matter, Danny wanted to be lost in them. She'd be foolish to let that kind of luck go.

"Are you okay?"

Danny met Ellen's eyes. "Not quite."

Ellen's eyes narrowed with concern. "Can I get you anything? You look flushed." She placed a hand on Danny's forehead. "Not a fever, but maybe you should lie down. I'll get you a pillow." Ellen started to stand, but Danny caught her arm.

"Wait."

"Yes?"

"It wasn't an unfortunate communication."

"Come again?"

"I want to see where this will go."

"This?"

Danny pulled Ellen close. Without wondering if it was wise, without a clue as to where it might lead, she whispered against Ellen's lips. "Kissing. Let's start with some kissing."

Ellen's lips parted, and this time Danny accepted the invitation, taking a moment to enjoy the first press of flesh before she moved her lips against Ellen's. Soft, firm, tender. The light touches sent waves of burning pleasure coursing through her entire body, but the anticipation she'd experienced since the moment she'd met Ellen had reached a fever pitch and light touches weren't going to cut it. She traced Ellen's lips with her tongue and groaned when Ellen invited her in. Instead of being satisfied, she was hungrier now. A taste wasn't enough. She lowered Ellen to the couch and slid down beside her. She flashed on the memory of Ellen's cleavage that had teased her all throughout the mixer. Her preppy sweater set hid her lovely breasts from view and Danny was desperate to remedy the issue. She reached under the sweater and traced her hand up Ellen's stomach, relishing the tiny hitches of breath her touch elicited. Slowly, gently, she traced first one nipple then the other with her fingers. Ellen responded with groans, but their lips never stopped touching.

Why had she waited for this? Ellen's body, her responsiveness, was amazing. Her fears, her trepidation dissolved in the heat of their passion. She'd been a fool.

"Hey, where did you go?" Ellen whispered.

Danny kissed the frown on Ellen's forehead. "Nowhere. Just kicking myself for waiting so long to do that."

"The kissing or the touching?"

"The everything."

"We haven't done everything. Not yet, anyway."

"Is that an invitation?"

"Do you really need one?"

Danny grinned. "Not anymore." Her fears fell away and she leaned in for another kiss. And everything.

❖

Ellen shuddered. With every kiss, with every touch, she fell deeper and deeper into the spell Danny Soto had cast. For so long she'd managed to shy away from intimacy. She could barely remember the name of her last lover, and she definitely couldn't remember a time when the very idea of sex had shaken her to the core.

But this wasn't sex. It was amazing, it was incredible, and she wanted to indulge every tingle, every sensation, but she wasn't quite ready to call it what it was.

"Are you okay?"

Danny's voice was soft, tender. Ellen opened her eyes and met Danny's. They were dark with lust, but laced with concern. "Yes. Everything is wonderful." She pulled Danny closer. "You are wonderful."

Danny leaned back and stared at her. Those eyes again. They were almost black now. "I want to kiss you again."

"Uh huh." Arousal robbed her of vocabulary, and Ellen let her eyes drift shut as she waited for Danny's lips. But instead of kissing, Danny whispered in her ear. "I want you to look at me when I kiss you." Danny traced the edge of her ear with her tongue and Ellen groaned. "Do you think you can do that?"

She would do anything to feel Danny's lips on hers. Climb mountains, leap tall buildings, swim oceans. But she couldn't. Danny's lips and hands were driving her crazy, but her eyes? The pool of emotion reflected in her eyes was a dangerous place to wade, and Danny was asking her to dive full in. She didn't know how to swim in the deep end, and learning this way, with this woman was too risky. She shifted in Danny's arms and eased away. Time to stop this before one of them got hurt.

Danny had other ideas. As she pulled away, Danny tugged her closer, "I've got you and I promise we don't have to do anything you don't want." Danny gasped the words while nipping at her neck, her ears, her forehead, everywhere but her lips.

"I want to do everything, but I can't promise you anything, and I don't think that's what you want to hear."

"I want you."

"You say that now." Ellen managed a smile. "You know, while you have your hand on my breast. Later, you may regret this."

Danny eased her hand away and waved it between them. "Tell me you don't feel this."

Every practical bone in her body yelled for her to say no. Or to say she felt physical arousal, but not any depth of emotion, but that would be a lie, and she knew when Danny spoke about feelings she meant more than lust. She should stop this now. If she didn't, one of them would get hurt, although she was no longer sure which one.

"I promise I won't try and move in tomorrow, talk about how many kids we'll raise, and plan for our retirement." Danny held her hands up. "And look, no hands on breasts."

"Look at you, charming me with no hands. You're simply amazing."

"You say that now because you really want my hands back on your breasts."

"Maybe."

"Say the word."

The playful banter felt nice, but if they kept it up, they would fall back into conversation and the sexual tension between them would fade. This was the moment, the tipping point. Ellen knew what she needed to do, and she opened her mouth to say the words that would define their relationship.

Eyes wide open, she said, "Kiss me."

Danny didn't hesitate, and she groaned as the import of Ellen's words aroused her almost as much as the feel of her lips—touching, taking, melting. She didn't wait for a tease or an invitation this time before returning to Ellen's breasts, taking one into each hand and kneading them, gently at first, but then increasing the pressure as Ellen pressed into her grasp. She coaxed her nipples to a fine point and shuddered at the ache between her legs, the gathering wetness signaling her own insistent response. She had to have Ellen tonight, and she no longer cared about where that would leave them tomorrow. "I want to take off your clothes. Take you to bed."

Hazy eyes met hers and she knew Ellen was in too deep to argue. She didn't wait for an answer; instead, she grasped Ellen's hand and carefully pulled her to her feet. She paused for a second as she realized she'd only ever been in the kitchen and the living room. She had no idea where in this huge house Ellen's bedroom was. "Point me in the right direction."

Ellen tugged her forward and they walked down a long hall to a staircase, up the stairs, and down another hall. Just when she thought they might never reach their destination, Ellen threw open the door to an enormous suite. Completely at odds with what she'd seen of the rest of the home's traditional decor, the room was furnished with sleek, modern furniture, and edgy artwork hung on the walls. French doors led to an expansive second-story deck, but the most prominent feature in the room was the bed, a king-sized platform, upholstered in black leather.

Ellen pulled her in for a kiss. "If you looked at me like you're looking at that bed, I'll fulfill your every wish."

Danny looked from the bed to Ellen. "Prepare to grant wishes."

"What's your first one?"

"For you to be naked." She jerked her chin. "On that bed. And not under the covers."

A grin. "I knew it was the bed you were after."

Danny pulled at Ellen's soft cotton sweater and she took the hint. She pulled it over her head and flung it to the floor. "Your turn."

Danny slowly unbuttoned her shirt as Ellen watched, unable to hurry as anticipation made her suddenly extremely uncoordinated. Ellen stepped to her. "I can't wait any longer," she whispered.

Danny dispensed with the buttons and pulled her shirt and the T-shirt underneath over her head. "Me neither." She reached around Ellen and unfastened her flimsy bra, letting it drop to the floor before pulling Ellen on top of her on the bed. The bed felt enormous. She patted the space beside her. "Don't wander too far. I might not find you again."

Ellen's smile was wistful. "Don't say that. If I get lost, please promise you'll look for me."

"I promise."

The view was amazing. Ellen's perfect breasts, nipples erect stared down at her while her wet thighs straddled her abdomen. Danny bent forward to kiss her, and the press of their flesh sent electric pulses straight to her clit. With every stroke of her tongue, with every pass of their lips, the intensity built, and she hazily wondered if she could come from kissing alone.

As if to answer her question, Ellen murmured against her lips. "Touch me."

Danny continued kissing her, but slid a hand between Ellen's legs and made slow circles in the slick wet of her arousal. Ellen arched against her touch and she took the sign to enter, savoring the tight, warm walls closing on her fingers.

"Feels…so…good," Ellen gasped.

"Yes." The one word was all Danny could manage, but she wanted more. She placed a hand behind Ellen's back and while still inside, rolled them both over. Ellen's blond waves fanned out on the pillow, and her expression was dreamy, eyes fading shut. Danny circled one stiff nipple with her tongue before kissing her way to the other. As if she'd flipped a switch, Ellen arched her hips and bucked against her hand. She grazed her teeth along Ellen's breast and sucked harder now, hungry for her climax. "You're so close." She murmured the words against Ellen's skin in response to the escalating groans of pleasure. Within seconds, she uttered her own moans as Ellen's fingers found her dripping clit, and teased it to erection.

"You're so wet."

"Excited. You…make…me." Danny moaned between each word, torn between giving and receiving pleasure. But as hungry as she was to make Ellen come, she wanted more. She kissed Ellen's closed eyelids. "Baby, look at me."

Ellen's eyes fluttered open and Danny stared into the midnight blue. Passion, excitement, promise. Maybe she was reading too much into Ellen's gaze, but in this moment, anything seemed possible. She leaned down and kissed her lips, their eyes still locked as the intensity of their touch brought them to the brink. She had no idea who crested first—their orgasms tumbled together and they both cried out, sounds that might have been words, but didn't need to be for her to understand what they meant.

Finally spent, she collapsed beside Ellen who had turned her head to keep their connection. Gazing into Ellen's eyes, she was thankful the intensity of their climax had robbed her of the ability to speak. She was certain if she could have managed whole words, she would have said too much.

Chapter Fifteen

Ellen opened her eyes to bright sunlight and a half empty bed. Had she managed to chase Danny away again after all?

Not a chance. She may be a little fuzzy from exhaustion, but not enough to forget what had caused her to be so drained. Danny kissing her. Danny touching her. Danny on the couch, on the bed, in the shower. She hadn't run away, she'd stayed and taken her to ecstasy. Over and over again. But where was she now?

A long stretch netted her answer when her fingers connected with a piece of paper. The note was short, but Ellen read it several times before tucking it between the pages of the journal she kept on her nightstand. *I couldn't imagine a more perfect evening. Was looking forward to waking up with you, but duty calls. Sweet dreams, Danny.*

Thoughtful, romantic, sweet. Ellen had to admit that if she'd done a casting call for girlfriends, Danny would be a super star. But she wasn't looking for a girlfriend. Girlfriends hung around, expected you to share details about your personal life. She'd spent more time on her personal life this week than she had in the last year, and while she didn't regret a second spent with Danny, she felt guilty for not visiting her mother as much as usual, and even more guilty for keeping secrets from Danny. But she'd promised to keep her mother's illness a secret even if she didn't understand why it was so important to her.

She couldn't begin to imagine how Vivian felt, checking in and out of reality on a daily basis. No more of the high society trappings she associated with civilized life. Now she was reduced to flirting with old men in what was really only a glorified nursing home. If her father had only stuck around instead of jumping ship when his wife lost her faculties, then things might be different. Mother could have stayed in this house. They could have gotten a private nurse to be here around the clock. But no, Bill had taken off at the first sign of trouble, and his only help was an encouraging phone call now and then. Whenever she pressed him about it, he would only say things had gotten too complicated.

Could she really blame him? She avoided complicated. Or at least she had until last night. Sleeping with Danny was fraught with complexity, but she'd done it anyway. And she didn't regret it. Not yet, anyway. If things went further, she didn't know what would happen, how she would feel. She didn't need the complications, but as she lay in the bed where she and Danny had shared a night of passionate pleasure, what she needed paled in comparison to what she wanted.

And what about what Danny wanted? Last night hadn't been a romp; it had been a journey. Things had shifted between them, and what had started days ago as harmless flirtation had veered into dangerous territory. Danny had been hurt by a woman who didn't share her sense of commitment, yet she'd shown no sense of caution last night despite the fact Ellen had made it clear she wasn't up for anything more than the physicality they'd shared.

But had she made it clear? She knew she hadn't been cautious either, with Danny's feelings or her own, and now she lay in bed, not knowing what last night had meant, but knowing it had meant something important. She was equal parts relieved and sad Danny wasn't here to talk it out.

Time to get up. Face the day and forget about the night. First step, coffee. She pulled on a robe and padded to the kitchen. While the coffee brewed, she stepped outside to get the paper, tripped, and fell on her face. Lying on the ground, looking back toward the house, she saw the culprit. An enormous vase of white roses lay on its side. Damn. She pulled herself up and stepped carefully around the broken glass. There had to be at least a dozen roses now adorning her front porch. She retrieved a broom, brushed away the glass, and gathered each of the thirteen white roses and the tiny envelope lying in the floral debris. She waited until she was back in the house before opening the envelope. The card inside was simple—block letters and a short note. "Last night was such a rush. Thanks for the view."

Simple and to the point. No silly "I love you" or "hey, let's move in." The comment about the view struck her as odd, but she had bared way more than her soul. Ellen read the note again and conceded Danny might be satisfied with great sex and no strings, and that wasn't complicated at all. A pang of disappointment struck her, and she shrugged it away. She had no business feeling sad that she and Danny finally seemed to be on the same page. She'd planned to call Danny this morning, tell her something about how she'd enjoyed the night together, but now the gushing emotion she'd felt upon waking seemed excessive. She'd still call, thank her for the flowers, but no need to get all emotional. She stuffed the pangs of longing she'd woken with and picked up the phone to dial Danny's number. Before she could enter the number, her cell phone buzzed with a text from Jill. "I know it's Sunday, but call me. We have a problem."

When Jill answered, she sounded out of breath. "Thank goodness you called. I ran by the office to pick up some signs for a picnic on campus, and I found an angry voice message on the answering machine. Sophia Falco called and she's on fire. Something about cops beating down her door, grilling her for information about murders. She wants you to call her back right away. I don't think it'll keep until tomorrow."

Ellen sighed as her peaceful morning slipped away. "Give me her number. I'll call her as soon as I manage to down a cup of coffee. Sorry you had to deal with this."

"Picking up the message and calling you was nothing. You have the hard part. Good luck."

While she brewed a pot of coffee, she pondered what Sophia could possibly want, especially on a Sunday morning. Funny, she'd just been thinking that unlike Danny, she rarely had to go rushing off to deal with an emergency during non-work hours, but here she was phoning her primary benefactor before her caffeine even kicked in.

"Sophia, it's Ellen Davenport. I heard you left a message at the office. Is there something I can help you with?" She barely got out the words before Sophia started her rant. When she finally finished, Ellen was furious. She promised Sophia she'd get to the bottom of the matter. She hung up and placed her next call to Danny, her mood completely altered.

❖

"What's going on?" Danny strode into the war room at police headquarters, wishing she'd stopped for a decent cup of coffee. She'd gotten the page from Sarah while still tucked in Ellen's bed. She'd longed to ignore the call of work, but she didn't want anyone thinking the fact she was dating Ellen was interfering with her ability to do her job.

Dating Ellen. She rolled the words around in her head and tried not to become too fond of them. She wasn't really dating Ellen. She'd taken her to her parents' house for a meal and then they'd gotten naked. The night of sex had been amazing, but the last thing she needed to do was make it into something it wasn't. Something she wanted it to be, but Ellen wasn't interested in pursuing.

And why wasn't she? Ellen was single and willing. What was it about her that made exploring something more so unpalatable? She made a mental note to ask next time she saw her. Nothing like being direct to get an answer you may or may not like. After last night, she had no doubt. She wanted to date Ellen. She probably should've determined what Ellen wanted before sleeping with her, but it wasn't the first time a pretty woman had knocked her judgment out of whack. But if she'd been reading signals right, then Ellen might want something more too. They hadn't just shared sex, they'd shared feelings, intimacy. She hadn't gotten laid last night, she'd gotten shot through the heart, and she'd been reeling from the effect all morning.

Sarah cleared her throat and Danny snapped to attention. Fine to be distracted on her personal time, but right now she needed to focus on the case.

"We've started contacting some of the alumnae who were in the same class as the majority of the victims."

Danny felt a knot of panic rise in her throat. "When did you start doing that? Does Ellen know?"

"Yesterday and I have no idea. Do we need to get a civilian's permission to do interviews? Is that how you do things in Dallas County?"

"Don't be an ass. It's just we kind of promised her that we wouldn't spread the word she'd shared information from their files without letting her know."

"I get it, but we were discreet. Besides, it's not like anyone's going to know where we got the information. We could've gotten their names from the university."

"Okay." Danny pushed the panic aside. Sarah was probably right. No, she was actually right. She couldn't let her promises to Ellen supersede the need to investigate this case, especially since her promises weren't really made in her role as a professional. "Did you learn anything?"

"Not much. These women circle the wagons at the first sign of an outsider. I'm actually a little surprised Davenport agreed to let us have the access she did. They aren't big on sharing."

"Maybe we should talk to Ellen about that. They seem to have a lot of respect for her. If she were to pave the way, they might consent to some interviews."

"Any excuse to talk to the pretty lady, right?"

"There you go, being an ass again." Danny dismissed her guilt. Sarah couldn't possibly know about their "date," and she wasn't about to share. For now, she'd do everything she could to compartmentalize her dual relationships with Ellen.

"Don't be so naive. Anyone who watches the two of you together can tell you are more interested in getting in her pants than getting information."

Was Sarah right? George hadn't picked up on her interest in Ellen until she put it out there by bringing her to Joe's party. "I think you just have a vivid imagination. You've had sex on the brain since the moment you walked in here."

"Nothing wrong with that. You want to grab a drink later?"

"Let me guess. If I say no, you'll assume it's because I'm all hung up on someone else."

"You got it. And not just someone. Maybe I'm asking because when this case is over, I plan to ask her out."

Sarah's expression was a challenge and Danny resisted rising to the bait. No way to win points in this conversation. Best way out was to feign indifference. "Remember to invite me to the wedding."

"Now who's being an ass? Besides, neither one of us is going to get involved with Ellen Davenport and I'll tell you why. She's—"

Danny's phone rang, blocking out Sarah's words. She started to answer, but paused when Ellen's number appeared on the screen. She'd wanted to talk to her since the moment she'd left that morning, but she'd been surrounded by Sarah and the rest of the team. She couldn't wait any longer. She ducked away with a murmured lie that her mother was on the phone and answered. "Hey."

"Are you alone?"

The question was suggestive, but the tone wasn't. Ellen sounded upset. Make that angry. "I'm at the station, but I'm not with anyone right now." She lowered her voice to a whisper. "I miss you."

"I got a call this morning from Sophia. Apparently, your team has been showing up on the doorsteps of Alpha Nu alumnae, asking a bunch of personal questions."

"Yeah, I was just talking to Flores about that."

"When were you going to talk to me about it?"

Nothing suggestive about Ellen's words anymore, unless Danny was looking for a fight. And she wasn't, but she couldn't help but get defensive. "In case you don't remember, we're working a case here."

"And your investigative skills are best used by bothering a bunch of middle-aged women?"

"Look, you know I can't share any of the details of our investigation with you. I've already shared more than I should."

"You look. You wouldn't have any of that information if I hadn't been nice enough to give you access. I trusted you to not go around sharing it with everyone else. I don't think you realize what a dicey position you've put me in."

"What? You have a bunch of rich old ladies angry with you? Poor Ellen, you have a hard life." Danny regretted the words the minute they left her lips, but she was pissed. She'd been a little put out with Sarah for questioning these women, but she knew it was the right thing to do, and Ellen should know what they were doing to investigate the case was way more important than the complaints of a few women who'd had police show up in their rich, quiet neighborhoods. "I'm sorry, that was harsh."

"I think last night was a mistake."

Thud. The words were a blind blow, and Danny couldn't think of anything to say. Last night with Ellen was the best thing that had happened to her in a long time. Last night had been what she hoped was the beginning of more nights together. To hear Ellen dismiss what they'd shared as a mistake roused every defensive instinct she had. "You're probably right."

Silence. Danny waited it out, not in the mood to back down. The tug of war went on for what seemed like minutes, but was likely only seconds. Ellen spoke first. "Okay then. Please have Agent Flores call me to discuss the data files. I think it's time I involve our attorneys."

"Okay."

"And, Danny?"

"Yes?"

"Thanks for the flowers. I appreciate the gesture."

"Flowers?"

"The white roses, this morning, on my porch?"

Danny nearly dropped the phone, but instead she summoned the wherewithal to wave Sarah over. She took a moment to whisper what Ellen had just said in Sarah's ear and then handed the phone to Sarah who placed it on speaker. "Ellen, this is Sarah. Listen very carefully to what I'm about to say. Lock your doors. Is there somewhere in your house where you can go to hide? Not for long, but just until I can get there?"

"Uh, yes, there's a wine cellar just off the kitchen." Ellen's voice shook. "What's going on?"

"Wine cellar is perfect. Now, is there a key hidden outside?"

"Yes, one of those fake rock things near the front porch. It's about a foot from the big flower pot with the lemon tree. Seriously, what's going on? You're scaring me."

"Lock your doors and go to the wine cellar. Take your cell and turn off the ringer. Don't come out until I text you. Tell me you understand."

Danny held her breath while she and Sarah waited for Ellen's response. She needed Ellen to heed Sarah's words, not to ask questions. She knew they were scaring her, but they couldn't afford to be afraid together.

"Okay. Please hurry."

"We will, Ellen. Don't you worry about a thing."

Sarah clicked off the call and handed the phone back to Danny, not even pausing before she started to shout orders. While Sarah assembled a team, Danny considered that the killer might be in the house already, or working his way inside. Last night had not been a mistake. It had been anything but, and she'd give anything to take the words back, redo the conversation to make it about anticipating the future instead of regretting the past. She watched through a haze as Sarah and George headed for their cars.

Follow them. The thought galvanized her into action and she took off running. She may not carry a gun, and she may not have a clue what to do in this kind of a situation, but no way was she going to sit and wait while Ellen's fate hung in the balance. Her only mistake in the last twenty-four hours had been thinking she could wait and see where her feelings would lead her. They'd already led her to love and she wasn't about to let that go without a fight.

Chapter Sixteen

Playing in the dank cellar as a child had been fun, but now Ellen wished she'd never known the place. Dark, cold, and completely spooky. Like Sarah's hurried instructions on the phone. It had been clear she wasn't supposed to ask questions and that scared her the most. Doing what she was told without question had never been one of her strong suits, a fact long lamented by her mother. Vivian Davenport specialized in ordering people around, and Ellen and her father had been the primary subjects of her mother's control. Ellen had spent her youth testing the boundaries of her mother's patience. It wasn't until she went off to college that Vivian became the supreme enforcer. "You will not now, nor will you ever do anything to besmirch the family's good name at university," She relished using words like besmirch. "I have a reputation and you must uphold it. You will be a lady of Alpha Nu and you will be the best Alpha Nu there has ever been. If not, you'll be cut off."

She should've taken her up on it, since she'd been cut off in one way or another since she'd been born. An only child, her most intimate relationships had been the ones she'd had with a progression of nannies, all of whom wound up being deemed unsatisfactory. Her child's brain recalled no problems with any of them, but her adult mind reasoned her mother's jealousy was probably the reason for the firings. Bill Davenport always went out of his way to balance his wife's harsh demeanor by being especially nice to the help. Ellen often wondered if he realized he cost many of them their jobs.

Doubtful. Bill Davenport had sailed through life, the absent-minded law professor, living on his wife's money. The only price he had to pay was devotion to her causes and dutiful attendance at all her society events. He'd lived his life this way until last year when Vivian was diagnosed, and then he cut all ties. He took a transfer to a university in Chicago and left with nothing more than the clothes on his back. No explanation, no apologies.

Her relationship with her parents had never been close, but losing both of them at the same time—one to a void, the other to distance, left Ellen lonelier than she cared to admit. Her solution had been to dive into work and her mother's care. Her friends and co-workers noticed the change and thought she was paying short shrift to her personal life, but she knew the truth. Relationships weren't all they were cracked up to be. If she was doomed to the same fate as her parents, then she was better off never getting involved with anyone in the first place.

Which made her think of Danny. Would Danny come to her rescue with Sarah, or had she washed her hands of her? She couldn't blame her if she chose to stay away after the stupid things she'd said. *This was a mistake.* Last night hadn't been a mistake, not in the least. Being with Danny had been the best thing that had ever happened to her. And potentially the most risky. She surveyed her surroundings. Risky in more ways than one considering she was hiding out in a dark cellar waiting for a team of police officers to come rescue her.

It hadn't taken her too long to figure out what was going on. The flowers. Danny hadn't even responded when she'd mentioned the roses. She assumed they were from her, but that was silly really. Danny rushes off to work, but takes the time to call a florist on a Sunday morning to have roses delivered, right away? With a note, even though she'd already left a note. And of course they were white roses. Ellen pulled up the mental image of Danny receiving a white rose from Angela at the mixer. They'd been smiling, almost flirty. She'd wanted to rip the rose from Danny's hand and shove it down Angela's throat. She'd been so excited to get a whole vase of the flowers from Danny she'd completely forgotten the recent warnings about strangers posing as flower deliverymen.

But there had been no deliveryman. She mentally retraced her steps. She'd walked out on the porch and tripped over the vase, breaking it in the process. She'd gone back inside to get a broom, walked back out, swept up the mess, gathered the flowers, and gone back inside where she'd read the card. She'd contemplated the message, then reached for the phone to call Danny when Jill rang. At least thirty minutes had passed from the time she'd discovered the flowers to the time she had spoken with Danny and not a single suspicious thing had happened during that time. The news warnings about flower deliveries had implied that the man making the deliveries might be dangerous, but it didn't appear the man had stuck around her place to do any harm. If he had, where was he? Was he watching her? How long had he been there? Had he strategically waited until Danny left?

Where was Danny now? Ellen stared at her cell phone, willing Danny to call her, tell her everything was okay, that the scare had been a false alarm. Fear aside, they would talk, figure out what last night meant. Where they would go from here. She couldn't wait any longer. She started typing a text, but got no further than "Are you here?" before a loud crash froze her fingers.

The drive to Ellen's place had taken forever. Danny didn't have the benefit of lights and sirens in her civilian pickup. When she finally reached the house, half the street was already blocked off. She left her truck parked at an angle and rushed toward the scene, badge in hand. The uniform posted at the farthest point raised a hand to stop her, but then quickly waved her in once he realized she was from the DA's office.

"Where's Agent Flores?" Danny barked at the patrol officer.

"She's inside. They went in a minute ago."

Danny considered her options. It was one thing to show up at a scene where a crime had already happened and that had been cleared, but she knew she wouldn't be welcome inside the house right now. Her appearance could cause confusion if they were still searching for the sick fuck who'd delivered the flowers. She pictured Sarah and George leading a team of guys in flak jackets, guns drawn. No, she'd have to wait it out. Even sending a text to Ellen was too risky. What if she'd left the sound on on her phone? A simple ping signaling a text message could be enough to get her killed.

She paced the street outside Ellen's house. Back and forth, back and forth. The uniform cops stationed outside stared, but she ignored them. They couldn't possibly understand that the woman she'd made love to last night was somewhere in that house, scared and in danger. They would judge if they knew. She'd lost what little professional distance she'd had and she was in full-fledged panic mode. When Ellen emerged safe and sound, she would have to deal with her own breach in protocol, but for now, she wore out the pavement with her worry.

"Soto!"

Danny swung around and almost smashed into Sarah. "Where is she? Is she all right?"

"Whoa, there, Counselor. Hold up a minute."

Danny pushed against Sarah's arms. "Let me by or tell me what's going on!"

Sarah grabbed her by the arm and steered her over to one of the patrol cars parked in front of the house. She opened the door and pushed her into the passenger seat.

Danny seethed, but Sarah wasn't giving her any space to get away. "What the hell are you doing?"

"Keeping you from making a fool of yourself. What do you think's going to happen if you run in the house and find Ellen? You going to sweep her up in a big hug, maybe give her a just married style kiss?"

Danny's shoulders sagged as she realized the truth in Sarah's words. She'd been about to make a foolish display of public affection that could jeopardize her job and embarrass Ellen. Sarah had saved her, but had she saved Ellen?

As if she could read her mind, Sarah said, "She's fine. Scared, but fine."

Danny sighed and shook the tension out of her shoulders. "Anything?" She relied on Sarah to understand her shorthand.

"Nothing. The flowers were placed on the front porch, in a vase, sometime this morning."

"Had to be after seven."

Sarah nodded, no judgment in her eyes. "She saved the card, but I doubt we'll get anything off of it."

"I need to see her."

"She's talking to George and Peter right now. They need to talk to her while the details are fresh in her mind."

Danny heard an undercurrent of caution. "You're not going to let me see her are you?"

"I need to talk to you first."

"Spill."

"She may not be everything she seems."

"I don't even know what that's supposed to mean."

"Did she tell you this is her mother's house?"

"She may have mentioned it used to belong to her parents. You have something against people who live with their parents?"

"Her mother is an Alpha Nu alum. In the same age range as our other victims. Same class as Marty Lawson."

Danny considered Sarah's words. Ellen had mentioned her mother. Or Sophia had at the mixer. Neither of them had mentioned she was Alpha Nu and Danny hadn't read anything into the exchange. Looking back, she realized if she hadn't been so wrapped up in Ellen, she might have asked more questions. "So what? Maybe she didn't want to make a big deal of it."

"Oh, she went to great lengths not to make a big deal of it. Yesterday, one of the detectives who was questioning alumnae found out about Vivian Davenport, who these women described as one of the most active Alpha Nus around. Peter checked the database that Ellen gave us, and guess what? She's not listed."

Danny racked her brain for a plausible explanation. What had Ellen said? Some members chose not to register and pay alumnae dues. "And you imply what from that?"

"Wouldn't mean much if the database hadn't been altered."

"Altered?"

"Vivian Davenport's name and contact information had been changed. Want to guess when?"

Danny fought to remain calm. "When were you planning to tell me about this?"

Silence.

"You weren't planning on telling me, were you?"

Sarah cleared her throat. "Eventually. Just needed a little more time to sort out the facts. Our bad guy showing up on your girlfriend's doorstep kinda got in the way."

"She's not my girlfriend."

"No? Well, I bet you wish she was. Seriously, Danny, I'm only trying to protect you and this case. How's it going to look if we miss clues because you're sleeping with a key witness?"

"She wasn't a key witness until this morning. I even talked to George about it last night. He confirmed that it didn't appear sorority members were involved in the killings in any way other than as victims."

"Things have changed, don't you think?"

"Really? You think Ellen's mom is a killer? That Ellen deleted her name because they're in on it together? Some crazy mother-daughter sorority sister serial killer team?"

"Settle down. I don't know what's going on and neither do you, but until we have more information, you need to keep your distance. For the investigation and for your job. Understood?"

Danny hung her head. Sarah was right and she hated her for it. Silly really, since it wasn't Sarah's fault. She'd gotten into this mess on her own, and it was up to her to put a stop to it. She just needed to do one thing first.

"I'll keep my distance, but I need one thing."

"Name it."

"I want five minutes alone with her."

"Name something else."

"I won't do anything stupid, but I need to hear from her that she lied to me." She hoped Sarah could read her desperation without requiring her to beg. She waited. After an excruciating few seconds, Sarah finally nodded.

"I'll bring her over here. You get five minutes. Don't raise your voice. Don't do anything crazy. Promise?"

"Promise."

Danny waited anxiously, unsure what she would say when she finally came face-to-face with Ellen for the first time after their night together. Her warm fuzzy feelings from earlier that morning didn't mix well with the blast of cold water Sarah had delivered. She didn't have to wait long before Ellen showed up at the car, led by Sarah and visibly shaken. Sarah motioned for Ellen to sit in the back and then fixed Danny with a stare. "Five minutes."

Danny turned in her seat, the awkward angle nothing compared to the awkward conversation they were about to have. First things first. "Are you okay?"

Ellen nodded. "Yes, but I don't have a clear idea about what's going on. One minute I'm talking to you on the phone and the next minute I'm hiding out in my own house, waiting for the cavalry."

"Maybe if you'd been honest with us from the beginning, you wouldn't be in this position." Danny winced inwardly at the harshness of her words, but she was determined to confront Ellen about her omissions.

Ellen puffed up. "I don't know what you're talking about, but I do know you're the one with an honesty problem. Telling me that you'd keep our records private, that you wouldn't expose our members to harassment."

"Don't get all indignant on me. I know why you wanted to keep the records private and it wasn't to protect your band of high and mighty sorority sisters. No, you had a different family member to protect, didn't you?"

"I have no idea what you're talking about."

Danny stared, but nothing about Ellen's demeanor gave her a clue as to whether she was telling the truth. Was the omission innocent or was she just a really good liar? Sarah said the files had been altered. No way did only one file get changed before Ellen turned them over and it coincidentally wound up being her mother's information? There was no innocent omission here. Ellen had deliberately misled them. Her. She'd deliberately mislead her, a fact made worse in light of the intimate night they'd just shared. Her stomach rolled, but she stuck to her promise to keep things professional. "You could be charged with interfering in a police investigation."

Ellen's bottom lip quivered, but Danny held strong, waiting for a response that would explain everything, redeem Ellen. Several beats later, Ellen shook her head. "I didn't do anything wrong. That you think I did means you don't know me at all and you are not the person I thought you were."

Danny pointed a finger over the seat back. "Don't you dare try and turn this around on me. The only thing I've done wrong is to get involved with you in the first place. But then again, I seem to have a knack for falling for the wrong women, and you are no exception."

Ellen placed a hand on the door handle. "I think we're done here. If you have any official questions to ask, you should contact my lawyer. I'll give her contact information to one of the detectives."

And she was gone. Danny sat in the front seat and watched Ellen march over to Sarah and do a little finger pointing of her own. Danny was more confused than angry. She wanted to believe that Ellen hadn't lied to her, but the evidence didn't add up. Facts don't lie, and the facts were that Ellen had kept valuable information from them. She'd come on to Danny from the beginning, and all Danny could think about was whether her salacious behavior might have been a cover. Distract her enough and she wouldn't notice what she was hiding. Well, that ruse was done. She'd work this case eyes wide open from here on out.

Sarah appeared at the car. "Did you get what you wanted?"

She couldn't remember the last time she'd gotten what she wanted, at least not on a personal level. Professionally? She'd gotten assigned to this case, had the opportunity to be a shining star. To think she'd almost thrown it all away over a fleeting affair was a wakeup call. "I'm good. Let's go catch this guy."

❖

"How long until I can get back in my house?" Ellen barked the question at George who stood on the front sidewalk, barring her entry. She hadn't been able to get away from Danny fast enough. Her initial relief at learning she'd come with the rest of the crew had faded in the face of Danny's abrupt manner, her accusing tone. Now, all she could think about was getting the hell out of here.

"Not sure," Ramirez said. "We need to process the scene. The Crime Scene Unit should be here any minute."

Ellen glanced around. A small crowd of neighbors had started to gather on the usually quiet street. In keeping with their tendency to act like crime never affected their lives, they all glanced away whenever she attempted to make eye contact. Silly, since she was the victim not the perpetrator, but she knew that they considered her tainted merely by virtue of having the police at her house. She shouldn't be surprised. Even Danny had treated her like a common criminal, like she hadn't been the one who'd been threatened by a killer who'd managed to elude law enforcement for weeks.

But she had lied, or at least omitted information, and Danny had no way to know her mother's ties to the sorority weren't relevant to the investigation. And they weren't, were they?

Her mother's words upon learning of Marty's death echoed. *I think you might be in trouble again.* What had she meant and who had she been talking to? She'd assumed it was more raving of her addled Alzheimer's mind, but what if what Vivian had had to say really was important?

She considered her options. Only thing she knew right now was that she wasn't staying at this house tonight. "Detective, I assume you're done with me? If so, I'm going to a hotel."

She watched George glance over in the direction of the car where Danny still sat, and offered a comment. "I already informed Ms. Soto that I won't be giving any more interviews today. I'm sure you can appreciate that I'm a bit shaken up."

"Sure, I understand. Just make sure we have all your contact information. Would you like an officer to drive you?"

Sarah Flores appeared at her side. "I'll take her. I have a few questions for her." Her tone was authoritative and her fierce facial expression made it clear she wouldn't accept any arguments. Ellen had no intentions of leaving with her, but she dutifully followed her to a spot a few yards away from the rest of the officers on site. She had a couple of questions of her own. When she was sure no one else could overhear, she asked, "Am I in danger? No one's given me a clear picture of what happened this morning. Right before your people burst into the wine cellar, I heard a loud crash. Is everyone okay?"

"A rookie was a little exuberant and knocked over a plant stand. He's in there now, cleaning it up. As for whether you're in danger? You might be. It's hard to tell since it's clear you're not being honest with us."

Ellen gestured toward the car where she and Danny had last talked. "I've said all I'm going to say about that."

"Then I'm not sure what we can do for you. But I do suggest you stay away from here for a while, change your habits." She followed Ellen's lingering gaze. "And stay away from her."

Ellen jerked to attention at the unexpected warning, and she could tell by Sarah's tone that she knew something had transpired between her and Danny. "You have nothing to worry about. If you or Danielle Soto has anything further to say to me about this case, you can contact my lawyer."

How dare everyone cast her as the bad guy? She'd been alone in her house when a killer supposedly showed up on her doorstep. A killer who knew where she lived. He may have been in the house last night when she and Danny got home, may have watched their every move. She felt a rising blush warm her face and waves of nausea coursed through her as she remembered what he would've seen. How long had he been watching her? And why?

She didn't have answers, but she was determined to find them. And she'd be damned if she was going to ask Danny Soto to help.

Chapter Seventeen

Monday morning, Ellen sat in the lobby of the law firm of Bradley & Casey, P.C., waiting for her appointment with Morgan Bradley. She hadn't actually been serious when she'd told Danny and Sarah to contact her lawyer, but the more she thought about it, it seemed like a good idea for her to find out if she really was in any trouble. She could have called her dad for legal advice, but he hadn't practiced outside of a classroom in years, and she had no interest in letting him know the mess she'd made. Morgan had been a student of her father's who had stayed in touch with him over the years. She honestly didn't think she needed a lawyer, but she didn't trust her own judgment lately. She'd done everything wrong when it came to Danny.

"Ms. Bradley is ready to see you now."

Ellen followed the attractive receptionist down a hallway to a small conference room. She took a seat and declined anything to drink while she waited. Seconds later, Morgan appeared in the doorway with a tall, handsome, dark-haired woman.

Morgan walked over to where she was sitting and took her hand. "Ellen, it's been so long. How are you? How is your family?"

"Great." She was purposefully vague, and quick to direct attention away from herself by sticking a hand in the direction of the other woman. "Hi, I'm Ellen Davenport."

Morgan made the introduction. "Meet my wife and law partner, Parker Casey. Based on what you told me on the phone, I asked her to sit in on this meeting. Parker used to be a homicide detective with the Dallas Police Department. I thought she might know some of the players."

Parker's handshake was firm and her smile gentle. They all sat at the conference table and Morgan dove in. "Ellen, why don't you recap what you told me on the phone and expand the details? Parker might have a few questions of her own, and I want her to hear your version firsthand."

Ellen steeled herself and then poured out the story, from the day Danny and George had shown up at her office to the scare yesterday morning. The only thing she held back was the personal relationship that had developed between her and Danny during the investigation of the case.

Parker asked the first question. "Sounds like you've cooperated above and beyond what anyone would expect. Any idea why Soto and Flores are threatening you with obstruction? Danny's been around a while, and she has a solid reputation as a professional—this sounds out of character for her."

Parker's tone didn't contain a hint of judgment, but Ellen knew she couldn't hold back the truth. Not if she wanted their help. "Things haven't always been professional between us. Danny and I have, well…"

It wasn't that she couldn't admit it, but she just didn't know what to call what had existed between them. While she struggled for words, she watched Morgan and Parker exchange smiles. Morgan placed a hand on her arm and said, "You can't always pick the perfect time and circumstance to meet someone you care about."

"Is it that obvious?"

"Pretty much so."

"Do you really think she intends to pursue you criminally?"

"I don't know. I mean, no. She was angry. The problem is there's more to the story. More I haven't told them. I don't even know if any of it matters or if it will get me in trouble, but I need to tell someone and I didn't know who else to call."

"Did your father suggest you call us?"

"I haven't talked to him about any of this." Ellen braced for their reaction to the secrets she was about to spill. "He and mother have separated. He's in Chicago. She's…" Saying it out loud was harder than she imagined. "She's in a home. Mother has Alzheimer's, early onset."

"Oh, I'm so sorry," said Morgan. "When was she diagnosed?"

"Last fall. I suppose the signs have been there for a while, but mother's really good at hiding weakness." She knew she sounded bitter, but she didn't have her mother's skill. What little family she had had imploded once the diagnosis became final. She spilled the entire story, including the fact she'd doctored the Alpha Nu database to hide her mother's association with the sorority and her mother's strange actions after she found out about Marty Lawson's death. When she was done, she folded her hands on the table. "Now you know everything. Everything I know, anyway. I keep going back to her outburst at the home, after she found out about Marty. That night it felt like she thought I was Marty. It seems like her words might be important, but I can't imagine how."

Morgan looked at Parker and nodded. Parker said, "It boils down to this. Do you want to cooperate with the police? I mean, they already know about the database issue and I assume you have nothing else to hide, right? And since your mother's been in a home since last year, she isn't likely to be directly involved in these murders."

"I want to do what's right. I just don't want anyone to get hurt in the process. I don't think Mother could handle a police interrogation right now. She has lucid moments, but anything can trigger a setback."

"She has no obligation to talk to the police," Parker said. "And it sounds like she's really not in a position to make a decision about whether or not to do so on her own. Is there anyone else we could talk to that might have some insight about what she was talking about?"

Dad. She'd purposefully avoided the thought, but Ellen knew her parents had been college sweethearts. Her mother's words led her to believe she'd been reliving a college memory, real or imagined. Her father may not know about secret sorority business, but he may have some ideas about which other Alpha Nus besides Marty that her mother had been close to while in college. "I may have an idea. What do I do if I come up with a name?"

"Let us be involved when you make the contact," Morgan said. "We don't want anyone thinking you're interfering with the investigation. In the meantime, do you want us to contact someone involved with the case to let them know they shouldn't talk to you without one of us present?"

"Anyone" and "someone" were placeholders for Danny. Ellen didn't know what to say. Did she want her lawyers to contact Danny and warn her off? Truth was, as upset as she was at Danny's irrational anger, she was just as mad at herself for the way she'd reacted. The last thing she wanted was to push Danny further away. "No. If anyone tries to talk to me about the case, I'll tell them to call you."

"Good plan." Morgan pulled a card from the holder on the table and wrote two numbers on the back before handing it over. "Both of our cell numbers are on the back. Call anytime." She placed her hand on Ellen's. "I mean it. Even if you just need to talk. Okay?"

Ellen felt the sting of tears prick her behind the eyes, but she silently commanded herself not to cry. She'd started the day naked and sated, tangled in sheets that smelled like Danny. From there she'd tripped and fallen over flowers delivered by a serial killer, gotten yelled at by her organization's biggest benefactor, been scolded by an FBI agent, and fought what felt like a fight to end all fights with the woman who'd touched her body and soul in the most magical ways the night before. She deserved to cry, but she wouldn't do it here. She may not do it at all. She'd managed to keep her feelings in check this long and she wasn't about to let go now. She would, however, call for reinforcement.

❖

Danny paced the war room at police headquarters, waiting for Sarah and George who were on their way. Other than the text from George this morning, she hadn't spoken with either of them since Sarah had practically thrown her off Ellen's property. Make that Ellen's parents' property.

A glance at the clock told her they were only thirty minutes late, but it seemed like she'd been waiting forever. Several times, she'd reached for her phone, tempted to text Ellen or hoping she'd left a message. No incoming messages. She resisted the urge to start an exchange. She wasn't confident that Ellen would respond even if she did reach out. She'd said some harsh things. They both had. A cooling off period was definitely in order.

She finally decided to pass the time doing something productive. She signed onto one of the computers in the room and pulled up Lexis to see what she could find out about Ellen's mother, Vivian Davenport.

No doubt Sarah and her team already had whatever information existed, but she was tired of relying on other people for information.

The house where Ellen lived was owned by Vivian and William Davenport. William "Bill" had, until recently, been a professor at Richards University Law School. He'd transferred to a small college in Chicago for the spring semester. So where was Vivian? Was she on an extended trip as Ellen had told the women at the mixer or had she moved to Chicago with her husband? She definitely hadn't been at the house on any of the occasions that Danny had been there. And last night the sounds of their lovemaking would have flushed anyone out of hiding.

Make that the sounds of their sex. Really, that's what she should call it since it was clear now that love hadn't been in the mix. Whatever she'd felt beyond the purely physical had been a figment of her imagination, and it was her own fault she'd gotten her hopes up for something more. Ellen had been clear from the beginning that she wasn't interested in anything more than a physical encounter. Now that she'd gotten laid, was Ellen done with her and ready to move on to the next? Last night she'd seemed so tender, so sweet, so romantic. Had it all been an act designed to warm her up and get her to relax her standards?

She had to let it go. Let Ellen go. Sarah and George could handle whatever further questioning was necessary. She needed to focus on her job because it was the one relationship she could count on.

While she was surfing databases, she typed in Angela Perkin's name. She'd never mentioned her to George after the mixer. Another consequence of her distraction. The intern from the mixer had given her the willies and she couldn't shake the image of Angela flirting with her while holding the creepy white rose like it was a magic wand. Tag on the conversation she'd heard in the restroom, and she figured Angela definitely merited a second look.

Not much to see. Angela owned a car and not much else. And the car wasn't much either. A twenty-year-old Dodge. Definitely didn't fit with Danny's idea of a rich sorority girl, but maybe her stereotypes were out of whack. Ellen had seemed so down to earth despite her money. Seemed was the key word. Something was off about Angela Perkins, but all Danny had was a gut feeling that kept her looking a bit longer. Angela didn't have much family that she could find. Mother deceased, no information about a father. Wonder who she'd been talking to on the phone the other night? From the snippets of conversation she'd heard, it didn't seem like Angela was thrilled with sorority life. So why pay the expensive dues and all the other trappings if she wasn't interested?

"Whatcha looking at?" George asked. He and Sarah stood looking over her shoulder.

"Not sure. I mentioned this intern to Flores the night of the mixer. She acted funny that night and I think she's worth looking into."

"Print out what you've got. We're meeting with the team in fifteen minutes to review everything we have," Sarah said. "I think we're getting really close, but not quite close enough. We need to have a serious brainstorming session." She turned to walk away, but Danny stopped her.

"Can we talk?"

Sarah looked between Danny and George, her gaze questioning.

"George, can you give us a minute?"

He nodded and left the room.

"I thought he was your friend," Sarah said.

"He is, that's why I'm trying to keep him out of this. You know in case I get kicked off the case for sleeping with one of the witnesses."

"Fair enough. And me? You don't care if I get tainted by your indiscretions?"

Danny cracked a smile. "Not really."

"Nice, Soto. Okay, what do you want?"

Danny pointed at the sheet she'd printed out about Angela Perkins. "I have a gut feeling this girl is up to no good."

"You already implied as much. You couldn't tell me that in front of George?"

"I don't know if Angela's intern duties mean she only works events or if she puts in time at the sorority's headquarters, but I want you to keep her away from Ellen. Can you promise me that?"

"You need to let this thing between you and Ellen go."

Danny bit back a sharp retort. "I have, but that doesn't mean I can't care about whether she's in danger. And what about that guy who was at the mixer the other night? Who's got eyes on him?"

"We do. Peter's run a full background check and a team of DPD officers have him on round-the-clock surveillance, but so far no action on that front. One of the things we're supposed to discuss at the meeting this morning is whether we need to quit watching and start questioning."

"Maybe there's no action because he knows you're watching."

"Could be, but the guys assigned to him are top-notch. Trust me, after this many kills, our guy is twitchy for the next one. He'll fuck up soon, but it might be worth asking him a few questions to rattle him a bit."

"Just as long as you don't rattle him right into Ellen Davenport. Promise me you'll watch out for her?"

"I promise. Already had one of the guys follow her yesterday so we know where she's staying. She saw an attorney this morning, by the way."

Danny wasn't surprised. It was her fault, after all. She'd practically threatened Ellen with arrest and right on the heels of a horrifying experience. Ellen had no reason to trust Danny or the police. She resisted the urge to ask Sarah where Ellen was staying, because she wasn't sure she could resist showing up on her doorstep and apologizing for her behavior. For Ellen's sake and hers, she needed to stay away.

❖

Ellen stared at her watch. Eight o'clock. The airport was full of Monday commuters who were returning after a day of work in Austin and Houston. She was fairly certain her father wouldn't have checked a bag, but no longer able to stand waiting in the car, she paced the baggage claim area at Love Field watching for his arrival.

When she finally spotted him, she was surprised she recognized him. His conservative haircut had been replaced by a fashionable style and he sported the beginnings of a beard. He wore jeans and a leather jacket instead of one of the frumpy suits her mother had always insisted on. The only thing truly familiar was the same haunted look in his eyes he'd had the day he told her he was leaving.

When he reached her side, they half hugged before standing in awkward silence. Ellen made the first move. "You check any bags?"

"No."

"I'm parked in the first garage."

"Great."

After they were seated in the car, the conversation stayed at the same pace. "Hungry?" Ellen asked.

"Not really."

"I got you a room at the Palomar. It's where I'm staying."

"Perfect."

Neither spoke the rest of the drive, and Ellen took the time to reflect on her conversation with him that morning. After leaving Morgan's office, she'd called him, sure that if anyone knew what her mother had meant by her strange comments at Cedar Acres, it would be him. She didn't know what she'd expected when she called—avoidance, apathy, or anger. What she hadn't expected was for him to tell her he was flying to Dallas. He hadn't offered any explanation for the sudden visit, and she sensed he wouldn't be pressed. He'd tell her when he was ready.

She left him at the desk to check in and went to her room. The first thing she did when she was alone in the room was check her phone. She had a message from Morgan who'd called to see how she was doing, but nothing else. She put the phone away, chastising herself for wishing Danny had been the one to check on her.

A few minutes later she heard a knock on her door. The man on the other side of the peephole looked like her father, but after yesterday's events she wasn't taking any chances. "Who is it?" she shouted.

"Bill Davenport. Open the door."

She unhooked the chain and opened the door enough to stick her head out and determine he was alone. "Come in."

He walked into the room and walked immediately to the mini bar. "I think we're both going to need a drink for this. What's your pleasure?"

"Gin." She may as well have the drink, since she had a feeling nothing she was about to hear would bring her any pleasure.

CHAPTER EIGHTEEN

"Did you fly all the way from Chicago just to have drinks from a hotel minibar?" Ellen studied her father. He'd been pensive since he arrived and she wasn't willing to wait any longer for him to say whatever it was he didn't feel he could say over the phone.

Bill Davenport took a deep drink from the glass of Scotch in his hand. "When you called this morning, you really took me by surprise. I had no idea what was going on back here. If I had, I would've talked to you about this sooner."

"I have no idea what you're talking about. Maybe if you'd stuck around instead of running off to find yourself or whatever the hell you're doing, you'd have known exactly what's going on around here." She was done with his vague comments and excuses. She'd watched him spend his whole life never standing up to her mother, but why did he choose the moment they needed him the most to take off?

"It's not as simple as that."

"Let me guess, it's too complicated for you to explain. That's all I've ever heard from you. If you didn't come here to explain, then why are you here?"

"I am here to explain. It just isn't easy. I've kept your mother's secrets for all these years. As much as you think I'm a disloyal rat, I'm actually pretty good at keeping secrets, even when they tear people apart. Now, are you ready to hear what I have to say? It's not pretty."

Ellen nodded. She had no way of knowing if she was ready or not, but she did know she had to have some answers about why her family was suddenly in the sights of a serial killer. "I'm ready."

"I met your mother at a joint Alpha Nu and Tau Zeta mixer our junior year in college. I had transferred in from another university, didn't know a lot of people. You know your mother. She was in the center of things, always in charge. I mistook her enthusiasm for her sorority for enthusiasm for life, and it was addictive. I was a little on the shy side back then, still am, but your mother helped me learn how to break out of my shell." He shook his head. "I never thought any of this would ever surface."

"If you don't get around to telling me what 'this' is soon, I'm going to scream."

"Sorry. I've never told anyone this story. Bear with me."

Ellen tamped down her impatience and waited for his next words. Within moments, she was transported back to her parents' college days. She'd never heard her father speak of that time in his life, and her mother only spoke about college to extol the virtues of Alpha Nu.

"These were the days before stories about binge drinking flooded the news. We didn't know and didn't care about the dangers of drinking to excess. We were a year away from graduation and we were invincible.

"Our mortality came to visit the fall semester of our senior year. During rush. Your mother was the president of Alpha Nu, and Marty Lawson was the pledge captain. Between the two of them, they ran all the recruitment activities for the sorority. They had a habit of picking a batch of girls who looked and acted just like them, with similar backgrounds and interests. But every year they chose one charity case. A girl who wasn't a legacy, didn't have the same pedigree as the rest. She may not be as pretty, she may not have much money, but she desperately wanted to be a part of the group. That was the key."

"The key to what? Things are no different than now. We admit girls who aren't legacies and we have programs available to help with dues. It's important to be diverse."

"Dear, this wasn't about diversity. Although I guess you could say it was about diversity of class. The one girl who wasn't quite worthy? Well, she paid way more than money for the price of admission. She was the gopher, the doer of unpleasant tasks. I'd venture to say the only thing she got out of the experience was the ability to list Alpha Nu on her resume if she made it through the process. In the fall of our senior year, your mother and Marty had their sights on one particular girl. They decided she would be the perfect Pledge Thirteen."

"That's an ominous name."

"Fitting though. Rush was always a crazy time. Personally, I hated the antics. Fraternity hazings were pretty rough compared to the pranks sorority sisters played on new initiates. The problem came when you mixed the two. On the last night before final pledge cards were sent out, the Tau Zetas invited the Alpha Nus to their house for a combined mixer. Beer wasn't the only thing flowing freely in the house that night."

Ellen took a deep drink of her gin, unsure she wanted to hear anything more her father wanted to say. Wasn't as if she didn't know her parents weren't perfect, but hearing about their crazy parties was a little too much information. She decided to urge the story along. "Was this Pledge Thirteen there?"

"Of course. Her duties for the evening included waiting on the officers of the fraternity."

Her parents rarely talked about their college days except to say that's where they'd met and fallen in love, but his comment sparked a memory. Ellen dug deep to remember. She'd been in high school, cast as Lady Bracknell in the senior play, *The Importance of Being Earnest.* Convinced she could find a better costume among her mother's castoffs than the one the theater department had provided, she semi-accidentally found and rummaged through a box of her parents' personal stuff in the basement of their home. Starved for something personal beyond the posed photos and framed certificates that decorated their home, she spent several hours pursuing the contents of the box. Snapshots, yearbooks, letters back and forth between them. The only thing she recalled about her exploration at this moment was a photo in one of the yearbooks featuring Bill Davenport, Chapter President, standing with his arms around two other officers of Tau Zeta. The significance sent chills up her spine. "She waited on *you.*"

"And others. Your mother thought it was funny. Even then she liked to watch me squirm."

"And yet, you chose to marry her." The bitching on both sides had gotten old a long, long time ago. And so had this story. "What horrible things did you and your pals make Pledge Thirteen do, and why are you telling me all this?" She had a sinking feeling this story was headed in a bad direction and she'd prefer not to endure the torture of his long, slow telling.

"I promise I'll get to it. Be patient with me. I'm wading through a lot of history here."

Ellen's sympathy stores were drained. "And I'm wading through a bunch of secrets. The police are mad because I've lied to them." Not to mention she'd lost Danny because of the lies. "I'm sick and tired of not knowing what's going on."

He cleared his throat and continued the story. "At some point during the party, she disappeared. Your mother threw a fit. Pledge Thirteen was supposed to be visible, show her allegiance to the chapter by waiting on us. Frankly, I thought the whole thing was silly, but it seemed harmless. She was supposed to bring us beer, tap the kegs, make sure everyone had snacks. Compared to the hazing my fraternity brothers put us through, it was tame."

"So what, she skipped out?"

"She was in my room. In my bed. With one of my fraternity brothers, Leonard Cenco. Jerry Jager, our pledge captain, found them there."

Long pause. Was she supposed to read the rest of the story from there? Fooling around wasn't out of the ordinary, especially at these functions. Watching him tell this story bit by painful bit was excruciating. Time to shake things up. "Were they fucking?"

His head jerked up and he frowned with distaste. That's the one thing he and her mother had in common—reluctance to say anything distasteful. But she wasn't backing down. "Seriously, Dad. You fly across country and you have to belt down a few drinks before you can manage to tell me why you're here. I'm going crazy not knowing what's going on. What the hell happened and why does it matter now?"

"I think Pledge Thirteen is involved in these murders. I think she's taking revenge."

"What?" She practically screamed the question. Nothing he'd said so far made any sense insofar as how it related to her current predicament, but his proclamation was over the top. "You need to fill in some blanks here."

"She claimed Leonard raped her that night. Actually, she claimed Leonard and Jerry both raped her."

"Oh my God." Ellen grabbed the sides of her chair as the implication sunk in. Nothing would take down a house like a rape accusation, especially if it occurred during a function on the chapter's property. It's one thing to say the house has a bad apple or two, but a sexual assault during an event with free-flowing liquor meant there would be hell to pay. As the president of the fraternity, her father would have been called on the carpet, probably lost his position, might have even been suspended.

But none of that had happened. The yearbook she'd seen had come out the summer of his graduation. He'd been proudly featured as president of a fraternity that had to be in good standing to make the book. This had to be the point of the story. Of course, it was. If Pledge Thirteen had been seeking revenge, it had to be because she didn't get justice at the time. A wave of nausea coursed through her as she remembered picking up the roses from the broken vase on her front porch. A baker's dozen of gorgeous white roses. Thirteen. A message for her? No, Pledge Thirteen was sending a message to her parents. But why kill Alpha Nus if it was the men of Zeta Tau who'd harmed her? She posed the question to her father.

"I don't know. Maybe it's because of what happened next. Your mother, Marty, and a few other girls took her upstairs to the game room and held a little session. Your mother paid her a tidy sum to leave the party and never come back. That's all she told me, anyway. But last year, while I was attempting to find things that might resurrect her memory, I came across a stack of her journals in the attic. I opened one and started reading and couldn't stop. Parts were mundane, but the rest detailed everything that happened that night. Every detail about how they threatened that girl with certain ruin of her reputation. They told her if she went to the police, they would give Leonard and Jerry an alibi. They were ruthless. They didn't have as much to lose as Leonard and Jerry, but Alpha Nu was everything to your mother. She had no identity without it. She couldn't bear the thought of the university shutting down the chapter."

"And you? I guess losing your cushy little fraternity life was too much to handle. You didn't dare rat out your friends?"

"It wasn't that simple. If someone had gone to the police, we all would've been investigated. Jerry denied he had sex with her at all. Leonard said it was consensual. We all knew who the police would believe. And…"

He stopped talking and hung his head. She could tell recounting this story was painful for him, but she had to know what he'd stopped himself from saying. "And what?"

"And your mother pointed out they had had sex in my bed. That evidence would be there. That the police would look at me as a possible suspect or at least an accomplice. My future would be ruined. I was already accepted to law school. A rape charge would have ended my career before it began."

His lack of sympathy for the abused girl and her mother's ruthlessness sickened her. "Where are the journals now?"

"I don't know."

"Try again."

"Really, I don't know. Your mother and I got in a terrible fight over them. She started saying she was going to tell people what was in them. She went a little nuts about it. I realized later it was probably the Alzheimer's talking, but I didn't know about it at the time. It was right before she was diagnosed.

"We've never really gotten along. I think the only reason we actually stayed together was this secret. She was so focused on what she wanted out of life, and I fit into that picture. If either of us had told anyone what had really happened, the walls would come crumbling down. Staying together was the only way we could trust each other."

Ellen shook her head. "Don't make this all about her. You had just as much to lose, and when she really needed you, you took off."

"I spent my entire life with this secret. She's not even really present anymore. I can't live tied to a memory. And she was threatening to expose me. I could've lost my job, my reputation. Once I learned about her disease, I realized if I wasn't around, it was much less likely the memories would be stirred. She wouldn't be as troubled and I could be free. And then you called."

And then I called. And brought the walls crumbling down. She'd called him for help, for comfort, but there was none of that here. She shuddered to think that she was a child of a completely loveless relationship. Two people who'd married and built a family out of an obligation to keep a secret. And she'd been keeping secrets too. Unknowingly, she'd interfered with an investigation by not telling Danny or Sarah about her mother and her involvement with the sorority. They might have been able to connect some of the events if they'd had this information. Well, she was tired of carrying other people's burdens. It was time to get rid of the secrets.

Chapter Nineteen

S he's bringing a lawyer?" Danny had rushed from the courthouse when she'd gotten Sarah's call. Now she listened to Sarah explain that she'd gotten a call from Ellen that morning. Apparently, Ellen was ready to talk, but didn't trust them enough to come forward on her own so she'd hired some hotshot lawyer to represent her.

Of course she didn't trust them. Danny knew she was the reason. Within the span of twelve hours yesterday, she'd gone from making love to Ellen to hurling accusations at her. She'd resisted breaking the wall Ellen had erected even though she'd longed to send a text, make a call. Ellen had made it clear she should stay away. So she kept her lonely distance. Ellen had every right to distrust all the things she'd said about wanting a relationship. People in relationships didn't issue ultimatums at the first sign of trouble.

But they weren't in a relationship. Ellen had made it clear from the start she wasn't interested in anything more than a good time. Which was probably for the best. Danny wasn't sure she could get past the fact Ellen had hidden information from her. It wasn't as if what she'd concealed had been something inconsequential, like a messy closet or a propensity to eat chips in bed. She'd deliberately concealed information Danny and the others needed to solve this case. The betrayal stung, and, as much as Danny tried not to take it personally, she couldn't help but compare Ellen to Maria. Was she doomed to repeat her mistakes?

No. She'd write their brief interlude off to lessons learned. Today, she would focus on the case, on her work—the only thing she could really count on.

"She should be here any minute. Do you want to get another ADA involved?"

Danny looked up at Sarah, surprised to see concern in her eyes. "Another prosecutor? Why?"

"You know, just in case it gets a little uncomfortable?" Sarah shrugged, but Danny got the point. An attorney for the state should be in the room, in case whatever hotshot attorney Ellen had likely hired wound up trying to push the cops around, acting like they should be able to cut a deal. But it should be her. This was her case. She could either buck up and see it through or admit she was both a personal and professional failure and bow out. She squared her shoulders.

"I'll be there. You and George take the lead. It'll be fine." She stood and started to walk to the coffee maker, but stopped and turned back. "Seriously, I'll be fine, but thanks for...you know..." She hoped Sarah got the point.

Sarah gave her an aw-shucks expression and waved her off. As Danny poured her cup of coffee, she considered how much her first impression of Sarah had been off. She'd assumed the flirty, cocky, arrogant side was all there was, but now she saw clearly the loyal, caring person beneath. The realization reminded her of Ellen's transformation from playful to passionate. Then painful. She shook away the thought, and spent the next few minutes wishing coffee had healing powers beyond caffeine.

She was halfway through the cup, when she heard Ellen's voice. Bracing for their first meeting since the revelations outside of Ellen's house, Danny turned to greet her, but instead of Ellen, a familiar tall redhead stood in her path. "Morgan?"

"Nice to see you again." Morgan extended a hand. "Parker sends her regards."

Morgan Bradley was more than hotshot. She was high power. If Sarah had been from around here, she would've known that Morgan was one of the best criminal defense attorneys in town. Maybe Ellen really did have something to hide. She'd been up against Morgan and her partner, Parker, a former cop, several times and, although both were pleasant to deal with pretrial, once they entered the courtroom, the battle was brutal. "Nice to see you too. I assume you're here for Ms. Davenport."

Morgan raised her eyebrows at the mention of Ellen, but her tone remained cordial. "I am. I was hoping you and I could talk alone for a minute before we get started."

Danny couldn't resist a look into the hall. Ellen stood facing Sarah, but neither of them were talking. She was just about to look away when Ellen looked at her. Despite the distance, Danny could see the pain in Ellen's eyes, the circles underneath. She desperately wanted to push past Morgan and go to Ellen, slip an arm around her waist, and whisper in her ear that everything would be all right. Whatever secrets Ellen had, whatever lengths she'd gone to to hide them, everything would be all right. She willed Ellen to read her mind because it was the most she could do for now.

She looked back at Morgan who didn't even try to hide a slight smile. "Yes. We can talk."

Alone in the room with the door shut, she waited for Morgan to say her piece.

"Ellen wants to talk to you, to tell you everything about her mother, but I thought it might be helpful to give you a little background to make it easier for you to understand how difficult this has been for her, and to spare her from experiencing too much emotion when she tells her story."

Danny's mind raced with possibilities. Was Ellen about to confess to some horrible deed? Was her mother involved in these killings? She steeled her mind to remain open and nodded for Morgan to continue.

"As you know, Ellen's mother has been an important player in the Alpha Nu alumnae group. What you don't know is that last year she was diagnosed with Alzheimer's and Ellen had to place her in a home."

Not what she'd expected to hear. Her heart ached for Ellen and the trauma that must have been. "I had no idea."

"Around the same time that her mother was diagnosed, her father, who was one of my law school professors, cut ties with the family and left town."

"Does Ellen think he has something to do with the murders?"

Morgan looked startled. "No, no, not at all. But we do think he might have some information that would be helpful to your investigation. He shared this information with Ellen and she wants to share it with you."

Danny drummed her fingers on the table. This entire exchange was not at all what she'd been expecting. So Morgan was here, not as a big shot criminal defense attorney, but as a family friend. Ellen's only tie to the murders was information her father had. If that was the case, why was Morgan really here at all? She asked as much.

"She was nervous so she came to me for advice. She said you threatened her with some talk about filing charges. Interfering in an investigation?"

Danny's face burned. "I was mad."

"It's hard when someone you care about isn't entirely honest, but I can assure you she was only trying to protect her family who I can also assure you didn't have anything to do with these terrible murders. In fact, I think her mother is likely to be one of the targets."

Danny barely processed anything past "someone you care about." Apparently, Morgan was enough of a family friend for Ellen to have shared the details of their relationship.

Relationship. There was that word again. "She told you."

"She told me no details, but I'm pretty observant. I'd suggest you get some other ADA to sit in on the interview to keep a keen defense attorney from questioning your role, but frankly, I'm not sure she could get through the telling without you in the room as well. She's had a rough couple of days. Remember, a killer was on her doorstep."

Danny nodded. Morgan was a fierce adversary, but she trusted her and she was right. No matter what, Ellen was a victim too. She'd hear what Ellen had to say and she'd keep an open mind.

Ellen finished telling the story her father had relayed and waited for the inevitable questions. Morgan, George, Sarah, Danny, and the other assistant district attorney who'd joined them, Molly Howard, all seemed to be rendered speechless by her story.

Danny was the first to speak. "Do you need a break? Are you okay?" Her voice was soft, gentle. Ellen met her eyes and stayed locked there. She wasn't okay, but she didn't need a break. She needed something else—forgiveness, comfort—but she couldn't ask for it here, not in front of all the others. She shook her head and broke the stare. "I'm okay, but can I have a glass of water?"

George stood and motioned for the rest of them to stay seated. When he placed a bottle of water in front of her, she took her time twisting off the cap, drinking deep, before she felt calm enough to face them all again.

Sarah asked the next question. "Your father didn't know the woman's name?"

"He said he didn't. He only knew her by that stupid nickname. If it's in the journals, he didn't read that far before my mother took them away. I believe he was telling the truth about that. I've racked my brain, but back then we didn't keep records of pledges who didn't complete rush. The woman he talked about could be anyone who was enrolled at Richards University that year. We could ask women who were members of the sorority at that time. They might remember some names."

"The ones we've talked to have been anything but cooperative," George said. "Do you know where your mother's journals are?"

"I don't. I've searched my mother's safe deposit box. I packed all the things she took to the home, so I know they aren't there. If they were in the house at all, I'm sure I would've run across them when we packed her things."

Danny leaned forward and placed a hand on her arm. "I hate to ask this, but may we search your house? There's a chance you may have missed them. After all, you weren't even aware they existed back then."

"If you think it will help. Do you need me to be there?"

"It would help if you were nearby, so the police could ask you questions if they need to, during the search. I'll be right there with you."

Ellen met Danny's eyes again. Not a trace of anger, not an ounce of distrust, only compassion. And strength. She drew it in. "Okay, I'll go. Let's do it now, before I lose my nerve."

Everyone stood and filed out, leaving the two of them standing in the room. Ellen saw Morgan, Sarah, and Molly, waiting just outside the door, acting as if they weren't listening in. Danny waited beside her, expectantly.

"I'm sorry."

"You have nothing to be sorry about," Danny said. "I'm sorry. I was so harsh on you."

She looked at Molly. "Is she replacing you on the case?"

Danny followed her gaze. "She's helping. You don't need to worry about that. I'm not off the case, no matter what happens."

"I feel like I really messed things up." Ellen willed Danny to know she wasn't just talking about the case.

"You didn't. I'm just glad you're safe. We'll get the journals, we'll find out who this woman is, and Sarah and George will make an arrest. Whoever did these murders, whoever threatened you, will go away for the rest of her life."

Danny's goals were so simple, so true. And none of them included anything outside of solving the case. She had no right to expect they would. In their every interaction, Danny had been exactly as she'd appeared. Not a bit of subterfuge. The attraction, the caring, the openness, all of it had been real, genuine. She clearly still cared, but her concern had morphed from that of a passionate lover to a pitying caretaker.

She didn't need pity and she didn't need a caretaker. At least she didn't need those things from Danny. Ellen struggled into a smile. "I'm not worried. Not with a herd of police and FBI here to watch out for me." She walked to the door and said, "I'll ride with Morgan so you don't have to worry about carting me around if I'm ready to leave before you are."

Morgan nodded and Ellen followed her out of the station without a backward glance, unable to bear the prospect of seeing relief on Danny's face now that their acquaintance was drawing to a close.

Ellen sat in her car, watching the police swarm her parents' house. She'd made Morgan drop her off at the hotel so she could retrieve her car. When she'd run up to her room to get the keys, she found a note from her father. He'd returned to Chicago that morning, despite her entreaty to him to stay. The police were going to want to talk to him, she was certain of that, but she decided that was their problem. She was tired of being left to pick up the pieces of her parents' failures.

Danny stood on the sidewalk, directly in front of the house. Several times Sarah, George, and Molly had come over to discuss some matter with her and they'd huddled in conversation. She looked completely in her element and Ellen wondered if she had the same blend of ease and command in the courtroom. Probably. Juries likely loved her sincerity, her passion. She certainly did. But she'd risked it all to keep a secret, one she never would've kept had she known the depths of the deceit she'd helped hide. It was one thing to think she'd been shielding her sick mother from unnecessary attention, but she'd unwittingly harbored a dangerous truth that may have brought death in its wake. She'd chosen poorly, but to her credit she hadn't had all the information. Now Danny had all the information she needed about her, her family, and their past, and she couldn't blame her for choosing to walk away.

"Ellen?"

She looked up to see the foursome headed her way. George spoke first. "Our teams have looked everywhere. Any secret compartments or hidden rooms, anything like that we might be missing?"

"The wine cellar is the only place in the house I know that's not readily visible to a visitor."

"If they're not here, do you have an idea of where they might be?"

Ellen shook her head. She didn't have a clue. Only one person knew where the journals were and she wasn't capable of telling them. Or was she? Vivian did have moments when she seemed present, but whether they'd be able to coax specific answers to specific questions was a gamble, and not completely without risk. Patterson had warned that pushing Vivian on her memory could have the unintended consequence of driving her deeper into forgetfulness. No one really knew whether the effects were long lasting, making it impossible to assess the risk. But what if her mother could tell them where the journals were? What if the journals led them to the killer? What if lives were saved?

It was time to start taking risks, to think about the bigger picture. She'd held back before out of concern for her mother, but those other women who might be on the killer's list deserved her concern as well. And if it turned out that the killer was Pledge Thirteen, and her mother had set this whole ordeal in motion, well, this was her chance to make it right.

Unconcerned about what the others might think, she reached for Danny's hand, and when Danny's fingers curled tightly into hers, she drew the strength to say, "Let's go talk to my mother. I think it's time we get some answers."

Chapter Twenty

I don't think this is a good idea." Mrs. Patterson stood at the front of the visiting room with her hands on her hips. Danny, Molly, Sarah, and George sat with Ellen, watching as she considered their proposal. "Asking her a bunch of questions about the past isn't likely to get you any usable information, and it could do more harm than good." She looked prepared to do battle to protect her ward.

Danny started to speak, but Ellen held up a hand. "How is she?" It was still early in the day and she hoped they'd managed to get here in time to catch her mother during a good spell.

"She's good, but what you're proposing could drive her deep inside. Is that really something you want to risk?"

Ellen slumped in her chair. She'd spent the last year taking care of her mother's every need, keeping her secrets. Now it was time for her mother to do something for her and for all of the women who might be in danger. Was she selfish for demanding reciprocity?

Danny spoke up. "What if we don't question her about the past? What if we only ask where she put the journals? If the information we need is in there, then we may not need to talk to her, at least not right away."

Mrs. Patterson cocked her head as if considering the idea. "That might work, but all of you can't be in the room. Too many strangers will only confuse her. Ellen, I think the questions would work best coming from you. One other person and no more."

Ellen looked around the room. She knew everyone there wanted to be the first to get whatever information her mother could provide, but she didn't care about what they wanted. Right now, all she cared about was her own need to have someone in her corner, and she knew exactly who she hoped that someone would be.

Danny read her mind. "I'll go with you."

Ellen nodded her thanks, scared if she said anything it would be too infused with emotion. She turned to Mrs. Patterson. "Do you know where she is now?"

"She's out in the garden. She's spent a lot of time out there since you were here last. I suppose she finds it soothing. Come with me. I'll show you."

They both followed Mrs. Patterson out to the balcony where Ellen had visited with her mother the day she learned of Marty Lawson's death. Danny joined her at the rail and, as their fingers brushed together, Ellen nearly melted into Danny's embrace. She didn't want to be here, didn't want to be on the front line of figuring out her mother's role in this tragedy, but she drew strength from Danny's presence. As Mrs. Patterson gazed out over the balcony, she turned and whispered, "Thank you."

"I'm not going to leave you," Danny said as she squeezed her hand.

If only she meant what Ellen needed her to mean.

"There she is." Mrs. Patterson pointed to the same spot Vivian had pointed out that night, the one that had her so agitated. Ellen gasped at the sight of her prim and proper mother, dressed in gardening boots and a hat, planting a rose bush. She'd never seen her mother performing any kind of menial labor, especially not something where she could get her hands dirty. "When you said she was spending time in the garden, this is not at all what I thought you meant."

"She's been quite vigorous about it. Even insisted on exactly what plants should be where. Her doctor was so happy to see her exhibiting enthusiasm for something, that we ordered whatever she wanted, even a stone plaque naming the garden. She did insist on paying for that herself and we took it out of her incidental fund. I hope you don't mind."

"Of course not. I'm just amazed to see her actually doing the work herself. Should we wait until she's done?"

"You'll have to wait until sundown if that's the case. She tends to be at her best when she's in the garden. Why don't you join her down there and see if you can bring up the topic of her journals. Gently. And I'll be nearby in case you need me."

"Thank you." Ellen waited until Mrs. Patterson walked away before she faced Danny. "You ready for this?"

"Are you?"

"I wouldn't have thought I was ready for anything that's happened in the last week, but I'm still standing."

"I can't even imagine what you're going through."

"I'm okay. I've had a whole lifetime to get used to hiding truths." And hiding feelings, she thought, but didn't say.

"It's taken its toll."

Danny's tone was sad, and despite the fact she didn't hear any recrimination, she knew she owed her an apology. "Danny, I'm so sorry. I never meant to lie to you. I had no idea—"

Danny gripped her hand. "Stop. We're good. I'm the one who crossed the line between personal and professional and I owe you the apology. I never would've been so emotional about you keeping information from us if we hadn't…" She cleared her throat. "Anyway, we're good now. Let's go talk to your mother. Okay?"

Ellen nodded. Danny may be good, but she was far from it. The best thing she could do would be to get this over with as quickly as possible, so she and Danny could go their separate ways.

Even in a garden hat, boots, and gloves, Danny could see that Vivian Davenport was an older, not quite as beautiful, version of her daughter Ellen. Where Ellen's lines were sophisticated, Vivian's were harsh. And her eyes were sharp, hard, not warm and inviting like her daughter's.

On the walk from the balcony, they'd decided that Ellen would take the lead. She'd introduce Danny as an old friend, hoping to make contact with one of Vivian's sorority sisters. That was as far as they'd planned since they didn't have any idea how far they would be able to get. Although their talk had been confined to how to handle the discussion with Vivian, Danny wasn't immune to the increased tension between them. They had both assumed their roles, she as attorney, Ellen as witness, but the feelings they'd shared still lay unresolved between them. Danny wanted to talk about it, but fear kept her quiet. Ellen had gone through, was still going through, a scary ordeal, and she showed no signs of wanting to reconnect in that way. Danny resisted the urge to interpret her need for comfort as a need for something more.

"Mother, I want you to meet a friend of mine. Her name is Danielle Soto."

Vivian smiled and waved a small trowel at them both. "A pleasure to meet you. I'd shake your hand, but as you can see..." She looked down at her mud-covered glove and giggled. Danny shot a glance at Ellen who looked shocked at the display, and she decided Vivian wasn't normally much of a giggler. Things didn't look good for a coherent conversation. "Nice to meet you too, Mrs. Davenport. You have a lovely garden."

"Indeed. I have worked very hard to maintain it. Do you like the begonias?"

Danny followed the direction of her pointed trowel. She wouldn't know a begonia if it bit her in the ass. She only knew what a trowel was because Mama Soto made her and her brothers work in the yard to earn allowance when they were growing up. She'd been relegated to raking leaves since she couldn't be trusted to know a weed from a plant about to bloom. She cast a look at Ellen who subtly pointed at a clump of red blooms. She nodded. "Yes, ma'am, those are a beautiful red. They'll look nice with the white roses."

Vivian winked and pointed at Ellen. "Marty thinks I'm crazy to plant the roses here, but I think it's a brilliant way to remember where I put them. I have trouble remembering everything I need to these days."

Her self-revelation was sad, but Danny forced a smile while she tried to decipher Vivian's statement. Vivian returned the smile and then dug back into her work. Ellen tapped Danny on the shoulder and mouthed "Marty" as she pointed at her own chest. It took a few seconds, but then realized that Vivian thought Ellen was Marty Lawson, her long time, now dead friend. But she still didn't get the other part of what she'd said, "It's a brilliant way to remember where I put them." What was the "them"?

While she considered what to say next, Ellen circled the garden plot, stopping when she reached the stone plaque in the far corner. Ellen stiffened as she stared at the ground, and Danny could feel anxiety coming off her in waves. She rushed over to her side and followed her gaze. The rectangular marble plaque was about a foot long and half a foot wide. Just big enough to contain a simple phrase, the name Vivian Davenport had chosen for her special garden. *Thirteen Roses.*

Ellen turned into her arms and Danny moved them a few steps away from the garden, holding her close. "It's okay," she murmured. "I've got you. It's okay."

"I have to get out of here. I can't handle this."

Danny leaned back and looked into her eyes. She wanted to leave with Ellen, take her home, curl up in bed with her, and hold her until her fears subsided. But she couldn't. Molly may ultimately replace her on the case, but she was still a member of this task force. She had work to do, a case to solve, and she wouldn't leave here until she got some answers. "I understand, but promise me you won't leave on your own. Sarah and George can get someone to drive you to wherever you are staying, keep you safe." As much as she wanted to be that person, she knew this was best. Ellen needed to get away from here, and Danny needed to stay if she wanted to find out what was going on.

She watched as Ellen walked away, and waited until she was out of sight before engaging Vivian again. She kept her voice light, her tone even. "You were telling Marty where you put them. You were talking about the journals, weren't you?"

"Of course."

Danny struggled to keep her surprise at the frank admission from her expression. "Are they safe?"

"Safe as buried treasure."

Danny followed her gaze to the stone plaque. Ellen had insisted that Vivian hadn't brought the journals with her to Cedar Acres, but what if she had? What if when she learned of Marty Lawson's death, Vivian had decided her secrets weren't safe and she needed to hide the journals? What if they were right there, underneath the macabre stone plaque in this memorial garden to a woman who'd been wronged and who was likely seeking revenge on the sisters of Alpha Nu?

❖

Ellen opened and shut the door of the mini bar several times before she finally pulled a tiny bottle of gin out and set it on the table in her room. It made her feel better just to have it close. She'd sat alone in the room for the last few hours since Sarah dropped her off. She'd dreaded the thought of being alone so much, she'd started to ask Sarah to walk her to her room, join her for a drink, but she'd thought better of it. Sarah was working and they were close to a break in the case. The last thing she needed to be doing was comforting the daughter of the woman who may have started this whole chain of events.

Besides, Sarah wasn't Danny.

She turned on her phone and pulled up Danny's number. She'd send one text. Just a few words to ask if things were going well, if they'd made progress, if anything her addled mother had had to say made any sense, helped in any way. She typed a message and deleted it several times before finally tossing the phone on the bed. Whatever she asked, whatever she said, it would be cover for what she really wanted to know.

Those hours they'd spent together, naked, vulnerable, aroused— did they mean as much to Danny as they'd meant to her? She desperately wanted to know and she desperately wanted the answer to be yes.

The sound of an incoming text startled her out of her reverie. *I'm in the lobby. Can I come up?*

Danny. *Yes.* She couldn't type the reply fast enough.

Room #?

3605

Danny was on her way up. She forced down the adrenaline flowing through her veins. She's probably here to talk about the case. Business. Try not to act like a love-struck teenager. She palmed the bottle of gin, thrust it back in the mini bar, and spent the next few moments tidying up the room. Satisfied none of her underwear was lying around, she sat on the edge of the bed waiting.

When she heard the knock on the door, she forced herself to remain calm. Danny was here. For the first time since they'd spent the night together, they would be alone. She wouldn't waste this opportunity to talk to her, to get her to talk, about what they'd shared, how it made them feel. Talking about feelings wasn't her strong suit, but she needed to reach out or she was going to lose the connection they had, and she was desperate not to lose it.

Danny alternately flashed her badge and face at the peephole and Ellen unhooked the chain and bolt and opened the door. She motioned Danny toward the chairs, but she remained standing, scrutinizing her face. Her silence was scary.

"What is it? Did something happen? Are you okay?"

Danny pulled her into her arms. "I should be asking you that question. Are you okay? Sarah said you didn't say a word all the way back here. I should've come with you, made sure you were okay."

"You have work to do. I get it."

"Pretty sure part of my job is taking good care of my witnesses."

Ellen bristled at the implication that Danny was here only in a professional capacity. She'd allowed herself to hope for something more, for all the somethings Danny had acted like she wanted before she found out she'd held back evidence and that her family was deeply involved in the tragedy of her case. She pushed her way out of Danny's arms. "Are you this affectionate with all your witnesses?"

Danny stepped back. "I was an ass before, and I'm sorry. I just wanted to make sure you are okay, and to give you an update. I thought you might be worried. We found your mother's journals and we're headed back to the station to go through them. George assigned an officer to guard Cedar Acres, just in case. I think that covers all the bases."

You're kind of being an ass now. Ellen quickly squelched the unfair thought. Danny was just doing her job. If she'd been upfront about her mother being in the target group from the beginning, Danny probably never would have pursued a date. Never kissed her. Never made love to her. Any affection she got from Danny now was residual to the connection they'd felt, and it wasn't going anywhere. Still, it hurt to have her in the same room and know nothing more would happen between them. Her pain spurred her to ask, "If you weren't working on this case, could you see past my faults? Could you give me another chance?"

She watched the struggle play out on Danny's face and wished she hadn't asked the question. For her it was simple. If she had to do it over again, she would've told the truth from the beginning, no matter what the risk. But that wouldn't have changed anything. If Danny had known her mother was a potential victim, she never would've asked her out, never would've let her emotions get in the way of her work. Ellen remembered every detail of what Danny had told her about Maria. How their breakup had affected her ability to work, her effectiveness. She wanted to be the person who stood beside her lover, but with all her baggage, she would only be in the way.

Lover. She never should've tried on the word, because it fit perfectly. She'd finally found someone who'd penetrated her resolve not to feel and she'd messed it all up. She shouldn't put Danny in the position of having to reject her. She should just walk away. "Don't answer that."

"Ellen, I'm sorry."

"Don't be. I like you. I like what we shared, but I get it. I really do."

"I have a job to do. I can't do it if I'm distracted. I've already compromised…" Her voice trailed off and several seconds passed before she took a deep breath and started again. "It's not just the stuff about your parents. It's you. You're a potential victim too, you know. The killer was on your doorstep. There are police down the hall, watching your room right now."

Anger flashed across her face and, even though Ellen knew it wasn't directed at her, she felt the force of Danny's emotion and asked, "Can't you give the case to someone else? Molly or one of the many, many lawyers at the DA's office?"

She knew immediately this was another question she shouldn't have asked. Why should Danny give up a chance to regain her stature at the DA's office over her? She'd almost messed up her career over a woman before. She wasn't likely to do it again. Besides, Ellen didn't want to be this person, who stood in the way of her lover's success. If she really cared about Danny, she should make letting go easy on her, but now that she found someone she really cared about and who she knew cared about her, she didn't want easy. She wanted to see if she could handle hard. If Danny was going to walk away, it would have to be her decision. She wasn't going to pave the way. She braced herself for Danny's response.

"This is my case. I need to see it through. Maybe when it's over, we can…talk. See where things stand."

The pain on Danny's face didn't ease the sting of her words. They were over and they'd barely just begun. Fine. At least she knew where things stood. "I understand." She didn't, but the two-word lie was easier than the rambling truth that she'd started to fall in love with Danny, and for the first time in her life, she didn't want to detour away from her feelings. Danny didn't feel the same way, and it was time to cut this, whatever it was, off before she made a fool of herself. "You should go."

"I'm sorry."

"Don't be. I'm not sorry for what happened between us, but it's over now and we both know it."

Danny stood still for a moment, and she looked like she had something more to say. After a few beats of silence, she walked to the door, hesitated for a moment, and then she was gone.

All the things she'd wished she said rushed to the surface. Don't go. Yes, I'll wait until this case is over. I love you. Would any of those statements have kept Danny from leaving? Fear they wouldn't had kept her silent. And alone.

Chapter Twenty-one

Danny walked out of the hotel slightly dizzy and in pain. She had planned to go to Ellen's room, make sure she was okay, and let her know they'd found her mother's journals. She hadn't expected to go through an emotional breakup scene. Her plan hadn't been well thought out, but it had involved asking Ellen to wait until they could unravel the complexities of the situation. Her lack of careful planning meant the episode disintegrated. Ellen made it clear she wouldn't wait, and she didn't even want her to stick around for a meaningful good-bye.

She trudged over to Sarah's car. She wished she'd driven herself, but the visit to Ellen had been a quick stop on the way back to the station to scour the journals she'd managed to recover from Vivian Davenport. George had taken the small stack of leather bound books lined with scrawling about Vivian's college days, and he and Peter were probably halfway through them already. She should be there, but she couldn't seem to stop making poor decisions about her work when it came to Ellen.

She slid into the front seat. "Let's get out of here."

Sarah started the car and drove, and Danny sighed at the silence. Her relief at not having to rehash what had just happened was short-lived. Sarah waited a few blocks before broaching the subject. "Is she okay?"

"The witness is fine. Maybe we can get someone from the Victim Advocate's office over to talk to her."

Sarah yanked the car over to the side of the road and turned off the engine.

"What the hell are you doing?" Danny didn't have a clue what had gotten into Sarah.

"Trying to figure out why you're so stupid."

Danny folded her arms, refusing to engage.

"I mean, there's this woman back there in complete meltdown. She clearly cares about you and you obviously care about her. I'm thinking your night together wasn't some chaste affair where you slept on the couch. Am I right?"

Danny didn't even look at her, instead engaged in a mental chant. Start the car and drive, start the car and drive.

Sarah jabbed her in the arm. "I never took you for a one-night stand kind of person, especially since I offered you that when we first met and you turned me down flat. And have you looked at me? Do you even know what you missed?"

Danny let her eyes edge over to see Sarah's face, and she couldn't help but let loose a grin when she saw Sarah's broad smile. "If you're so great, why are you single?"

"Probably the same reason you are. You're married to your job."

"If I cared about my job enough, I wouldn't have gotten in this mess in the first place. I'm single because the women I fall for have honesty issues." As the words left her lips, Danny realized it wasn't fair for her to compare Maria's wanton disregard for their commitment with the actions Ellen had taken to protect her family.

Sarah echoed her thoughts. "She didn't do it to hurt you."

"Why are you defending her?"

"Better question is why aren't you? A woman like that, beautiful, smart, funny—if she was into me, I think I could cut her a little slack."

"She's over it. All she wanted was a fling anyway. She got that. Time to move on." Danny didn't feel the words, but she wanted to. What she could feel was Sarah's eyes on her, and again she wished she'd brought her own car rather than ride the rest of the way under the intense scrutiny of her FBI profiler training.

When they arrived at the station, George was poring through the journals and calling out names to one of the junior detectives searching the Alpha Nu database. He looked up when they arrived. "We've found the names of all of the victims. They all attended Richards University around the same time. Even Joyce Barr. As for the rest of the entries, they're all over the place, but I think we found the time period we're looking for. Mostly, she's writing about getting ready for the new pledges and planning all the things they're going to do with them and to them."

"Rush," Danny said. "That's what they call it."

"Dumb name," he replied.

Danny poked Sarah in the ribs. "Any response from our in-house sorority consultant?"

Sarah shot her a drop-dead look. "It's like a week of speed-dating. You go through a whirlwind of courtship and then you 'rush' to the sorority you want the most."

George grunted. "How sweet. Except it appears that once you rush to the one you want, you get abused into submission. Not much different from the military, promising glory and fame and then making you do a hundred push-ups in the dirt while it's raining like a motherfucker."

"I'm not saying what happened to this Pledge Thirteen was okay, but I'm telling you that most of the time, the initiation involves some light hazing that doesn't actually scar anyone for life. To some of these girls, belonging to the sorority gives them the support system they need to make it through school."

Danny piped in. "I didn't belong to a sorority and I got through just fine."

"I bet you went into school with a group of friends already. And I'm thinking you have a ton of family support. Family that loves you, cares about you, wants you to succeed."

Sarah's words hit hard as she thought about Ellen's parents, their loveless relationship, and their apathy toward their daughter's happiness. "Okay, maybe this Pledge Thirteen stuck around because she needed the sense of community more than she cared about the personal abuse. We need to figure out who she is and find her." She didn't say what they were all thinking: before she kills again. No one had yet discussed the fact that they'd been focused on a male killer this whole time, but if Pledge Thirteen was seeking revenge, they may have overlooked some obvious clues. "She's not going to be in the database since she left before officially joining the sorority. We should each take one of the journals and see what we can find. If her name's not in one of them, let's go back to beating down doors. One of the women of Alpha Nu has to know who she is."

Danny started flipping through the pages of the volume George handed to her, hoping the name they were looking for would be in the journals. She knew how painful it would be to Ellen to have her family secrets exposed to the women she worked with and for. Even here, supposedly focused on work, it seemed she couldn't stop caring about Ellen, her feelings and her future. She forced her mind back to the writing in front of her and read about three pages of useless gossip before being startled when Sarah cried out and waved her journal in the air.

"You sit on a tack or something?"

Sarah shoved the book toward her. "What's the name of that intern that got you so worked up the other night? The one at the mixer?"

"Perkins. Angela Perkins."

Sarah stabbed at a page in the journal. "Why is her name showing up in here?"

"Give me that." Danny ripped the journal from Sarah's grasp and stared at the open page. The name Angela Perkins jumped off the page. She waved George and Sarah to silence and started reading. Two pages in and she knew she'd found Pledge Thirteen. She could almost hear Vivian Davenport's laughter at the antics they'd put Angela Perkins through.

But what did this mean? The Angela Perkins from Vivian's college days couldn't possibly be the same girl who was interning at Alpha Nu's offices. Was she a relative?

"Where are those papers I gave you about the intern?" The fact she didn't know what was going on fueled a growing sense of panic, and she barked the question at Sarah. "And someone call whoever's on guard at Ellen's hotel and tell them to make sure she doesn't go to her office. Not until we know more."

She watched a uniformed cop dart from the room and assumed he was either off to warn Ellen's guard or he just wanted to get away from the shouting crazy lady. She knew she was spinning out of control, but she also sensed the answer to their questions was within reach. When Sarah handed her the printouts from her earlier investigation of Angela Perkins the intern, she scoured the pages. She wasn't entirely sure what she was looking for, but she was sure the answer was right in front of her.

George and Sarah stood behind her waiting as she flipped through the pages that contained the meager details of Angela's life. Old car, not much money. Dad unknown. Mom deceased.

Mom deceased. Danny ran her finger along the page. She recalled being startled that Angela's mother was significantly older than her daughter. She looked further. Wendy A. Perkins. She shoved the papers back at Sarah, pointing at the name. "I'm willing to bet everything I own that that 'A' stands for Angela. Use your fancy FBI database to figure that out and we need a cause of death, right away. Also, see if young Angela has a gun registered to her."

"You think an intern is killing a bunch of women to avenge her mother's rape at a sorority house over three decades ago?" George asked.

She didn't blame him for being skeptical. "I don't know, but until we come up with something different, I think we should check this out."

He nodded. "Fair enough. I'll get a couple of the guys to bring her in and we can talk to her." George paused and looked at his feet before asking, "You want in when we talk to her?"

She knew what he was really asking. He was giving her a graceful way to admit she was too close to the investigation to be in on the interview of a potential killer. Right now she was torn between looking that devious little intern in the eye and speeding as fast as she could to Ellen's hotel to make sure she didn't put herself in harm's way. He was right, but she wasn't ready to completely let go. "I'll call Molly and have her come over, but I want to be here when you interview her. I'll stay behind the glass." She lowered her voice so only George and Sarah could hear. "I need you both to promise me nothing will happen to Ellen or her family."

Sarah nodded and pulled out her cell phone. "We left a guard at Cedar Acres earlier, but I'll have a couple of agents from the local office check on Ellen." She turned to George. "Okay by you if we help out?"

George grinned. "Look at the fed playing nice. Better stop it or I'll have to take back all the mean things I've said about you guys behind your backs."

"Guys, can you focus?" Danny didn't try to hide the growl behind her command as images of horrible things happening to Ellen flooded her mind. The note with the flowers was etched in her memory. *Last night was such a rush. Thanks for the view.* If Angela was the killer, it would've been easy for her to find where Ellen lived. Was she after Ellen or Vivian? Whoever delivered the flowers, whoever wrote that note had watched them. On the deck, through the windows, on the bed. Danny shivered, horrified at the realization that the intimacy they'd shared had been a show for a killer. The emotion that coursed through her was a strong signal she had no business working this case any longer. Once Ellen's life had been placed in danger, she'd become too personally involved.

Hell, who was she kidding? Once she'd made love to Ellen, she'd crossed any line of professionalism she might have maintained. She might be able to fool the others into thinking all she cared about was Ellen's immediate safety, but the truth was she cared about way more than that. She wanted a future. A future Ellen clearly didn't want based on how easily she'd dismissed her that afternoon.

All the more reason to focus on the case. She may not be able to see it through, but at least for now, it could occupy her mind and crowd out all the wishing for things she couldn't have.

Chapter Twenty-two

A m I under arrest?" Ellen squared off with the suited agents standing in front of her hotel room door. Tired of being cooped up inside, she'd decided to make a trip to the office. She'd had a nagging feeling all day that the answer to finding the killer was somewhere in the sorority's records. It had to be and no one was better equipped to find the answers than she was, but when she opened her door she found that the uniformed guard down the hall had been supplemented by a pair of FBI agents who were insistent that she stay put.

"No, ma'am. We just recommend for your own safety that you stay here while certain developments are investigated."

Developments? Something big was happening. Ellen considered ducking back in the room and texting Danny to see if she could find out what was going on. But she'd told Danny to go. The last thing she needed to do was send mixed messages, especially when Danny had already made a choice to focus on her work instead of anything that might develop between them.

She stared at the agents' stoic faces and crossed arms. These guys weren't going to tell her anything. She'd have to leave the room if she wanted to have a chance of learning what was going on. Leaving the door propped open, she stepped back to grab her purse and keys. "You guys may be concerned about my safety, but I'm concerned about my sanity. I won't be gone long. Hope you don't get too bored waiting for me." Without another word, she shut the door, pushed past them and hurried to the elevator, hoping the car would arrive before she lost her nerve.

She drove straight to the office, but she parked on the street instead of in the depths of the underground parking garage. She didn't seriously think she was in any danger, but too many movie scenes of trapped victims dying lonely deaths in parking garages flooded her mind. Wouldn't hurt to be a little bit cautious. As she fished for coins for the meter, her phone buzzed with an incoming text.

Call me. 911. Agent Flores.

Nine one one indeed. The agents at the hotel must have ratted her out and now Sarah was going to try to coax her back to the hotel. She started to drop her phone back into her purse, but hesitated. Sarah was probably with Danny. And even if she wasn't, she might tell her what was going on. She punched in the numbers and waited impatiently for Sarah to answer.

"Flores."

"It's Ellen. Are you going to threaten to lock me up?"

"No one wants to lock you up, but we are concerned about you."

"If you want me to barricade myself somewhere, I'm going to need a good reason. Something better than a vague reference to developments in the case."

"Are you at your office?"

"I'm on the street in front of the building, but I haven't gone in yet."

"We have reason to believe your intern, Angela Perkins, is a suspect in the killings."

Ellen's response was immediate. "That's crazy."

"It's definitely crazy, but it's not without foundation. It appears her deceased mother may have been Pledge Thirteen."

"Deceased? Was she killed?"

"She committed suicide when Angela was fifteen. Guess who discovered her dead body?"

Ellen visualized a young girl finding her mother's corpse and gasped. "Oh my God. That poor girl."

"Maybe. I guess even Bundy had a bad childhood. Still not a great reason to go around killing people."

"She's supposed to be working this afternoon."

"I know. We have a couple of guys at your building and they are picking her up for questioning. Promise me you won't go up there. We don't want her to see you right now."

Ellen stared up at her building. Was Danny in there right now, about to help interrogate Angela? The image of Angela's smug smile as she handed Danny a white rose at the mixer flashed in her mind. Had Angela stood outside her house, delivered the flowers? Had she watched them making love? The very idea caused her to double over.

"Ellen?"

She leaned against the car. She had to pull herself together. "I'm here."

"Promise me you won't go up there?"

"Tell me one thing. Is Danny there?"

"What? No, she's at the station. You could call her, you know."

Sarah made it sound so easy, but it wasn't. She chose to ignore the advice. "I'm going for a drive. Will you keep me posted about what you find out about Angela?"

"You bet."

Ellen got back in her car and left downtown on I-35. She hadn't started out with a plan other than to get as far away from her office, house, and the stifling feeling of having her every move being watched. She drove an hour and a half to Hillsboro before pulling over and parking at the local outlet mall. As she stared out her window at the shoppers strolling around the complex, she wondered if they were all as carefree as they appeared, or if they were like her. Weighted down by a past full of secrets.

Danny sat next to Molly and they both watched on the closed-circuit monitor as George and Sarah took turns questioning Angela. They started with easy, background questions designed to make her think they were talking to everyone connected with the sorority, especially those who were at the mixer the week before. They even mentioned the guy they had followed from the mixer and been watching ever since to gauge her reaction.

She was eerily cool, offering a mix of concern and naiveté about the tragedy that had befallen some of the older members of the sorority. After about an hour of careful and kind questioning, Sarah took on the role of bad cop, questioning Angela about her whereabouts on the days of the murders, starting with the most recent delivery of flowers to Ellen's house.

Danny was constantly amazed how many people stuck around this long for questioning without asking for an attorney. Usually they at least asked something like "Am I in trouble?" or "Should I hire a lawyer?" to which the rote response was "If you didn't do anything wrong, you have nothing to hide" or "Sure, you can get a lawyer, if that's what you really want, but if you didn't do anything wrong…" But Angela didn't ask any such questions nor did she show any signs of cracking even when Sarah started asking about phone records and who she might have been talking to, disparaging the older members of the sorority, the night of the mixer. All of her responses were easy and calm.

Danny was so intent on watching the slow and careful grilling, that she barely noticed the tap on her shoulder.

"Ma'am?" A young uniformed cop stood behind her holding a folder.

She stood and motioned for him to follow her a few steps away so Molly could continue to watch the interview undisturbed. "Yes?"

He held up the folder and spoke in an earnest tone. "Detective Ramirez asked me to get this important information and bring it to him. Any idea if he plans to be out of there soon?"

Molly lifted her head at the mention of "important information" and walked over to stand beside her. Danny wondered if the folder contained Angela's mother's autopsy. They'd managed to find the reported cause of death from an archived newspaper obituary, but she hoped the autopsy would give them something more to work with. She was itching to open it, and if Molly weren't standing right there, she would have ripped into it. She could still do it. She was Molly's boss, after all. Time to decide which was more important, being the prosecutor or the lover. Ellen may have asked her to go, but it wasn't in her nature to give up so easily. If she wanted to fight for a chance with her, she needed to draw some lines and one of them was right in front of her.

She motioned for the officer to hand the file to Molly and walked back over to the monitor. She would see this part of the case through, but she'd start positioning Molly to take over the ultimate role once they were sure they had the killer. Lover. That was her choice. She only hoped Ellen would give her the chance.

"Danny, you're going to want to take a look at this." Molly held the folder in one hand and made urgent motions with the other. When Danny reached her side, Molly shoved the folder into her hands and started rattling off details at a brisk pace. "And check out these photos."

Danny flipped through the photographs, one by one. Half a dozen angles all showed the same thing. The same kind of hangman's noose that had been found at each of the murder scenes. If they hadn't been sure before that young Angela was involved in the murders, now they had motive. She'd come home one day after school to find her troubled mother swinging from a beam in their home. A scene like that could devastate anyone and, for someone who had been raised by a troubled woman, she had apparently broken, although she managed to maintain a psychopathic guise of normal.

She handed the photos back to Molly. "Knock on the door. George and Sarah need to see these."

"There's something else." Molly pulled a sheet of paper out of the folder. Danny watched as she traced the lines with her finger. It was a birth certificate. For a Collin Perkins. Mother, Angela Perkins. Father, unknown. She pulled the paper from Molly's hand and scoured the page for the date of birth. When she found it, she knew she held the most important piece of evidence they'd found to date. Collin Perkins had been born almost nine months from the date Pledge Thirteen had been paid to leave Alpha Nu. If Angela Perkins senior had been raped like she claimed, Collin Perkins, the child of that rape, definitely had the strongest motive to avenge her death. She knew she was jumping to conclusions, but Sarah and George weren't getting anywhere with the other child of Pledge Thirteen, and she was certain this piece of evidence was key.

"Do we know where this guy lives?"

Molly looked through the file. "Same address as Angela. Looks like the house is still in their mother's name. He probably inherited it and lives there with his little sister."

"No way we have enough for a warrant, but I think we're on to something. Get Sarah and George and let's meet in the war room." Danny turned to walk away with the folder still in her hand, but stopped short. Prosecutor or Lover? Could she be both? She handed the folder back to Molly. "You're the new lead on this. I'll clear it with Alvarez. I'm in the room, but you call the shots. Okay?"

Molly nodded and only barely hid a smile of excitement. They were about to have a big break. Danny could feel the pulsing energy and didn't blame Molly for wanting to be a part of it. Within a few minutes, they were all settled in the conference room. Danny let Molly explain what they'd found.

Sarah responded first. "I think George and I should go pay Collin a little visit. Maybe he'll invite us in and we can get a free look around. We see anything of interest, we can let you know and you can get a warrant to do a full search."

George nodded. "I told Angela we were getting her dinner. She has a thing for Yale, the cop who brought her in. I'll let him hang out with her while she eats, get her to stick around for a while. Danny, where will you be if we need you?"

She started to answer, that she'd be right there, waiting on their call to draft a warrant, but that was Molly's job now. Besides, there was somewhere else she'd rather be. Someone else she wanted to see. She told George to call Molly about the warrant and Molly to call her if she needed any help with the process. Satisfied she had made the right decision, she left the station and headed to her car.

CHAPTER TWENTY-THREE

It was after dark when Ellen pulled up to the familiar complex and waited for the valet to approach. She had no idea how she'd wound up here. She'd spent the time parked in Hillsboro wondering how her life had gotten so messed up in the course of a few weeks. Then she realized she'd been living a lie for years. A lie where her mother was a philanthropic socialite and her father a respected intellectual, ostensibly the perfect pair. What a crock. Vivian was a mean-spirited bitch and Bill was a coward. To top it off, they'd never loved each other and she now seriously doubted whether they'd ever really loved her. Suddenly her propensity to steer clear of anything more meaningful than a fling seemed normal. How could anyone expect her to be any different with these two as an example?

She wished she were different. If she were, she would have told Danny that she would wait for her to finish with the case. She would have told Danny that she wanted to try. She would have asked her to be patient. If she were different, there were so many things she would have done.

But she was the child of her parents, and that was likely why she'd unconsciously driven here, hoping that her mother was mentally present and that she could get some answers about why she'd done the things she'd done.

She handed her keys to the valet and walked through the doors of Cedar Acres. Probably best to check in with Mrs. Patterson before she talked to her mother. She had no idea if there'd been any fallout after the garden scene. Normally, she would've checked in sooner, but after the recent revelations, apathy was the strongest emotion she could summon when it came to her mother's well-being.

Mrs. Patterson wasn't in sight and the receptionist was on the phone, so she waited on a couch near the front counter and watched the residents shuffle around the facility. Based on the crowd, it looked like they were all flooding out of the dining hall. She tried to remember the last time she'd eaten and was surprised to recall it had been cereal from room service that morning. She'd lost her appetite after Danny had left her hotel room, and right now she felt as though she'd never be hungry again.

Several minutes passed and she was about to interrupt the talkative receptionist when Mrs. Patterson appeared at her side.

"Ellen, how nice to see you. I was headed out, but I saw you sitting here. I hope nothing's wrong."

"Nothing specific. How is my mother?"

"Well, it's been interesting. Since the visit from your friends, she's been more aware than normal. I know we were worried about setting her back, but it appears as if you may have jogged her consciousness in a good way."

Ellen considered the possibility that she might be able to have a prolonged conversation with her mother about her past, about what she had set in motion with her actions, about what she'd made of her life in the aftermath. Now that the possibility was real, she was uncertain. Did she really want to hear the truth?

"She's in her room if you'd like to see her. I'm sure she'd love the chance to talk to you."

Ellen wasn't sure about that, but she knew she needed to close out this chapter of her life before she could start anything new. And she desperately wanted something new. "I'll go see her now."

Vivian sat in a wingback chair reading by the light of a Tiffany lamp on the table beside her. Ellen noted the novel in her hand was the same one she had insisted someone had swiped from her room. The soft light from the lamp didn't hide the deep age lines that etched her once spa-pampered face and the black patches under her eyes. If she didn't know her, Ellen would've thought she looked like any other lonely old woman.

Ellen observed her in the quiet for a few moments before Vivian looked up. "Why hello, dear. I didn't hear you come in."

"Do you know who I am?" Best to start this process with a clear understanding of where things stood.

"Of course I do. Why don't you come in and sit down?"

Ellen edged into the room, but remained standing. "The last couple of times I was here you thought I was Marty Lawson."

"Poor Marty. She died, you know."

Her words were sad, but something was off, like she didn't realize the horrific way Marty had met her end. "I know. Do you remember how she died?"

"Are you here to quiz me? Because you really should sit down for that." She scrunched her brow. "I don't seem to recall exactly how she died, but I do recall it was recently and untimely. She was always very healthy and fit."

Ellen felt the buzzing of her phone. She pulled it out and looked at the new text, seeing the "where are you?" before she noticed the sender. Danny. She itched to type a reply telling her where she was and arranging a time to meet, but she needed to air things out with her mother first. She quickly typed, "call you later" and turned off her phone to prevent any other interruptions. For all she knew, Danny's text was merely Sarah's attempt to find out where she'd gone to elude the agents who'd been keeping her prisoner. No way was she going to risk losing the opportunity to take advantage of her mother's lucid moments. Her haste kept her from sugarcoating her next words.

"Marty was murdered."

"No, no." Vivian's hands flew up to cover her face, and the book she'd been reading thudded on the floor.

Ellen ignored her natural instinct to spare her mother the details and pressed on. "Do you have any idea who killed her?"

Vivian sobbed. "How could I possibly know?"

"Do you remember Angela Perkins?" When she saw her mother's puzzled look, she added, "Pledge Thirteen? Your senior year in college?"

The look on her mother's face left no doubt. She remembered Angela Perkins very well, but she still resisted admitting it. "I don't know where you heard that term, but I think we should talk about something more pleasant."

Ellen considered her options. She could do what she'd done all her life and go along with her mother's wishes. Unpleasant topics were unmentioned, swept under the table and dealt with only if absolutely necessary. Ignoring the past would definitely be the easier route. No confrontation, no unpleasant and uncomfortable drudging up of feelings. Letting buried truths stay buried might make this moment easier, but how would she ever find depth in her own life if she continued to mimic what she'd been taught? Weren't some things worth getting messy over?

She sat on the small couch and faced her mother, ignoring her clear expression of annoyance. "You have every right not to talk about the parts of your life that are yours alone, but when your past decisions affect me and so many others, you lose that right. I need to hear your version of what happened all those years ago, so if you have something redeeming to say, now's the time."

Ellen leaned back on the couch and folded her arms. Vivian opened her mouth, but instead of words, she emitted a sharp cry. Ellen followed her wide-eyed gaze and gasped when she saw a hulking man standing in the doorway. He wore the same uniform as all the other employees, but the gun in his hand clearly signaled he wasn't there in a care-taking role. With his free hand, he placed a finger over his lips and then shut the door behind him and walked further into the suite.

"Don't stop." He spoke the words to Vivian while pointing the barrel of his gun between them. "You were going to tell her about your college days and how hospitable you were to all the Alpha Nu pledges."

Ellen watched the scene play out, desperately trying to process what was going on. Had Sarah and Danny been completely wrong when they thought Angela, her intern, was the killer? What was this man's connection to the sorority and the deceased Angela Perkins? Tired of the lies, tired of the secrets, she braved a question. "Who are you?"

His smile was devoid of feeling and his eyes were blank as he spoke with a halting voice. "I'm Collin Perkins. Pledge Thirteen was my mother."

❖

Danny knocked on the door of Ellen's hotel room for the third time, but still no answer. She glanced around the hallway. Maybe Ellen had left and her guard had followed, but she was fairly certain she'd heard Sarah instruct them that someone should remain here watching the room at all times.

When she finally turned to leave, she spotted a uniformed cop coming toward her. He spoke first. "She left."

"Where did she go?"

"I don't know. A couple of feds showed up earlier today and tried to talk her out of leaving, but she wouldn't hear any of it. She left and they followed. I figured they had eyes on her, so I stayed here like I was told."

Right, and that's why you were right here when I showed up. Danny realized there was no sense arguing with the guy. She opened her phone and searched, hopefully, for a text from Ellen, a missed call, something to let her know where she'd gone. Nothing. She sent a text, a simple "where are you?" The reply, "call you later" was quick. She stared at her phone for a few seconds, pondering her next move. She started to call, but what she had to say needed to be said in person. She pressed in the numbers to Sarah's phone and when she answered, barked into the phone. "I hope your guys know where she is."

"Danny? Where are you?"

"At Ellen's hotel."

"She's not there?"

"No, she left a while ago according to the cop on duty. He says your guys are following."

"I know she wanted to go to her office earlier, but I talked her out of it."

"Well, where did she go?"

"I don't have a clue. I'll text you the number of the lead agent assigned to watch her. Listen, I was about to call Molly. We've had Collin's place staked out for a while, but he hasn't shown up. We're going to see if there's a trash bin on the perimeter of the property that we can check for clues."

"Make sure you stay away from the house without a warrant." Danny didn't want any potential evidence to be tossed because they'd violated the fucker's constitutional rights in their excited quest to apprehend him.

"I know the drill. We'll call Molly right away if we find anything."

Danny hung up and considered what to do next. Calling the agents assigned to protect Ellen was extreme. They probably had her safely in their sights, and she risked the possibility of coming off like an interfering worrywart. If she showed up to talk to Ellen, they'd know for sure she was only interested for personal reasons.

So what? She needed to talk to Ellen before she lost her nerve. She checked for Sarah's text and then called the agent's number, practicing what she would say while she waited through the rings. When he answered, she summoned her most authoritative voice. "This is ADA Soto. I'm working with Agent Flores. I need to verify you have Ellen Davenport in sight and can give me a location."

The few beats of silence echoed on the line, and Danny didn't try to hide the rising panic in her voice. "Tell me you know where she is."

"Actually, we don't. She parked in front of her office building and we thought she was going to go in. While we were scoping out parking, she apparently took off. We didn't have a chance at following her. She hasn't been to the office, her hotel, or her house, but we have all three places staked out just in case."

Unbelievable. "What time did you lose her?"

"About three hours ago."

Anything could happen in three hours, but Danny's thoughts included only the bad things. "When the fuck were you going to report that you'd lost her?"

"It's not like we haven't been looking. She could've gone anywhere."

Danny didn't bother replying. She clicked off the line and immediately redialed Sarah's number. Again she started talking the minute the call connected. "Your guys lost her. Hours ago. She could be anywhere, she could be—"

Sarah interrupted before she could get any further. "We found something."

"What?"

"In Perkins's trash. We found something."

"Is there some reason you aren't telling me what it is?"

"I've already called Molly so she can start working on the warrant. I need you to promise me you won't do anything stupid if I tell you."

"I promise." The lie was easy. She could hear the urgent undercurrent of fear in Sarah's voice. She'd promise whatever she had to in order to hear what had her all worked up.

"We found the address for Cedar Acres on some papers in Perkins's trash. It was handwritten on probably a dozen sheets of paper and…"

Sarah kept talking, but her words were a blur. How could she have been so stupid? She hadn't even considered Cedar Acres as one of the places Ellen might go, but her gut told her that was exactly where she was. Right in the path of a serial killer. She didn't care if Sarah or anyone else thought she was stupid. Finding Ellen before Collin Perkins did was the most important thing she would ever do.

Chapter Twenty-four

Ellen looked from the gun in Collin's hand to her mother's face and watched Vivian's mind flutter shut. Her mother was gone again and she was completely alone. Whatever was about to happen, she wouldn't be able to count on her for help.

"Get over there, both of you." Collin pointed his gun toward the back of the room, and Ellen's mind raced with ideas about escape. Her phone was in her purse, turned off. There was an internal house phone on her mother's nightstand, but the ten feet between her and it may as well have been a mile.

She stared at his uniform, ill-fitting and bunched in all the wrong places. She doubted he worked here, which meant he had probably cased the place and stolen a uniform for this very day. Or he'd traded clothes with some poor soul who actually worked here. She shuddered at the sight of a duffle bag in his hand, imagining it contained whatever he needed to carry out his revenge. Did he really think he could kill them both here without being detected?

Danny. Would her earlier terse text to Danny be the last words they shared? She couldn't bear the idea this would be the end and she resolved to survive whatever this was. Maybe she could draw attention to her mother's suite and warn whoever came to check things out. She started by knocking over a lamp on the way to the far side of the room.

The loud clank on the floor caused Perkins to shake his gun in their direction and hiss, "Quiet, or I'll make some noise you'll regret."

Already regretting everything about being here, Ellen turned her attention to her mother. Vivian's vacant look had been replaced by stark fear, her eyes focused on the gun. Ellen reached for her arm and guided her away from Collin. "It's okay, Mother. Nothing to be afraid of."

Collin laughed at her whispered words. "By the time I'm done with her, she'll be afraid all right. If you think she's going to get off easy like the others, you're dead wrong." He laughed again at his own joke and Ellen fought to hide any visible reaction to his sociopathic cruelty.

Danny's vague description about how each of his prior victims had died surfaced, and she tamped down the images in her head. She couldn't afford to focus on what might happen. She had to concentrate on saving her mother and herself. They were in a fairly small space, surrounded by many other rooms. If they were going to get out of here alive, she had to draw attention to their situation and make it very uncomfortable for Perkins to stay here and carry out his plans. Standing directly in front of Vivian, she raised her voice. "The only one who's going to be dead is you. The police know exactly who you are and what you've done. Do you really think they don't know you're here right now?"

Not a flinch. He covered his mouth with a meaty fist and his whole body shook. Took her a minute to realize he was laughing. Hard. "These old people can't hear anything, so you can stop making noise. And, as for the police? You think I don't know how to take care of them? The stupid one they put here won't be guarding anyone ever again."

Ellen struggled to hide her fear. Unless she could get them out of the room, they were certain to die here. He obviously didn't care if he was detected as long as he got to carry out his mission. He was going to shoot them both unless she figured a way to distract him long enough for them to escape.

The journals. Maybe if she could get her mother to talk about them, he would stop long enough to hear what she had to say. Hell, she'd even go as far as to say they were still here if it would get him out of this room and allow them even the slightest chance of escape.

Summoning every reserve she had, she said, "Collin, what my mother did to yours was unforgivable. She even wrote it all down. Would you like to read her journals?"

A flicker of interest flashed in his eyes, but the gun didn't waiver. He glanced at Vivian whose expression had returned to a blank stare, and she pressed on. "I know where she hid them."

"Tell me."

She shook her head. "She was so ashamed of what she did, she buried them in a garden outside. I have to show you." She watched his face, his expression changing as he slowly considered the possibilities. When he finally offered a plan, she didn't like it at all.

He pointed the gun at her and asked, "You have a phone?"

She waffled for a minute as she considered lying, but if he went through her purse and found it, there would be consequences. "Yes." She motioned toward her purse and watched in dismay as he dug through the contents and fished out her cell. Dismay changed to despair as he placed it under his boot and crushed it. Next he fished a strand of rope and a roll of duct tape from his bag, tossed it to her, and instructed her to use it to tie Vivian's hands and feet and tape her mouth. Ellen was as gentle as she could be, confident that her mother's memories of this would be buried with the rest of her past. She only hoped she would live to have memories of her own.

Danny called Ellen at least a dozen times as she flew down the highway to Cedar Acres, and each call was answered on the first ring by Ellen's recorded voice. There could be any number of reasons why she wasn't answering, but her mind raced to the worst conclusion—that she couldn't because Collin Perkins had her.

When she finally turned into the drive at Cedar Acres, she didn't wait for the valet, instead slamming on the brakes and abandoning her truck in the first open space. She ran into the lobby and looked frantically around. Her surging adrenaline was completely at odds with the easy Muzak and the slow moving residents, and after a minute she realized, she didn't know where to go from here. The place was enormous. Vivian and Ellen could be anywhere.

She fished her district attorney badge from her pocket and strode up to the receptionist who was chatting on the phone. After an impatient few minutes, she took the receiver from her hand and placed it on the cradle, shoving her badge under the woman's nose. "Police business. I need you to tell me the room number for Vivian Davenport."

The talkative woman assumed a know-it-all posture and asked, "Do you have a warrant, Officer?"

Danny growled, but didn't bother correcting the misimpression. "Where's Mrs. Patterson?"

"She's gone for the night."

"Does she know you sit up here and talk on personal calls all evening? Pretty sure I can let her know. Bet you'll be looking for a job somewhere else."

She typed a few strokes on her computer. "She's in room 277, but if you tell anyone that you got it from me, I'll deny it."

Danny didn't stick around to reply. She took off to the elevator bank she'd seen in the lobby and dashed into an open car, jamming the number two button over and over until the doors finally slid shut. As she traveled slowly to the second floor, she contemplated her next move. She didn't have a gun, but Collin certainly did. Sarah and George were probably on the way with backup. She should wait for them. If she had any sense, she would wait for them. But Ellen might be here, and common sense didn't matter where Ellen was concerned. All that mattered was keeping Ellen safe. She couldn't bear the thought of never being able to tell her how she felt.

The hallway was sermon quiet. She checked the signs on the wall and determined that Vivian's room was located at the very end. She tiptoed down the hall, careful not to make any noise. When she reached Vivian's door, she held her breath and listened. The seconds ticked away and she heard nothing. Now that she was here, her earlier bravado disappeared. She wasn't scared for herself, but she didn't want to do anything stupid, anything that could get Ellen hurt, or killed. Bursting through the door would be a loser move.

She leaned against the wall and considered her options. She'd barely gotten past a few initial thoughts before her phone buzzed. She covered it to block the noise and glanced at the screen. *We have Collin in sight. Cedar Acres. Where are you?*

So he must not be here in the room. She thumbed her reply to Sarah. *Inside. By Vivian's room.*

Stay put. I'll call you when we have him.

Danny sighed with relief. This would all be over soon. Ellen and her mother would be safe. The killer would be in custody. She would let Alvarez know she wanted off the case and she would be free to explore whatever Ellen was prepared to explore with her. She pushed away from the wall and considered whether she should wait here or find another place to keep vigil. As she considered her options, she heard a faint groan. She pressed her ear against Vivian's door and listened. Seconds later, another groan and then a thud. Was Vivian in trouble? What if Collin had made it to her before he slipped away? What if she was inside, dying from wounds he'd inflicted?

Without another thought, she turned the door handle. Locked. She pushed against the door. It gave slightly, but she'd have to really throw some weight into it to break it down. Glancing down the hall, it appeared everyone was in for the night. If she broke the door down, she'd wake them all, but she'd have to take that chance. She backed up and charged full force against the door. She spilled into the room as it gave way. It took her a moment to get her bearings. A figure lay on the bed. Bound and gagged. She rushed to her side and found Vivian on the bed, barely breathing, but still alive and with no visible signs of injury. She gently peeled the duct tape from her mouth and murmured gentle comforts while she untied her bonds.

"Marty," she croaked.

"What?"

"Marty. He took Marty. I think he might kill her. She promised to show him where I buried the journals."

She had no doubt that the "he" Vivian was talking about was Collin, but a more important question topped her list. "Has Ellen been here tonight?"

"She's taking him to the journals. I think he might kill her."

Danny struggled to process Vivian's ramblings. Was Vivian talking about Marty or Ellen? Only took her a second before she remembered being in the garden with Vivian. Vivian kept calling Ellen, Marty. Ellen had said she'd confused them before. Was she confusing them tonight too?

She grasped Vivian's shoulders and looked into her eyes, willing her to be clear. Before she could formulate a question, she saw a picture of Ellen on Vivian's nightstand. She picked it up and showed it to Vivian. "Is this the person who is taking him to the journals?"

Vivian nodded, fear in her eyes. Danny dropped the frame and picked up her phone, typing as fast as she'd ever done. *He has Ellen. Going to garden. Tell me she's alive.*

Within seconds, her phone rang. Sarah started talking in a hurried whisper the minute she clicked on the phone. "Listen to me. We have them in our sights. We have an entire team of snipers on it. You have to trust me."

"I'm coming down there."

"You'll be a distraction. Stay where you are."

"He tied Vivian up. Ellen probably distracted him or he would've killed her."

"Now it's our turn to save her. You have to trust me," Sarah repeated. "Oh, hell, hold on."

Danny heard muffled voices while she waited for Sarah to come back on the line. Finally, unable to stand not knowing what was going on, she hissed into the phone. "Tell me what's happening."

"We have…wait…she's…"

Sarah's voice was punctuated by bursts of static and Danny shouted, "Sarah, tell me what's happening!"

"No! No! Hold your fire!"

"Sarah!"

Nothing. A moment passed while Danny processed that Sarah was no longer talking to her, but before she could say anything else, the line crackled with the sharp shots of erupting gunfire. Danny took off running, certain she was too late.

❖

Ellen stood in the dark garden trying not to flinch at the cold metal pressed against her neck. This had been a huge mistake on her part. She'd assumed there was no way she and Collin could make it out here without running into someone in the halls of Cedar Acres, but the few people they'd passed had been residents too out of it to notice her distress. They probably assumed she was one of them in the company of a staff member.

She wished she was one of them, unable to process what was happening, let alone what was about to happen when Collin learned that there were no journals buried in the garden. He'd waste no time returning to her mother's room to finish what he'd started.

"Start digging." Collin punctuated his words with a hard shove and she dropped to the ground. Clawing the hard ground with only her hands would at least buy her some time, and she dug at the rosebushes with what she hoped was conviction. A few minutes later, she had amassed a sizable hole. Collin pushed her aside and peered into the ground.

"Where are they?"

"Deeper." She kept digging while casting about for a way to distract him from her futile task. "She's been punished enough."

"She who?"

"Vivian. My mother. She has Alzheimer's. She barely knows who she is from day to day."

"Your poor mother. Having to live out her life in a fancy retirement home. How sad for her." Collin's words were icy and mocking. "Want to hear about my mother? Want to hear what she remembered?"

Ellen forced herself to look him in the eyes. What Sarah had told her about Angela and how she'd found her mother's body, had been haunting enough. What horrible memories did this man have of his mother who'd apparently been so scarred she passed her desire for revenge along to her children?

"I can't even imagine what it's like to lose someone you love."

He placed a hand over his mouth and his body shook. Like earlier, she realized he was laughing and she was confused.

"I didn't love her. She was a horrible person and I was her bastard child. She comes to me at night still and tells me how much she wishes I was never born."

"Then why would you kill for her?"

He cocked his head and his eyes became vacant once again. "To cleanse."

Ellen instantly understood. He felt like he had to take action to be rid of the memories, but his twisted mind could only see murder as the appropriate response. Maybe if she offered comfort, understanding, she could get through to him and distract him from his path.

Any compassion she had was doused when he kicked her side. "Why aren't you digging?" She fell into the dirt, writhing in pain, his voice scratching and clawing at her. "Did you lie to me about the journals? I'm going to kill your mother, and there's nothing you can do to stop me. And then I'm going to kill you!"

Ellen stayed on the ground. Her last sight before she closed her eyes, was his huge hand raising his gun and the metallic click of the weapon being cocked. Loud shots, unintelligible screams and yells, the acrid smell of gunfire. She curled into a fetal position and let the whirl of senses float over her. The only feeling that stung was longing—for what Danny had offered and what she'd so easily dismissed. Nothing else mattered. All that mattered was that she was about to die and she'd never taken a chance on life, on love.

Chapter Twenty-five

Danny strained against Sarah's strong grasp. "Let me go!"

Sarah wasn't budging. "No. You need to wait until the scene is clear."

She sagged as Sarah's arms held her more fiercely in what was now an embrace rather than a restraint. The journey from Vivian's room to the grounds had taken forever, but this waiting, without knowing if Ellen was alive, was unbearable. "Is she…" She couldn't finish the sentence.

"You have to wait here."

The uncertainty in Sarah's tone rattled Danny and she suspected Sarah was keeping bad news from her. "Tell me what happened!"

Sarah shook her. "I don't know, but if she is okay, she's going to need you. George is over there now. He should be right back."

A deep voice from behind them chimed in. "Actually, I'm right here."

Danny felt his strong hand on her shoulder and turned to face him, struggling to read his expression. He didn't leave her hanging. "She's going to be fine. She wasn't shot, but he did rough her up a bit." He paused. "He's dead, but she's still pretty scared." He pointed toward the garden. "The paramedics will be here in a minute. I want them to check her out before she goes anywhere, but right now she wants you. We moved her over to one of our cars."

He pointed and Danny took off running again and closed the distance quickly. *She wants you.* The words were what she'd longed to hear, but when she reached Ellen, she pulled up short. If George hadn't already told her Ellen was okay, she would have come unglued at the sight of her pale face and blood-splattered clothes. Danny sat next to her on the car seat and drew Ellen's head into her lap, not caring if the cops standing nearby heard what she had to say.

"Ellen, baby, it's over." She squeezed her hand to emphasize the point and prayed she would quickly show some sign of life. George's assurance that she was okay wasn't enough. She leaned down and whispered. "I've got you. You are going to be fine. It's over." She stroked Ellen's hair while she waited for a response. The smallest one would do.

When Ellen's eyes fluttered open, she sighed with relief.

"I'm okay." Ellen's voice was thick and throaty.

She tried to push into an upright position, but Danny gently held her back, resisting the urge to offer too much information. "Relax. Everything's okay. Just sit here with me for a few minutes."

Ellen leaned back and closed her eyes for a moment, but then they shot wide open and she struggled to sit up. "My mother! He tied her up. I need to check on her."

Danny pulled Ellen into her arms. "Your mother's fine. I just saw her. In fact, she's worried about you. And Collin…" She hesitated as she cast about for an indirect way of saying he wasn't going to be a problem anymore before she settled on the truth. "Collin is dead. Angela is in custody. You and your mother are safe."

"Do you have to go?" Ellen whispered.

"What?" Danny couldn't quite process the non sequitur.

"Work." Ellen's eyes were clear now. "I guess there's going to be a lot for you to do now."

"Oh." Danny read the shade of wistfulness in Ellen's eyes and hoped it was for her. But this wasn't the time. Ellen was in shock, possibly injured. She needed to get her checked out, at least let her rest before she said what she wanted to say. "No. No work for me. I only came here because I wanted to tell you something and it had nothing to do with work."

"Tell me."

Danny heard a noise behind them. She looked over her shoulder and saw the approaching paramedics. She bent down and kissed Ellen's forehead. "Later."

"Tell me."

"Ellen, these guys are going to make sure you're not injured. If they take you in, I'll ride with you. Okay?"

Ellen's voice was calm, but insistent. "Danny Soto, I love you. Now, if you don't tell me you love me, I won't be going anywhere."

She loves me. Danny leaned back and looked into Ellen's eyes. Strength, conviction, and a hint of a smile. She'd known from the beginning that Ellen was special, worth any risk their relationship might demand. She'd gone looking for Ellen today to ask her to take a chance on them. She'd gone crazy when she thought Ellen might be in danger, the thought of losing her had been devastating. Now Ellen, who had every reason to fear emotions she'd been raised to avoid, had said the magic words. She had absolutely no doubt that she loved Ellen, that she would love her for the rest of her life, and that this would be the first of many times she spoke these words. "I love you."

CHAPTER TWENTY-SIX

Ellen jerked awake when she heard keys open the lock, but then settled back into bed when she realized she was still safely tucked away in Danny's apartment. After the ordeal with Collin and a thorough examination at the hospital, Danny had brought her here and tucked her into bed. She'd spent the last few days trying to stay awake so she could avoid the nightmares that had plagued her since Collin had been gunned down in the garden at Cedar Acres. This morning, after making a few calls, she'd climbed back into bed and exhaustion had finally taken hold.

"Hey, sleepyhead. How are you feeling today?"

"Lazy." Ellen stretched and yawned to emphasize her point. She glanced at the clock, shocked at the late hour, but relieved that it wasn't as late as she thought. "I can't believe I slept until noon. You must think I'm a slug."

Danny sat on the bed beside her. "I think you've been through a lot. Sorry, I had to leave, but I made sure a couple of folks I trusted were posted outside."

"I hate that I'm still scared."

"Perfectly normal." Danny leaned down and kissed her. "I want you to feel safe."

Ellen pulled her back for another kiss, murmuring against her lips. "I'm feeling something completely different right now."

"Is that so?"

Ellen deepened the kiss and then uttered a breathy, "Oh, yeah." Danny had held her the past two nights, but with her body bruised and mind racing, the action had been more about comfort than passion. She toyed with the buttons on Danny's shirt. "What are you doing right now?"

Danny's smile was knowing. "What do you want me to do?"

"Say it, Soto."

"I'm going to make love to you."

"Yes. Yes, you are." Ellen watched as Danny quickly undressed and then joined her under the sheets. She arched into Danny's embrace. She needed her touch, her heat, not just to erase the horror of the last week, but as a foundation for their future. As Danny raised her nightshirt and took a hard nipple into her mouth, she melted into Danny's embrace. "I love you."

Danny raised her head. "I love you too." She leaned on one elbow and with her free hand drew lazy, languid circles on Ellen's stomach, up her chest, and around each breast. "We've done this before, you know."

"Huh?" Ellen gasped as the light touches promised more, and then eased away leaving a trail of arousal in their path. She could feel her clit pulse and flood with wetness, and she was certain she could go insane if Danny kept touching her this way.

"The first time. We were making love, even then."

"Yes." Danny was right, but it was different now. All the obstacles she thought were insurmountable had turned out to be no more than self-imposed boundaries. She wanted nothing more than to be with Danny for the rest of her life and she would never let anything come between them. This time when they made love, she was making a promise and she knew Danny was too. With her eyes wide open, she guided Danny's hand between her legs. "I need you. Now."

Danny kissed her hard while stroking through the wet folds of her arousal. Ellen reached for Danny, not at all surprised to find her just as wet, just as ready. They thrust and ground against each other, seeking closeness, seeking release, all the while looking deep into each other's eyes until the height of climax sealed their promise.

❖

"Come back to bed." Danny patted the space beside her. She'd fallen into a cat nap after they'd spent the last several hours making love, and woken up to find Ellen getting dressed.

Ellen kept brushing her hair. "Come with me. I have an appointment at four."

"Doctor's visit?" Danny was instantly worried that an afternoon of physical activity had taken its toll. "Are you okay? I mean you were ready for this, right?"

Ellen sat on the edge of the bed and smiled down at her. "No, not a doctor's appointment. And I promise I was ready for *this*." She kissed her. "I'm ready for *thi*s again, but I have something I have to take care of. I would like it if you came with me." She stood and walked over to the dresser where Danny had cleaned out a couple of drawers for her to use. Danny watched her finish dressing, and all she wanted to do was convince Ellen to take off her clothes and get back in bed.

Later. Right now, whatever it was Ellen wanted her to do, she would do it. "I'll take a quick rinse in the shower and be ready. Don't leave without me."

Twenty minutes later, she walked Ellen to her car. "You sure you don't want me to drive?"

Ellen pointed at the passenger side and Danny got in. Once Ellen was settled in the driver's seat, she said, "I'm sure. I'm going back to work next week, and you won't be around to take care of me every day." She smiled. "That is unless you plan to quit your job."

"Well, actually, that's something we should probably talk about."

"What?"

Danny hadn't been sure how to bring up the subject, or anything related to the case without dredging up the stuff of Ellen's nightmares, but here in middle of the day, out in the sunshine, it seemed like the best time to broach the subject. "I've taken myself completely off this case. Molly has been working with Sarah and George on the case against Angela, and she'll handle the trial, if there is one."

"Oh, Danny."

Ellen's expression was pained and Danny knew she thought this was a replay of her backslide after her breakup with Maria. She rushed to dispel the idea. "It was an easy choice. And it wasn't really a choice at all. I'm your lover. That comes first. It will always come first. I can't be objective and I don't want to be. I spent the morning going over all my notes with Molly."

They stopped at a light and Ellen put the car in park and pulled her close. "I don't ever want to get in the way of your work. I know how important it is to you."

"Nothing's as important as you are." She meant the words and it felt good to speak the commitment out loud.

"So, we can talk about the case?"

"Of course. I just haven't talked to you about it because I didn't want to upset you."

"I don't think these nightmares are going to go away unless I can replace them with real facts."

Danny nodded. Made sense. "Here's the short version. Angela and her dead brother were both really fucked up, but they came by it honestly. Wendy Angela Perkins told her son Collin that she got pregnant at that party and that he was the bastard child of her rape. Later, she had Angela, but Angela's dad didn't stick around either, and it's likely she blamed her daughter for that.

"Not sure why, but she engendered some kind of sick loyalty from those kids, and when she hung herself, leaving a note about the evil Alpha Nus and how they'd ruined her life, they vowed to take revenge. Angela did the research and Collin did the killings."

"What took them so long to get started? I thought Angela was fifteen when her mother committed suicide."

"Not sure yet. From all accounts, Collin had a few screws loose. He obviously needed his sister's help. Maybe they waited until Angela could pledge Alpha Nu and find out more information about all their potential victims. In any case, it took them a little bit to get the routine down. Joyce Barr was probably their first. They hung her, but then decided to get fancier and just use the noose as a symbol. Who knows how long they would've gotten away with it if you hadn't supplied the motive? George and Sarah found a list at Collin's house with seven more names on it—all women who were at the Alpha Nu mixer the night Pledge Thirteen got ushered out of the sorority. They think he had originally planned to leave your mother for the end, but when we brought Angela in, they realized they were out of time."

Ellen shook her head. "Wow. I can't believe something that happened so many years ago could fester for so long and result in so much loss."

"It's over. At least for us. They have so much evidence against Angela, I doubt the case will ever go to trial. More likely, her lawyer will try for a plea and argue mitigating circumstances because she really is crazy."

"I almost took her out myself when I thought she was flirting with you at the mixer."

Danny grinned. "Is that how it's going to be? You're going to beat up any woman who talks to me?"

"Maybe."

Ellen pulled over and parked, and for the first time since they'd gotten in the car, Danny noticed her surroundings, genuinely puzzled. "We're at your house? I mean your mother's house."

"Yes, we are." Ellen opened the door. "George said it was released as a crime scene, right?" Danny nodded, and Ellen climbed out of the car. "Come on."

As they started up the walk, Danny heard the sound of a car pulling up behind them. She turned and spotted a Lexus SUV parking behind Ellen's car. "You expecting someone?"

"Actually, I am." Ellen didn't provide any other detail until the other woman joined them on the sidewalk. She was buxom, blond, and beautiful, dressed in a fancy suit. She was exactly the kind of woman Ellen would be friends with, and a few weeks ago, Danny would've felt insecure that this expensively dressed socialite was here to meet Ellen. But not now. Now she was certain that what she had with Ellen was deeper than anything money or social standing could buy. She reached out a hand to begin the introductions. "Danny Soto."

"Aimee Howard. Sorry I'm late. Baby issues. They never want to eat when you want to feed them." Her handshake was firm and her smile was friendly. Danny liked her instantly.

"Danny," said Ellen, "Aimee's the realtor I've hired to sell Mother's house."

Danny raised her eyebrows. She wanted to ask a ton of questions, but didn't know how personal she should get in front of Aimee. Ellen read her mind. "I've told Aimee everything. She thinks we can get a good price and a quick sale."

All Danny heard was the word "everything." "Aimee, do you mind if I speak to Ellen for a moment alone?" She didn't wait for the answer before she walked a few feet away. Ellen whispered something to Aimee and joined her.

"Everything okay?" Ellen asked.

"Are you sure you want to sell? Don't you want to wait and see how you feel when things have settled down, when more time has passed?"

"I've never wanted to be here and I only moved in out of a misguided promise to my mother. My happiest memory of this place is making love to you here, and even that's marred by the fact we were probably being watched."

"Where will you live? Obviously, you can stay with me as long as you want." Danny fumbled the words. She'd love for them to live together, but she knew her apartment was too small, and it definitely wasn't what Ellen was used to.

"Well, the two dresser drawers you've given me are pretty roomy, but I'm thinking of somewhere different. How about you?"

"Me?"

"Darling, Aimee's a realtor. She not only sells houses, she helps people buy them. I think it's time we both had a fresh start. You up for buying a house with me?"

A house. Their house. Where they could live and make love and raise a family of their own. Waking up with Ellen every day, falling asleep in each other's arms each night. Danny was up for it all and she didn't want to wait another moment for their future. She swept Ellen into her arms and kissed her soundly. "I'm up for anything, for everything with you."

THE END

About the Author

Carsen Taite's goal as an author is to spin tales with plot lines as interesting as the cases she encountered in her career as a criminal defense lawyer. She is the author of nine previously released novels, *truelesbianlove.com*, *It Should be a Crime* (a Lambda Literary Award finalist), *Do Not Disturb*, *Nothing but the Truth*, *The Best Defense*, *Slingshot*, *Beyond Innocence*, and *Battle Axe*. She is currently working on her tenth novel, *Switchblade*, another installment in the Luca Bennett mystery series. Learn more at www.carsentaite.com.

Books Available from Bold Strokes Books

Love and Devotion by Jove Belle. KC Hall trips her way through life, stumbling into an affair with a married bombshell twice her age. Thankfully, her best friend, Emma Reynolds, is there to show her the true meaning of Love and Devotion. (978-1-60282-965-7)

Rush by Carsen Taite. Murder, secrets, and romance combine to create the ultimate rush. (978-1-60282-966-4)

The Shoal of Time by J.M. Redmann. It sounded too easy. Micky Knight is reluctant to take the case because the easy ones often turn into the hard ones, and the hard ones turn into the dangerous ones. In this one, easy turns hard without warning. (978-1-60282-967-1)

In Between by Jane Hoppen. At the age of 14, Sophie Schmidt discovers that she was born an intersexual baby and sets off on a journey to find her place in a world that denies her true existence. (978-1-60282-968-8)

Secret Lies by Amy Dunne. While fleeing from her abuser, Nicola Jackson bumps into Jenny O'Connor, and their unlikely friendship quickly develops into a blossoming romance—but when it comes down to a matter of life or death, are they both willing to face their fears? (978-1-60282-970-1)

Under Her Spell by Maggie Morton. The magic of love brought Terra and Athene together, but now a magical quest stands between them—a quest for Athene's hand in marriage. Will their passion keep them together, or will stronger magic tear them apart? (978-1-60282-973-2)

Homestead by Radclyffe. R. Clayton Sutter figures getting NorthAm Fuel's newest refinery operational on a rolling tract of land in Upstate New York should take a month or two, but then, she hadn't counted on local resistance in the form of vandalism, petitions, and one furious farmer named Tess Rogers. (978-1-60282-956-5)

Battle of Forces: Sera Toujours by Ali Vali. Kendal and Piper return to New Orleans to start the rest of eternity together, but the return of an old enemy makes their peaceful reunion short-lived, especially when they join forces with the new queen of the vampires. (978-1-60282-957-2)

How Sweet It Is by Melissa Brayden. Some things are better than chocolate. Molly O'Brien enjoys her quiet life running the bakeshop in a small town. When the beautiful Jordan Tuscana returns home, Molly can't deny the attraction—or the stirrings of something more. (978-1-60282-958-9)

The Missing Juliet: A Fisher Key Adventure by Sam Cameron. A teenage detective and her friends search for a kidnapped Hollywood star in the Florida Keys. (978-1-60282-959-6)

Amor and More: Love Everafter edited by Radclyffe and Stacia Seaman. Rediscover favorite couples as Bold Strokes Books authors reveal glimpses of life and love beyond the honeymoon in short stories featuring main characters from favorite BSB novels. (978-1-60282-963-3)

First Love by CJ Harte. Finding true love is hard enough, but for Jordan Thompson, daughter of a conservative president, it's challenging, especially when that love is a female rodeo cowgirl. (978-1-60282-949-7)

Pale Wings Protecting by Lesley Davis. Posing as a couple to investigate the abduction of infants, Special Agent Blythe Kent and Detective Daryl Chandler find themselves drawn into a battle over the innocents, with demons on one side and the unlikeliest of protectors on the other. (978-1-60282-964-0)

Mounting Danger by Karis Walsh. Sergeant Rachel Bryce, an outcast on the police force, is put in charge of the department's newly formed mounted division. Can she and polo champion Callan Lanford resist their growing attraction as they struggle to safeguard the disaster-prone unit? (978-1-60282-951-0)

Meeting Chance by Jennifer Lavoie. When man's best friend turns on Aaron Cassidy, the teen keeps his distance until fate puts Chance in his hands. (978-1-60282-952-7)

At Her Feet by Rebekah Weatherspoon. Digital marketing producer Suzanne Kim knows she has found the perfect love in her new mistress Pilar, but before they can make the ultimate commitment, Suzanne's professional life threatens to disrupt their perfectly balanced bliss. (978-1-60282-948-0)

Show of Force by AJ Quinn. A chance meeting between navy pilot Evan Kane and correspondent Tate McKenna takes them on a roller-coaster ride where the stakes are high, but the reward is higher: a chance at love. (978-1-60282-942-8)

Clean Slate by Andrea Bramhall. Can Erin and Morgan work through their individual demons to rediscover their love for each other, or are the unexplainable wounds too deep to heal? (978-1-60282-943-5)

Hold Me Forever by D. Jackson Leigh. An investigation into illegal cloning in the quarter horse racing industry threatens to destroy the growing attraction between Georgia debutante Mae St. John and Louisiana horse trainer Whit Casey. (978-1-60282-944-2)

Trusting Tomorrow by PJ Trebelhorn. Funeral director Logan Swift thinks she's perfectly happy with her solitary life devoted to helping others cope with loss until Brooke Collier moves in next door to care for her elderly grandparents. (978-1-60282-891-9)

Forsaking All Others by Kathleen Knowles. What if what you think you want is the opposite of what makes you happy? (978-1-60282-892-6)

Exit Wounds by VK Powell. When Officer Loane Landry falls in love with ATF informant Abigail Mancuso, she realizes that nothing is as it seems—not the case, not her lover, not even the dead. (978-1-60282-893-3)

Dirty Power by Ashley Bartlett. Cooper's been through hell and back, and she's still broke and on the run. But at least she found the twins. They'll keep her alive. Right? (978-1-60282-896-4)

The Rarest Rose by I. Beacham. After a decade of living in her beloved house, Ele disturbs its past and finds her life being haunted by the presence of a ghost who will show her that true love never dies. (978-1-60282-884-1)

Code of Honor by Radclyffe. The face of terror is hard to recognize—especially when it's homegrown. The next book in the Honor series. (978-1-60282-885-8)

Does She Love You? by Rachel Spangler. When Annabelle and Davis find out they are both in a relationship with the same woman, it leaves them facing life-altering questions about trust, redemption, and the possibility of finding love in the wake of betrayal. (978-1-60282-886-5)

The Road to Her by KE Payne. Sparks fly when actress Holly Croft, star of UK soap Portobello Road, meets her new on-screen love interest, the enigmatic and sexy Elise Manford. (978-1-60282-887-2)

Shadows of Something Real by Sophia Kell Hagin. Trying to escape flashbacks and nightmares, ex-POW Jamie Gwynmorgan stumbles into the heart of former Red Cross worker Adele Sabellius and uncovers a deadly conspiracy against everything and everyone she loves. (978-1-60282-889-6)

Date with Destiny by Mason Dixon. When sophisticated bank executive Rashida Ivey meets unemployed blue collar worker Destiny Jackson, will her life ever be the same? (978-1-60282-878-0)

The Devil's Orchard by Ali Vali. Cain and Emma plan a wedding before the birth of their third child while Juan Luis is still lurking, and as Cain plans for his death, an unexpected visitor arrives and challenges her belief in her father, Dalton Casey. (978-1-60282-879-7)

Secrets and Shadows by L.T. Marie. A bodyguard and the woman she protects run from a madman and into each other's arms. (978-1-60282-880-3)

Change Horizons: Three Novellas by Gun Brooke. Three stories of courageous women who dare to love as they fight to claim a future in a hostile universe. (978-1-60282-881-0)

Scarlet Thirst by Crin Claxton. When hot, feisty Rani meets cool, vampire Rob, one lifetime isn't enough, and the road from human to vampire is shorter than you think… (978-1-60282-856-8)

Battle Axe by Carsen Taite. How close is too close? Bounty hunter Luca Bennett will soon find out. (978-1-60282-871-1)

Improvisation by Karis Walsh. High school geometry teacher Jan Carroll thinks she's figured out the shape of her life and her future, until graphic artist and fiddle player Tina Nelson comes along and teaches her to improvise. (978-1-60282-872-8)

For Want of a Fiend by Barbara Ann Wright. Without her Fiendish power, can Princess Katya and her consort Starbride stop a magic-wielding madman from sparking an uprising in the kingdom of Farraday? (978-1-60282-873-5)

Broken in Soft Places by Fiona Zedde. The instant Sara Chambers meets the seductive and sinful Merille Thompson, she falls hard, but knowing the difference between love and a dangerous, all-consuming desire is just one of the lessons Sara must learn before it's too late. (978-1-60282-876-6)

Healing Hearts by Donna K. Ford. Running from tragedy, the women of Willow Springs find that with friendship, there is hope, and with love, there is everything. (978-1-60282-877-3)